Dragon Crown Books presents

NEVADA
NIGHTMARE'S
EVE

Weird Tales of the Silver State
from the Twisted Minds of Sharon
Marie and Stephen H. Provost

SHARON MARIE and STEPHEN H. PROVOST

Front cover main image: Tonopah Cemetery, Stephen H. Provost
Back cover image: Black Rock Desert, Sharon Marie Provost
Cover and interior design: Sharon Marie and Stephen H. Provost

©2025 Sharon Marie and Stephen H. Provost
Dragon Crown Books 2025
All rights reserved.
ISBN: 978-1-949971-76-7

ScreamCatcher Horror, a division of Dragon Crown Books

Images

Unattributed images are in the public domain.

Contents

Introduction

Nevada Nightmare's Eve is the culmination of several projects Sharon and I have undertaken since my arrival in Nevada a few years ago. During our travels to various shows and events, we've been asked several times whether we have any Nevada-themed horror collections, and the answer was always "no." Until now.

We decided this past spring that we needed to produce such a collection, but in true Dragon Crown fashion, we wound up going the extra mile. We started out with the goal of writing one book—this one—but were unsure whether we would be able to produce enough stories in a short period of time to fill a single volume.

Boy, were we wrong.

Not only did we come up with 18 stories for this book, but we wound up with approximately two dozen additional stories—so much material that we decided to create an entire series of four volumes. Two are anthologies featuring other outstanding Nevada authors, past and present, alongside our own work. We released the first, Nevada Nightmares, Vol. 1, in September 2025, with the second to follow shortly. The fourth volume will be a companion to this one, featuring our own stories exclusively. Publication will come in 2026.

SHARON MARIE and STEPHEN H. PROVOST

We are extremely excited about this work because it builds upon the success of our Nightmare's Eve series, and Sharon's award-winning Shadow's Gate in particular, with some of our strongest material across the board. As always, we have strived to include a potpourri of horror stories and thrillers from a variety of subgenres, from highway horror to ghost stories, from folklore to cosmic horror, and some quirky stories that could only be set in the Silver State.

Nevada is unique in providing the kind of settings and conditions that are perfect for ghost stories, terrifying tales, and mind-bending excursions into the world of nightmares. These journeys are not for the tenderhearted. If you panic at the sight of blood, despair at injustices visited upon the guileless, shrink from the idea of vengeance, or quiver at tales of hopelessness and eternal torment, we advise you to close this book at once. It might cause irreparable damage to your innocent soul.

But if, like us, you are drawn to the anguish of the human heart, the mysteries that dwell in the murky black, and the terrifying nature of the world we live in, read on. We invite you to join us on this exploration of Nevada's dark side... if you dare.

Stephen H. Provost
September 18, 2025

Sharon Marie Provost

Ladies of the Night

I 'd always been skeptical about anything I couldn't prove scientifically: ghosts, UFOs, cryptids... but I sure as hell didn't believe in demons or the devil. Still, I couldn't get what Andre said out of my mind.

He had a theory that seemed both groundbreaking and horrifying to contemplate. I'd never heard anyone speculate that the old ghost stories of ladies in white or, in Old West towns, ladies in red, were anything other than ghosts of women who had died tragically.

Part of me wondered if he was teasing me. Or high on some drug. But it was Andre. He'd always been as straitlaced as they come. Logical. Intelligent. The epitome of a "good boy" and far from naïve. Something told me I shouldn't go, but I had to find out what had him so worked up. I should have listened to my intuition.

All the tales of ladies in white involved some young beautiful girl clothed in a white dress who had been hit by a car or killed in some other tragic accident. They were always seen along long, dark isolated stretches of road in the countryside or wandering around in cemeteries.

The ladies in red from the Old West were, much as you'd expect them to be, soiled doves. They were prostitutes who worked in the countless brothels, outnumbered only by saloons, that filled up western mining towns. They were beloved, beautiful young women who'd been murdered by jealous patrons. Not surprisingly, they were reportedly sighted in or near the old hotel rooms where they were killed.

Andre had been assigned to do a research paper for his American history class. Only he chose to investigate the true stories behind the ghost legends that attracted paranormal enthusiasts and tourists around the country. He had neglected to get his subject approved by the professor, so he was taking a really big chance: The project was worth 50 percent of his final grade.

He'd used spring break to travel across Nevada on his quest. His "breakthrough," as he'd called it, came after he stayed in the Lady in Red's room at the Mizpah Hotel in Tonopah. He'd called me up, begging me to make the four-hour drive down from Carson City so he could discuss it further. He'd given me the basics over the phone, but it seemed utterly preposterous.

He swore he had proof and was about to ask someone special to talk to us and confirm it once I arrived. The cell signal became spotty just after I passed Fort Churchill, and our call had

6

disconnected. But the last thing I heard him say was "Jocelyn, they're succubi."

The cell signal had not returned until the moment I entered Tonopah. I checked my phone to see if Andre had left any messages, but he hadn't. I tried calling him, but I only got his voicemail. I didn't know if I was supposed to meet him at the hotel or somewhere else.

I parked in the back lot of the Mizpah and entered the ornate lobby, adorned with plush Victorian furniture, brass chandeliers, old slot machines, a Big Six wheel, and a grand piano. I took the elevator to the fifth floor and went to Room 504, the "Lady in Red Suite."

I knocked on the door, but there was no answer.

Andre had sounded frantic, trying to convince me of his hypothesis. He'd probably worked himself up into such a dither that he'd crashed while waiting for me to arrive. I pounded on the door, calling out in a loud voice, "Andre! Open up. Damn it! I drove all the way down here. Don't leave me standing out in the hall. Andre!"

The door to Room 502, to my right, opened up. I flicked my head that direction to apologize for disturbing the occupant, but I couldn't turn my eyes away from her. A beautiful woman with long, wavy raven-colored hair, porcelain skin, and piercing eyes of... I'm not sure what color... brown, red, reddish-brown? They were glowing and indescribable, and I'd never seen their match before.

She wore a black silk sheath dress with a slit in the skirt all the way to the top of her thigh, and the V-neck cut down nearly to her navel. The dress conformed to every perfect curve of her voluptuous body. Her lips were painted a dazzling blood red, in perfect contrast.

"Is there a problem?" she asked in a sultry voice.

"Umm... no... not exactly. I'm just trying to get my friend to open up. He was waiting for me here, or at least, I thought he was," I stammered.

"You must be Jocelyn. Andre had to run out on an errand, but he said you'd be arriving soon. I'm Persephone. Would you like to come in and wait here? I'm sure he'll check in when he gets back." Persephone stepped back and opened the door wider, inviting me in with a sweep of her arm.

I hesitated for only a second before entering her room, and sat on the chair she offered me by a small table. "I'm sorry, but he didn't mention you to me, at least not by name. Are you the person he said we would be talking to about... about his thoughts?" I hesitated to verbalize the truth. I wasn't accustomed to being scrutinized by people for having outlandish beliefs.

Persephone's light laugh lit up the room as much as her smile did. "Yes, he wanted me to give you guys the history of the Lady in Red Room. Did you know that her ghost is not only seen in that particular named suite but in this room and Room 503 as well?"

"Why is that?"

"Well, take this all with a grain of salt—as you should with all ghost tales supposedly based on real people—but there is quite a story behind this particular ghost. Some people believe her name was Rose, but her identity and the truth have been lost to time."

"Isn't there a ghost named Rose at the Union Hotel in Dayton and others around Nevada or other towns in the West? For that matter, isn't there a Lady in Red that supposedly haunts the Jackson House Hotel in Eureka?"

"As I said, believe of this what you will. However, Rose does seem to have been a common name at the time. There is no known proof to back up this story, but here it goes. Supposedly during Tonopah's heyday, a prostitute named Rose had a palatial suite up on the fifth floor that encompassed the three rooms I discussed. She would bring her 'visitors' up here via that beautiful elevator to entertain them. She was known to be very kind and giving, still is, even to this day."

"Still is?"

"I'll get to that part later. According to legend, one of her jealous lovers strangled and stabbed her in a fit of rage, breaking her pearl necklace in the process. Her ghost has been encountered in the Mizpah ever since, whether that was because she became trapped here from the tragic nature of her death, or by choice. Eventually, her large boudoir was split up into three rooms. All the rooms experience activity, even though 504 got the name, but it's actually my room that generally has the most. That's actually how I met your friend.

"There's been a variety of different experiences, but the most commonly reported is men hearing a woman whispering 'sweet nothings' in their ears or a guest finding a pearl under their pillow."

"That's all very fascinating, but what does it have to do with Andre?"

"He was trying to research the history of the Lady in Red and determine the validity of the paranormal experiences. He knocked on my door and asked if I'd had any encounters. Andre is a very sweet boy. He was very apologetic for disturbing me."

"That certainly sounds like him."

"I told him that I hadn't experienced anything, but that I knew about the legend and have met many people with stories about this place."

"Not to be rude, but why did he want me to meet you? He could've passed along all this information you just gave me. Did he tell you his hypothesis?"

"About what?"

"Never mind. What was this errand he had to run?"

"I didn't ask. I just agreed to greet you if you should arrive while he was out."

I sat in silence, waiting for Andre's return. I didn't trust Persephone, but I couldn't put my finger on why. I knew I should probably just leave and wait for him downstairs or sit out in the hallway, but I didn't want to leave her company.

"Aren't there other spirits that are said to haunt this hotel as well? I think I remember hearing something about children in the halls on the fourth floor and two men in the basement?"

"Who cares about them? They're just ghosts... er... I mean boring run-of-the-mill ghosts."

"So what's so special about Rose then?"

Persephone's eyes flashed anger, if only for a second. Her tone had grown harsh. "Oh, there's nothing plain or boring about her!"

"I didn't mean to offend you. Am I missing something here?"

The tension in her body eased. Persephone sat down on the bed and regarded me with a cool stare. "I can see why the two of you are friends."

"What do you mean by that?"

"You're tenacious. A bulldog. The proverbial dog with a bone."

"Where's Andre? Shouldn't he be back by now?"

"I'm not his keeper," Persephone said in a sharp tone.

"I should go look for him. See what other people have to say." I turned to my left to retrieve my phone, which I had set on the table.

"You're not going to let this go, are you?" Her voice was right next to my ear. "Stay a while longer."

I awoke with a start. All traces of light had faded from the sky. I looked around the empty room, trying to remember where I was, and then I saw the old furniture. I realized I must have fallen asleep in the chair in Persephone's room. I pressed the button on my phone and found that three hours had passed. Where was Andre? And where was she?

I left the room and turned to knock on Andre's door, only to find it ajar. I walked in and found Persephone draped across his bed like a temptress.

"There you are! I thought we'd lost you," Persephone purred, a wicked smile on her face.

"Did you drug me?"

"How would I have done that, darling? I didn't give you a drink or anything to eat."

I shook my head, trying to shake off the confusion I felt.

"No. But... I don't know. I guess I was just more tired from the drive down than I'd realized. Where's Andre?"

"He's right there, silly girl," Persephone replied, pointing to an armchair in the corner of the room I had neglected to notice upon entering.

"Hey, Joce." Andre's glum demeanor stood in stark contrast with the enthusiasm he'd shown that morning.

"What's wrong?" I knelt by his side and peered into his face, trying to glean whether he was giving me a warning. But he wouldn't meet my eyes.

"I'm sorry. I didn't know. I shouldn't have called you."

"What didn't you know? You don't have anything to be sorry about. I will always come if you need me."

Andre turned to look at Persephone, pain in his eyes.

"You hear that, Andre, she'll always be there for you," Persephone smirked.

I glanced back and forth between the two of them, trying to figure out what I was missing. Clearly, I was on the outside of an inside joke they'd shared.

"Just spit it out! What in the hell is going on here?" I demanded. "Tell me, or I'm leaving." I rose and took two steps

11

toward the door.

"Oops... better hurry up. She's going to leave." Persephone scoffed.

I turned, my eyes blazing as they tried to burn a hole right through her.

Andre rose and took my hands, leading me to sit down in the chair he'd just vacated. "I think you should sit, and I promise I'll explain."

"You had better hurry up. I don't appreciate being the butt of your joke."

"There's no joke about it. I don't find any of this funny. I'm still trying to accept it myself, and I don't quite know how to tell you."

"Plain and simple... just spit it out, Andre."

"I think you should start at the beginning. Wasn't it Julie Andrews who said 'It's a very good place to start'?" Persephone's laugh cut me to the bone. The fuzziness in my head was beginning to clear, but my stomach felt hollow.

Andre sighed and began his story, "You know I've been researching old ghost stories, like the ones we used to tell at summer camp or read in those old kids' books, *Scary Stories to Tell in the Dark*. I was specifically looking into the lady in white stories. A young woman, dressed in a long white dress or nightgown, would be seen along a long, dark isolated stretch of road or wandering through a cemetery."

"Yes, I remember. Somebody, usually a man, would stop and give her a ride, only to find she was no longer in the car when he reached her destination. Or she'd disappear into thin air when she got out of the car. Or he'd tell somebody about her and be told she was a ghost of a young girl who had been killed on the road. Blah blah blah. Get to the point!"

"Yes, you're right. Well, ever since we moved here to Nevada to go to college, I've heard all kinds of stories about a lady in red. Another ghostly woman that appeared out of nowhere in a man's room, or a disembodied voice would speak to him in the room. Other times, he'd stop to assist a distraught woman near a room who needed help, only to have her disappear."

"Once again, I'm aware. Except this time, she's a murdered prostitute."

"Well, don't they seem eerily similar to you? I thought there might be more to it."

"I don't really believe in ghosts, unless you have something to show me, but I suppose if they did exist, one would expect the phenomena to be similar."

"That was my initial thought, but then I heard stories about otherwise healthy people who became very ill and/or died unexpectedly in hotels. Car crashes on those roads for no apparent reason. I began to wonder if they were somehow connected, so I started asking questions when I got here."

"Too many questions!" Persephone snapped. "You put your nose where it didn't belong."

I looked at Andre, trying to guess where this was going, but his stoic face gave nothing away. "What happened?"

"There had been a guy staying next door. We struck up a conversation one evening down in the bar. He told me about finding a pearl under his pillow and hearing a voice saying, 'Come over here, darlin', and let me give you some sugar.' He seemed very tired, but I didn't think too much of it. Later that evening, I heard a noise out in the hall.

"I looked out through the peephole and saw him fumbling for his key, trying to get into his room—and she was with him." Andre gestured toward Persephone lying on the bed. "The next day, I didn't see him at all. The following morning, there was a disturbance: The paramedics were called because he'd been found dead in his room. That night, I found Persephone in the bar, and I started asking her questions."

"And I gave you answers, did I not?" Persephone asked, her eyebrow cocked.

"Yeah, you sure did," Andre grumbled. "You told me a pack of lies."

"Lies that you should've accepted and walked away."

"I caught her attaching herself to another man after our discussion, and I followed the two of them up to Room 503. That's when I decided to call you. Somehow, she realized that I knew her secret and came after me that night while I was in bed. I woke exhausted and terrified, but thrilled with my discovery. It was a total adrenaline rush. I thought, if you were here, that we'd be safe. I never would have called if I thought I'd be endangering you. I swear!"

"Came after you how? Safe from what? I could have sworn you said 'succubi' before we got disconnected, but that doesn't make sense."

"Oh, but it does. Do you know what succubi are?"

"Some kind of demon or vampire, I don't know. But it's all make believe."

"Succubi are female demons. Medieval Judeo-Christian beliefs, mixed with folklore, came to describe succubi as female demons who seduced men in their dreams to collect semen. This they passed on to incubi, male demons, who corrupted it and used it to impregnate women, producing a demon-human hybrid called a cambion. Cambions serve demons and lure mortals to the abyss to be tortured."

"You're getting kind of out there, Andre. You know I don't believe in God any more than I do the devil."

"What you believe doesn't matter. You don't have to believe in something in order for it to hurt you."

"Amen to that one!" Persephone giggled.

Andre resumed with barely a breath, "Like I was saying, sometimes those succubi would end up draining the emotional, mental and physical energy of a man until he would become deathly sick or even expire, just as the women who birthed the cambion do."

"This sounds like a lot of bullshit to me. But what does all this have to do with ladies in white or the lady in red from this room?"

"They, the demons, figured out how to use our own folklore against us. They've created a symbiotic relationship with the inhabitants of these cities where the legends persist."

"That's preposterous! How?"

"The shopkeepers and motel owners of these historic cities perpetuate these myths about ghosts in order to attract tourists. The innkeepers thrive while simultaneously providing the demons with victims. The succubi feed off unsuspecting tourists while providing them otherworldly visions and experiences, and then use them for procreation, an act otherwise denied to them."

"Why would the people in the city agree to this?"

It was Persephone who answered. "Who says they did, knowingly? And in case you've forgotten, your society is greedy and self-serving, yet you call *us* demons. Why wouldn't they agree when it serves their purposes?" She raised her eyebrow questioningly.

"You know those vampire shows you love?" Andre said. "The ones where the vampires glamour victims to do whatever they say? The demons can do that, or just enter your mind through your dreams and make you do what they want." He looked defeated.

"That's impossible."

"Is it?" Persephone asked with a twinkle in her eye.

I felt fear and trepidation to hear any more of this nonsense, but those feelings were dull and... distant. I wanted to leave, but

I had to find out if this was real. To warn the world. To save Andre.

"Why would you tell Andre this? Isn't it taking a chance that your secret will get out?"

Persephone bit her lower lip and snickered as she tried to hold back her triumphant smile until the right moment. "It's time, Andre. Tell her the best part."

"The ironic part of all this... ghosts do exist."

"What?"

"Hey, we deserve a break too. A vacation every now and then. We can't have our little ruse go up in flames if the hauntings stop, so we need someone to fill in for us when we're otherwise occupied," Persephone explained.

"Why do you believe anything she's told you?"

Andre looked at me, his eyes full of pain and tears.

"You don't mean?" I pulled back in my seat, horrified, denying the possibility.

"But how can I see..."

Then it all came to me, like a ton of bricks falling on my head.

"Yep! Yep! Ding ding ding! Winner, winner! Chicken dinner! She's got it, folks!"

"You... you... you're telling me all of this because I'm..."

"Deader than a doornail," Persephone cried out with glee. "Just like Andre."

"Why do you take such joy in this? You're a demon. Why even bother with a ruse?"

"You mortals with all your goddamn TV shows, like *Supernatural* or *The Originals*. You seemed to be figuring out our secrets, and we can't have you ruining our jam. So we used your own creativity against you. We took your obsession with the paranormal and combined it with your ghost folklore to create a win-win situation.

"Well, I suppose you two aren't on the winning side, but the people of Tonopah are, and so are all the other towns with one of our kind in residence. I guess you can't win them all. There is an upside, though. You didn't believe in God or anything else. You thought you'd just, *poof!* disappear, when you died. Now you get to spend eternity here with your best friend. You can thank me anytime."

I've spent every last moment over the past ten years facing my demon, trying to take one step toward freedom. I haven't succeeded yet, but I guess I have all the time in the world to try.

"Ladies of the Night" by Sharon Marie Provost is based on the legend of the Lady in Red who is said to haunt the Mizpah Hotel in Tonopah. Though her identity has never been positively confirmed, she is thought to have been a prostitute who met her end in the hotel. The author spent the night in the room where she is said to have died, more than once. This story appears here for the first time.

Stephen H. Provost

Shadow Sentinel

When I was a young man, I lived for a time at Carson City, my brother and I often visited the St. Charles Hotel to partake of the whiskey and catch ourselves up on the gossip of the day. It was a suitable place to do so, being the headquarters of the Pioneer Stage Company, whose most reliable driver, a gentleman named Hank Monk, resided on the premises.

He would, from time to time, pass along accounts of his adventures crossing the Sierra, the most celebrated of which was his record-time delivery of Horace Greeley to Placerville for a lecture.

It is, on the surface of it, a laughable story indeed. Greeley was starting off from Carson, with Hank as his driver, and conveyed his urgent desire that no time be lost in making the trip.

Monk cracked his whip and started off at an awful pace. The coach bounced up and down in such a terrific way that it jolted the buttons all off of Horace's coat, and finally shot his head clean through the roof of the stage, and then he yelled at Hank Monk and begged him to go easier—said he warn't in as much of a hurry as he was a while ago. But Hank Monk said, "Keep your seat, Horace, and I'll get you there on time!"—and you bet he did, too, what was left of him!

That was the official story, since old Hank, naturally, wished to receive full credit for the swift delivery of his charge. But there is more to the tale, which he asked that I conceal until he had passed from this earth. This having recently occurred, I am no longer so constrained.

The truth of the matter is that Hank was so perturbed by Greeley's demands that he had made up his mind to proceed at a more leisurely pace just to spite him. It was then, near Strawberry, a popular stage stop about halfway along the route, that something fearful occurred: A giant figure resembling a great ape with the torso of Hercules and feet larger than a grizzly bear's (this was his description) suddenly crossed in front of him. It stopped there dead and stared directly at Hank from out of the shadows. As he watched, it raised its right hand high overhead and pointed at the stage with its left. A whooping sound issued forth from its mouth, followed by a series of pops and grunts... and what sounded like words, though he could not make them out.

The horses spooked and reared, and the creature resumed crossing the road until it disappeared in a tangle of trees due south. The horses, seeing it go, bolted forward at a gallop, runnin' like they were under the whip at Saratoga. They kept going that way clear on through to Placerville, and for most of the way, Hank swore he heard heavy footsteps behind him, following.

Greeley never said anything about it, so I have to conclude he blocked it out of his mind from the horror of it or had been sworn to silence by Hank. In any case, who would have believed him? He was a man of some note with a reputation to preserve.

The driver himself told me he never saw the creature again, but he never felt comfortable driving past Strawberry after that. But though he had nothing more to share with me, my curiosity was piqued, and I couldn't keep it at bay without investigating further.

If ol' Hank had fired up his horses for fear of this creature, it stood to reason that I might find corroboration of the creature's existence from other drivers known for their punctuality.

One such person was Charley Parkhurst, who had run the route between Carson and Placerville as well. But before I could track Charley down, I ran into another individual with an interesting story to tell. Like Hank he swore me to secrecy, and he seemed downright terrified at the prospect of the story getting out. I assured him I wouldn't say a word about it until after his death.

The man's name is John Thompson, but most folks know him as "Snowshoe," on account of the way he used snowshoes to convey the mail across the Sierra in winter. The truth of the matter is he used skis, but they weren't called that back then.

Anyhow, it's not commonly known, but before he slipped on his first pair of skis, Johnny also set up a business of crossing the mountains on a sleigh, just like Saint Nick, but he gave it up after encountering a creature very similar to the one Hank had described.

The main discrepancy between Hank's story and the one Johnny told me was that the creature actually conversed with him, in English, no less, although with a very strange accent punctuated by clicks and other sounds foreign to our own speech. He spoke slowly, Johnny said, not because he struggled with the language, but with an air of grave importance.

He came upon the creature in this manner: The snows were heavy that year, so he was forced to stop after driving his sleigh a certain distance beyond Lake Bigler. Seeking shelter as the clouds darkened, he diverted his sleigh from the road. He could discern from the skies overhead that the storm moving in would be treacherous. A little ways to the south, below Lover's Leap, he found a large-mouthed cave with several stones strewn across the entrance and judged it would provide a suitable refuge.

Inside, he came upon a curious sight: the skeleton of a grizzly bear, which he said measured ten feet in length and had been picked entirely clean of its meat. This was not some ancient fossil. Rather, the animal had been recently slain, as evidenced by its fur-covered skin, which lay draped over a stalagmite protruding from the cave floor nearby.

Johnny wanted to leave the place then and there, but storm clouds had been stalking him all day and had finally caught up to him, adding large quantities of swirling snow to the thick blanket already on the ground. Whatever had killed the grizzly was no longer in evidence and, he reasoned, would not be returning in what could almost be described as a blizzard. Similarly, he would have been a fool to venture back out in it.

Against his better judgment and despite his most valiant efforts he allowed himself to nod off—only to be awakened sometime later by a commotion just outside the cave. He ventured tentatively toward the opening, concealing himself behind a substantial rock, and saw to his horror another grizzly, perhaps even larger than the skeleton within, rearing up on its hind legs only a few feet outside the entrance.

To his relief, it was ignoring him, distracted as it was by something beyond his field of vision. He realized he'd been holding his breath involuntarily when he gasped at what happened next: A hairy figure—large, but not quite as large as the bear—had launched itself at the grizzly, striking it in the stomach like a charging bison and sending both of them flying backward.

In a moment, however, they both regained their feet and began circling one another like pugilists.

At first, Johnny told me, he was of the opinion that the attacker was a second bear, concealed as it was by the blinding snow. However, the storm began to abate while he was watching the two behemoths in mortal combat, and he realized then that the assailant was no bear. It was, instead, the same sort of creature that Hank had described to me—perhaps the very same creature, in fact. Could there possibly be more than one such creature of that kind on Earth? John did not know.

What he was quite aware of was being trapped there in the cave while the bear and whatever it was continued their struggle just outside. He fully expected the grizzly to prevail, being, after all, a grizzly. Yet he watched in utter amazement as the other creature, being faster and more nimble, continually avoided the bear's deadly claws and rained down blows upon it. This, unsurprisingly, enraged the grizzly more, but its fury only exhausted it as its forelegs flailed wildly and jaws snapped repeatedly on nothing but air and snowflakes.

As it tired, the other creature rushed around behind it and launched itself up onto its shoulders, wrapping both arms around its neck and pulling back hard.

The bear came crashing to the ground, but the creature did

not loosen its grip in the slightest. The bear's forelegs flailed even more madly than before as it choked and gasped for air.

So entranced was Johnny watching them, and so astonished when the creature prevailed, that he just stood there, his feet fixed to the earth, as the creature grabbed the bear's carcass by the shoulders and began dragging all 600 pounds of it into the cave. The creature had not set both feet inside when it lifted its nose in the air and began sniffing feverishly.

John attempted to shrink back into the shadows, but the animal's sense of smell was so acute that it had already turned in his direction. ("It," Johnny could now attest with full conviction, was a male.) He was, in that moment, sure that his demise was imminent, but in the next, he was just as convinced he was still sleeping and in the midst of a dream.

The creature did not attack him as it had the grizzly. It merely looked at him like a scientist studying a test subject in an experiment. Then, it spoke.

It wanted to know what Johnny was doing there and why he was sufficiently slow-witted to attempt crossing the Sierra in the midst of such a blizzard.

John told him he had been charged with bearing correspondence between men on opposite sides of the mountains. He was honor-bound to fulfill this duty—or endeavor with all his strength to do so—even should he perish in the attempt.

The creature told him that the mountains had been put there by the Great Spirit to separate the two lands and their peoples, to prevent them from making war on one another. In these mountains, he placed guardians, his race of people, to preserve the peace. Men, he said, called them "Bigfeet" and the "Hairy Ones" out of ignorance, having forgotten to honor the Great Spirit. Humans, he said, had a boorish tendency to apply names to others based on their appearance, and this was one more example of that. The creature and his people called themselves the Shadow Sentinels in their own tongue, and were sworn to their own purpose, just as Johnny was sworn to convey the messages of men across the mountains.

The Sentinel told Johnny he admired his dedication to this task; it was for this reason, he explained, that he had not crushed his skull and picked his bones clean as he had done with the grizzly.

What had the grizzly done to offend him?

The Sentinel said it had caused no offense but had attempted to remove him from the cave he was now occupying. He further explained that it provided him with plentiful nutrients, which were scarce during winter. As to why he hadn't slaughtered Johnny for the same reason, the Sentinel shrugged his massive shoulders, cocked his head to one side, and said human flesh was not to his taste, comparing it to Brussels sprouts. Johnny decided not to mention that the vegetable was one of his favorites.

Would the Sentinel kill him to prevent him from crossing the mountains?

The creature raised a hand to scratch his temple, considering, and took such a long time doing so that Johnny began to consider making a run for it. (He decided, ultimately, that the Sentinel would merely use its long legs and superior strength to catch and dismember him in any case, so he stayed where he was, fidgeting with his fingers.)

After what seemed like an eternity, the Sentinel finally responded. He would strike a bargain with Johnny, allowing him alone to pass... but only on foot. Should he see any artificial conveyances crossing the divide, he would smash them to bits and kill anyone inside. He did not speak with relish or regret, but as one simply stating an inevitability. As an afterthought, he then informed Johnny, stoically, that he had discovered his sleigh and broken it into splinters. He would collect the letters in his cargo later and bring them to Johnny, or Johnny could retrieve them himself. It made no difference to the Sentinel.

Not being in a position to debate the matter, Johnny accepted the creature's proposal. Thereupon, the creature offered to help him make modifications in his skis so as to better traverse the mountains more effectively. Having big feet, he explained, had its advantages, such that he knew the optimal surface area for traveling through the snow. It was simple evolution, he said, as though he had actually read *On the Origin of Species*. For all I know, he had.

From there, he let Johnny take his leave unmolested.

John crossed the Sierra many times after that without seeing the Sentinel again. He once sought out the cave, but never could find it again. He considered that he had, most likely, become disoriented in the blinding snow and forgotten how to find his way back to it. Yet he found no cave at all beneath Lover's Leap, no matter how thoroughly he searched. When the station owner at Strawberry told him there was not, and never had been, a cave in the vicinity, it sent a chill through his entire being. He began to doubt all the more, with the passage of time, whether the entire episode had ever occurred. Suspecting he had been seduced by a dream or taken by some enchantment, he was gripped by an oppressive sense of foreboding concerning both the creature and the cave. He wanted nothing more to do with the matter.

In later years, he told my friend and former colleague, Dan De Quille, that he had never for a single moment been lost while crossing the Sierra, and that, further, he had never seen a grizzly bear in twenty years of delivering the mail to Murphy's and Hangtown on the California side. He passed along this judiciously modified version of these events a few years after he confessed the truth to me, which led me to believe he either wished to keep it otherwise private or had convinced his own mind that they had never happened.

Yet I still had questions.

This peculiar lack of courage, even terror, in one who had repeatedly traversed the mountains under the most adverse conditions seemed peculiar. His insistence of burying the topic in the recesses of his own mind near the end only served to fire my curiosity further.

Had the creature simply honored his part of the bargain with Johnny? Had he died? Disappeared? Or had it, in fact, been a dream or exaggeration? Yet Johnny was not given to hyperbole, and it would have been difficult to imagine him inventing the strange creature's fight with a grizzly bear out of whole cloth.

I was about ready to let the matter drop when I remembered my intention to contact Charley Parkhurst. Being absentminded, I remembered it only because I happened to run into Charley, who was in attendance at my lecture in Gold Hill. It was not difficult to recognize the famed coach driver, wearing his favorite wide-brimmed hat and chomping on a fat cigar as he was wont to do.

I was waylaid by a number of former acquaintances following the lecture, most of them wanting more stories from the Sandwich Isles, which I had communicated from the stage. I feared, in the press of the throng, that Charley might slip out before I could approach him. I needn't have been concerned, as it turned out, because he approached me. We had not been acquainted before then, but he grasped my hand as though he were an old friend and congratulated me on my performance. I had to admit that I had come a long way since my first public appearance, at which I spoke so haltingly and timidly that no one in the back row heard a word that I was saying.

Yet before I had begun to lecture, I had been a newspaperman, and the instincts associated with my former profession came quickly to the fore. My innate curiosity demanded of me that I find out, once and for all, whether Charley had ever encountered the creature that had so affected both Hank and Johnny. When I inquired, he lowered his voice and said that he had, but suggested that we adjourn to somewhere more private in order to discuss it. To this, I agreed, and we reconvened a short time later in the offices of the *Territorial Enterprise*, which my former editor, Joe Goodman, opened to us at my request.

Like the two other men I had spoken with, Charley was never one to back away from a challenge. He was, by reputation, a master of the whip, which he employed to good effect on horse and man alike. Word was, he could separate a man's cigar from his mouth at fifteen paces, but he would not allow *himself* to be separated from his cargo, which frequently included silver bullion from Virginia City and gold from California. The contents of the Wells Fargo box being what they were, the stages often attracted the interest of highwaymen in search of an easy mark.

If they lay in ambush for Charley, though, they soon made a rueful discovery. One such bandit, who was known by the name of Sugarfoot, once sought to waylay Charley's stage, and came to regret it in the short life that followed. Upon demanding that the box be thrown down to him, he was set back on his heels when Charley cracked his whip and his six horses bolted. Somehow keeping hold of the reins and thus retaining control of his team, Charley drew his six-shooter and began firing away. Charley escaped unscathed, with his cargo intact, while Sugarfoot was hit by a bullet and subsequently expired from the wound.

Charley lost an eye when he was kicked in the face while shoein' one of his horses, and he wore an eyepatch ever after, but he kept drivin' his horses over the mountains, regardless of the danger.

I have shared these details here to provide the correct context for what I will say next: that this same fearless, hard-drinking, tobacco-chewing stage driver was put into a state of panic—at his own admission—by something he encountered on the road. This something, he insisted, was no highwayman, but a beast he described in the exact same terms that had been used by Hank and Johnny.

The creature, he said, chased him down from Carson Pass, spooking his horses so badly they stumbled off the road. I had heard this story before, and it had become something of a legend on both sides of the Sierra: After the horses stumbled, the coach went careening away, its wheels nearly coming apart as it struck an embankment of jagged rocks. Through it all, Charley hung on to those reins, even when the horses dragged him over the ground on his stomach. Through the sheer force of will, he managed to steer the horses back to the road, saving the coach, his team, and his passengers. It was on this singular event that Charley built his reputation, but now I came to learn that a single aspect of it was untrue. According to the story as I'd heard it, the team had been spooked by a group of wild pigs crossing Charley's path, and that is precisely what Charley himself told everyone. Now, sitting alone in an empty newspaper office with me, he told a different story: one in which no pigs were present, but the Shadow Sentinel was the cause of his team's distress.

He had done so, he said, because of an agreement he had made with the Sentinel in an earlier encounter. Charley had agreed to keep the Sentinel's existence a secret if the creature, in turn kept a secret he had revealed.

I, of course, pressed Charley as to the nature of this secret, but he would not under any condition reveal it. He seemed more concerned that he had told me the Sentinel's secret, thereby violating their oath. I wondered if Charley had told others of the creature's existence, and that this was the reason it had chased him down the pass, but if so, why should he have concocted the story of the pigs? This suspicion of mine was laid to rest when

Charley confirmed that I was the first living soul with whom he had shared the truth of the tale, and I saw, too, that he regretted doing so. A look of terror appeared on his face as he told me the oath had been bound to a curse: that his tongue would be silenced forever should he ever speak of the Sentinel.

Then he did something quite unexpected: He put his head into his hands and began to weep. I was at a loss about how to respond to this, but I took his hand and assured him that I would not repeat what he had told me. My curiosity had been satisfied, and I felt no small remorse at having been so determined to wring the truth from him. Others had told me of the creature, and I had not needed his testimony to confirm what other credible sources had already provided. Had I foreseen the profound effect upon Charley of having shared his experience with me, I would have certainly refrained from posing the question at all.

That was the last time I saw Charley Parkhurst, and I expected that whatever secret he held so tenaciously would go with him to his grave.

And so it did.

Charley died in 1879 at the age of sixty-seven and it was then that the truth was revealed beyond the grave. The coroner's report revealed, to everyone's wonderment, that Charley was, and always had been, a woman. Her given name was Charlotte, and she had concealed this from everyone in order to pursue a career as a driver. Further, a newspaper account from *The San Francisco Chronicle* declared that "an examination attested the fact of the dead woman having once been a mother."

The cause of death, the same coroner's report revealed, had been tongue cancer—which at once brought to mind Charley's reference to the curse laid upon him should he break his oath to the Sentinel: that his (or her!) tongue would be silenced forever.

Yet why had the Sentinel chased him, or her, down Carson Pass that day? This was a question that remained unanswered until some years later, when I discovered a small item in an obscure newspaper that referred to a sighting of the creature. With that creature, it was said, a smaller member of the same species had been seen.

A child.

I could not confirm what I concluded from this revelation, yet I knew instinctively beyond a doubt that this child Sentinel was Charley Parkhurst's daughter, and that his mother had left the despondent father to care for it alone.

This story was written from the perspective of Mark Twain. His love of writing satirical "quaints," presented as fact, seemed perfect for a story about Sasquatch. Hank Monk, Snowshoe Thompson, and Charley Parkhurst were all contemporaries of Twain during his time in Nevada. The historical background contained here is based on real incidents and details from their lives. Twain's own account of Hank Monk's lightning-quick journey across the Sierra with Horace Greeley in tow is recounted here. (Greeley, a candidate for president in 1872, lost in a landslide to Ulysses S. Grant—whose autobiography Twain later published.) John "Snowshoe" Thompson was, in fact, famous for delivering mail across the Sierra on skis and did, at one point, use a sleigh to complete the task. Lover's Leap is a real granite outcropping near Strawberry, a few miles west of Lake Tahoe (referred to here by the name Twain preferred, Lake Bigler)—although the photo at the beginning of this chapter is from a different Strawberry just a few miles away. Charley

Parkhurst, as stated, began life as a woman named Charlotte who lived her life as a man. The incidents involving the bandit "Sugarfoot" and the out-of-control stagecoach on Carson Pass are both historical. Parkhurst, incidentally, voted in the 1868 presidential election under her given name. The revelation that she was a woman came as the result of a coroner's inquest, which also revealed that she had given birth to a child—the basis for my final, fictional twist. The brief quote from The San Francisco Chronicle *concerning the revelation of her gender is accurate and reproduced here verbatim. "Shadow Sentinel" by Stephen H. Provost appears here for the first time.*

Sharon Marie Provost

Ancient Wonder

T he surface of the playa glimmered in the first rays of sun, reflecting the mountains towering over the alkali flats. In the middle of the Black Rock Desert, most people would have assumed that what looked like water was actually a mirage, merely heatwaves rising from the earth. But the normally barren, dry ground was covered in water from the recent string of severe summer thunderstorms, creating a primordial goop just under the surface that was nearly impossible to trudge across.

The serene pool was suddenly disturbed by vibrations underground, creating rings that expanded out across the face of the water. The salty ground split open, and an enormous 40-foot eel-like creature broke the surface. It began to move across the playa toward the dry shore where two men stood.

"Dr. Hinckley, you have to come out here now!"

"What? Where? Bromwyn, is that you?"

"Yes, sorry. I should've told you it was me. I forgot you don't have caller ID."

"Edward. I've told you to call me Edward. You haven't been my student for two decades now. And you've more than earned your right to be seen as my colleague."

"Okay... fine, Edward. Just listen to me. I know this is going to sound insane, but I literally found a living dinosaur. Well, not dinosaur. Forgive my excitement. I mean prehistoric creature, but still."

"And we're not talking about the Loch Ness Monster or Tahoe Tessie or any of those other hogwash cryptids?"

"You know that's my own private research. I would never try to involve you in that."

"Then why involve me in this?"

"You are the pre-eminent authority in paleoichthyology. You're the only man I'd trust with this information."

"First things first. Where are you exactly?"

"Northern Nevada in the Black Rock Desert."

"Well, that's a promising start. It may be a desert now, but Nevada was submerged under the ocean hundreds of millions of years ago. And they did find the largest ichthyosaur fossils there. But you said living... not fossil? Did I hear that correctly?"

"Would I call you up like a madwoman if it were just a fossil? Wait... don't answer that. But still, I'm serious. It's the biggest discovery since... since... since ever. You've got to jump on a plane and join me."

"Why, may I ask, are you out there in the Black Rock Desert? You aren't there for that crazy Burning Man Festival, are you? I swear you should've been a hippie back in the '60s."

"Yeah, yeah, I know. No, the festival is next week, but I did come out here to commune with nature. That's just it, though. We have to figure all this out before the festival happens."

"And why is that?"

"Well, if I am right, there could be a real and present danger... for everyone involved. If they've managed to survive for hundreds of millions of years undetected, we need to protect them. And I don't think any of us knows the diet of a large prehistoric fish, not in the modern world at least."

"And what is 'them' exactly? I study prehistoric fish, but you are in the desert."

"If I had to guess—mind you it was from a long distance— I'd say a previously undiscovered ancestor of the lungfish. That's what makes it so special—and plausible, at least in theory. The Black Rock Desert is a playa, an old dried-up lake bed that refills with water when it rains. Nevada may be a desert, but it has a vast system of groundwater, some of it hydrothermal."

"The prehistoric ancestors to lungfish were marine animals."

"Yes, but their modern descendants have adapted to freshwater. Maybe this one did as well."

"I suppose that's possible."

"Lungfish have gills to extract oxygen underwater, as well as primitive lungs for breathing air. Species in Africa and South America can survive protracted droughts by encasing their bodies in a mucus cocoon to conserve moisture and burying themselves in the mud. Then they enter a dormant state, dropping their metabolism to one-sixtieth the normal rate. They can live for years that way.

"You may not be familiar with the Black Rock Desert, but this playa goes through periods where it returns to a lake state multiple times each year. Plus, with all that warm groundwater bubbling to the surface out there, it may add to their ability to stay alive. It seems unbelievable, but it is technically possible. Right?"

"I suppose. I'm the last one to say that anything is impossible. In this year alone, we've had several significant discoveries in the world of paleoichthyology. But what you're saying goes beyond finding new species of extinct fish."

"Can you do me a favor and just look at what I've collected? I have pictures—before you ask, I took them myself—and I've done a lot of research on lungfish. Just take the day and think about it. Then call me tomorrow, or better yet, jump on a plane. Please?"

Edward never could say no to Bromwyn. She'd been the most accomplished student he'd had in 40 years of teaching. She might be a bit of a hippy and subscribe to a preposterous belief in the existence of cryptids, but she was incredibly knowledgeable and a thorough researcher.

"Send it all to my home email. I'll look at it tonight, and then I'll be in touch. No promises though, Bromwyn."

"Okay. Great! I totally get it, but trust me, we're going to be famous. Fuck *Jurassic Park*! That's just a movie. This is reality." Bromwyn hung up without saying goodbye in her hurry to get the information sent to Edward.

When Edward got home that night, he put a Hungry Man dinner in the microwave while he went to his office to retrieve his laptop.

He pulled a beer out of the fridge and logged in to see this "groundbreaking" proof.

Bromwyn had sent him a long email detailing all her experiences and her research on lungfish, along with six pictures and a video. Edward resisted the urge to jump straight to the photos, instead reading her email first:

Edward,

Thanks for agreeing to look at this. I wouldn't have reached out if I wasn't confident of its validity. I guess I should start at the beginning. Like I told you, I went out to the Black Rock Desert on vacation.

When I got there, I found much of the playa was closed to the public. I went into town that day to get some ice, and I asked them why. The "story" is they close roughly 33 percent of the playa, the section that will be part of Burning Man, to help preserve the environment before the large onslaught of people.

That made sense to me, but at the same time, something felt off. They seemed nervous about me asking. I rose early the next morning, before the sun, and I couldn't see what harm I could do just taking a walk out there. I took my sketchbook and sat down to draw the beautiful scene before me.

I saw ripples appear in the water, like when a drop of water falls into a pool or the effect from a strong vibration. At first, I thought it had started to rain, but my notion was soon dispelled by another sight: A gigantic fish that looked like an eel rose out of the water, and it began to skim across the surface. It must have been 40 or 45 feet long.

When the water got too shallow, it began to "crawl," using its lobed fins and body to pull itself across the sandy muck, even rising off the ground in a quadrupedal fashion. I know this all sounds fantastical, but I haven't even gotten to the most shocking part yet.

While I claimed this discovery, that's not quite true. Other people already knew... at least two men, for sure, wearing BLM shirts, were out there when the creature

SHARON MARIE and STEPHEN H. PROVOST

arose, and it came to them.

To be fed, Edward. Like a goddamn dog.

They fed it a cow. A live fucking cow! It scarfed it down like it was candy.

I mentioned danger. That danger extends not only to the fish itself, but to all the people who will be there during Burning Man. I'm assuming they fed it to keep it alive, but also so that it doesn't eat all the partiers coming to the area. Full belly, happy fish, right?

The forecast calls for record-breaking hot, dry days over the next week, so the playa should dry up quickly. If my hypothesis is correct, the creature should go dormant again until the moisture returns. But what meteorologist do you know that's accurate about the weather at all times? It rained there a couple of years ago during the festival and created a real mess. What if that happens again, and the giant eel, or whatever it is, awakens from its dormant state at the wrong time?

I know this all sounds incredible, but you'll see what I mean when you look at the pictures and the video. Lungfish are the closest living relatives to the tetrapods, meaning all four-limbed vertebrates: amphibians, reptiles, birds, and mammals. That would explain this fish's ability to ambulate.

Lungfish have hard plates in their mouths in order for them to eat their usual diet of hard-shelled invertebrates like snails, mollusks, and shrimp. This prehistoric creature is sure to be carnivorous as well, and it probably dined on other large fish, giant squids, and who knows what else. We can't let humans be the replacement in their modern diet.

I'm anxiously awaiting your call. Just come here, Edward. Book a redeye.

—Bromwyn

Edward took a deep breath after finishing the letter. He didn't know what to think. Bromwyn had never been one prone to histrionics or exaggeration.

If she's that scared, there must be something to it. But what?

There was only one thing to do: It was time to look at her evidence.

Edward clicked on the first picture and was startled to see an immense marbled dark-grey with black fish with an elongated body. It had a long tail that tapered at the end with long spaghetti-like thin pelvic and pectoral fins. Its body, reminiscent of an eel, was at least ten times longer than its head.

True to what Bromwyn said, it appeared to be about 45 feet long, which became apparent in the pictures as it approached the men on shore when the cow was used for scale. His breath caught in his throat as he flipped from one picture to the next. Her discovery was breathtaking and terrifying at the same time when he saw the cow in its gaping maw.

He wasn't prepared to watch the video, but he had to see it move for himself. He couldn't imagine what would ever bring Bromwyn to manufacture evidence, but he had learned to never trust anyone fully. He was by no means a video expert, but he felt confident he'd notice anything hinky.

But there wasn't anything to question.

Except maybe his sanity.

Bromwyn was right. He needed to get there immediately so he called the airline and booked a redeye to Reno, Nevada. The flight left in a few hours, so he hastily typed out an email to the president of the college claiming a family emergency. He packed his duffel bag with all the equipment he'd need for documentation and testing before calling an Uber to take him to the airport.

As he buckled his seatbelt on the plane, he texted Bromwyn, "I'm on my way. Can you pick me up at the Reno Airport at 10 a.m.?"

Edward awoke bleary-eyed five hours later to the roar of the thrust reversers fighting to slow the plane down. Zephyr winds over the mountains had fought against the plane's descent, so the pilot had to come in hard and fast, the jet bouncing down the runway before the brakes engaged... hard.

"Whoa, Nellie!" the flight attendant said with a laugh.

I didn't know I was going to the rodeo.

Edward grabbed his bags from the overhead bin and surged to the head of the line to exit the plane. When he came down the escalator to the lobby, he saw Bromwyn's beaming face waiting for him.

"Thank you so much for coming. I didn't know what else to do. To be honest, I don't know if two paleoichthyologists are enough to convince somebody to do something, but we have to try." Bromwyn wrapped him in a bear hug and grabbed the small backpack he'd stuffed with a few changes of clothes.

Bromwyn stopped at Starbucks to get them both coffee before she started the nearly three-hour drive back out to the desert. They discussed their game plan for gathering more proof: Finding out how many people knew about the creature—and *what* they knew.

"It's not going to be easy, Dr.... Edward. They're clamping down real tight on access to the playa since yesterday because it's so close to the festival. We're probably going to have to sneak in."

"Are you kidding? I'm a scientist who studies prehistoric

fish, not Indiana Jones. In case you didn't notice, I'm going to be 65 this year."

"A hot, spry 65 at that, Edward." Bromwyn playfully punched his shoulder and laughed, winking when he raised his eyebrows at her. "It won't be quite as bad as you're imagining. I do have a friend that lives not far from the playa on a ranch. He's willing to lend us his quads. We'll just have to start out before dawn so we're not seen by anyone."

"That doesn't sound like a lot of protection from a prehistoric sea... or should I say, *lake* monster, now does it?"

"Well no, but it'll be worth it in the end. We'll stay back from the water's edge. Deal?"

"So what's in that cooler in the back? Beer and some sandwiches, I hope."

"Not exactly. More of a snack for Phoenix."

"And who exactly is Phoenix?"

"Oh yeah, the fish. I'm calling him Phoenix the Playa Leviathan. I thought it was cute to symbolize the rebirth of an ancient species believed to be extinct."

"Leviathan is right, but believed to be extinct is not quite correct though. We didn't even know it *had* existed."

"Well, it's close enough. There's a reason I never had pets or children. I never said naming someone was my strong point."

Edward guffawed until he was hoarse. "May I see this snack for Phoenix?" He reached into the back and grabbed the handle, tipping the cooler slightly as he pulled it up front.

"Watch out!" Bromwyn yelled when water sloshed out onto both of them.

Edward set the cooler on the floor between his feet. "What's in there?"

"Fish. Live fish, hence the water."

"And why do we need live fish for Phoenix?"

"I figured that was the best way to call him out. It seemed logical that a struggling fish might capture his attention, just like it would with a shark. It's Plan B, just in case he doesn't come out on his own at dawn."

"You've thought of everything, haven't you?"

"I had this real hard-ass professor back in college. He taught me to be thorough."

"Sounds like a good man."

"The best," Bromwyn said with a smile.

Bromwyn and Edward rose at 3 the next morning and rode out to the northern edge of the playa. When they arrived, the faintest traces of light had just begun to appear in the sky. The playa was still awash in an inky pool of darkness.

"Where were the men that day?" Edward asked as he pulled out a pair of night vision goggles.

"Where the hell did those come from, Mr. I'm Not Indiana Jones?"

"It's all part of my obsession with being thorough. One must also be prepared. So I made a little stop at Cabela's before I went to the airport."

Bromwyn tried to squelch a laugh, but it escaped with a loud snort. "I would've paid money to see you in there."

"Hell! That's not the half of it. I don't think any of the employees will soon forget the senior running in with a limp five minutes before closing yelling, 'It's an emergency! Where can I find your night vision goggles?' They probably think I'm some kind of pervert."

Bromwyn couldn't stop laughing, her face turning red as she tried to catch her breath. "Stop it! Stop it! You're killing me. And we're supposed to be here incognito, not broadcasting our location far and wide."

"You asked. Now back to the matter at hand. Where were they and where did you see Phoenix come up? There's still quite a bit of water out here. What are they going to do if it doesn't dry up soon?"

"The men were over there to the west." Bromwyn pointed to an area about a half a mile to the north of the 12 Mile Playa Access Point. "And Phoenix came up out there, pretty much in the center of the pooling."

Edward began searching the alkali flat along the area she had pointed out. After a few minutes, he put down the goggles and turned to Bromwyn. Except she wasn't there. He'd been so engrossed in his search, he hadn't noticed her get up and wander away.

"Bromwyn! Get back here now," Edward whisper-yelled. "The coast is clear. Now's our chance."

Bromwyn had wandered about 50 feet away from him, where the water was up to the ankles of her Xtratuff boots. She was bent over, looking at something.

"What are you doing anyway?"

Bromwyn stood up with a smile on her face and a wiggling fish in her hand. As she turned toward him, she didn't notice the large serpentine fish rising out of the pool on the playa.

"Bromwyn!"

"Fuck!" Her eyes widened in terror when she felt the water drip on her back seconds before the fish grabbed her and pulled her beneath the silty water. Edward ran to grab her hand before it disappeared from sight, but he was too late.

Edward stood, dumbstruck, staring at the place where she'd disappeared. He knew he had lost her, barring a miracle... a miracle that never came. As the sun began to rise high in the sky, he made the only decision he could. He jumped on the quad, still choking back tears, and rode back to the ranch. He'd found Bromwyn's car keys in her pack on her quad, so he drove into town to the Washoe County Sheriff's Office.

Edward ran into the office and up to the desk. "Help! I need to speak to the sheriff now. This is an emergency!"

The woman looked at him as if he were high. He couldn't blame her. She was probably used to dealing with way too many pot-smoking party animals.

"My name's Dr. Edward Hinckley. I'm a paleoichthyologist, and something has happened to my colleague."

"Just a moment, sir." The woman rose and casually made her way back to get the sheriff, who was already staring at him through the blinds of his glass-enclosed office. The woman rolled her eyes as she relayed the information. Then the sheriff rose, hitched up his pants, and cleared his throat before coming out.

"What's this emergency, sir? We don't take kindly to pranks here. We're about to enter our busiest season of the year, and we don't have any time to be dealing with bullshit. Am I making myself clear?"

"Do I look like a teenager pulling a prank? I'm 65 years old for fuck's sake. I, likewise, do not have time to convince an officer of the law to do his job. Do you have a supervisor?"

"I am in charge here. Shall we take a seat in my office and file a formal report? Mind you, filing a false report is a crime."

Edward followed the sheriff back to his office and took the proffered seat. "My colleague, Dr. Bromwyn O'Kelly, is dead. You need to cancel that Wicker Man, or whatever you call that stupid festival, immediately before more people die."

"Slow down here. Are you talking about Burning Man? And just why exactly would we do that? Do you know how much money has been spent on preparations and how many thousands of people are on their way here as we speak—from all over the world, I might add?"

"I get it. I do. But do you want to be responsible for the

biggest scandal the world has ever seen? I will hold you personally responsible for any deaths that will occur if you don't stop this."

"Have you been drinking or taking any illicit drugs?"

"No, of course not."

"Then why don't you start at the beginning. Who is this murderer you're rambling about?"

"Not who. What! As I'm sure you heard me tell your secretary, I'm a paleoichthyologist."

"Forgive my ignorance, I'm just a lowly country bumpkin here." The sheriff affected a mocking country drawl as he spoke. "But what the fuck is that?" he asked, his voice thundering through the small office.

"I study prehistoric fish: their physiology, behavior, evolution, and ecology. It is crucial to our understanding of modern biodiversity, and to our conservation of underwater ecosystems."

"Well la-di-da! What the fuck does that have to do with people dying?"

"My colleague discovered a prehistoric fish, an ancient wonder one might call it, living here in Nevada in your Black Rock Desert. We were out on the playa near 12 Mile early this morning to study it when the fish grabbed her."

"How exactly were you out at 12 Mile? That area's been closed to the public by the BLM since July 24th. So you're admitting to a crime before you even get to this emergency you're all riled up about?"

"Well yes, I guess that's true. We rode on quads out to the area where she first saw it. We had no intention of harming the environment. In fact, we were trying to do the opposite. Our whole mission was to save this ancient wonder, as well as anyone whom might be harmed by it. It's not evil; it's just trying to survive like any animal in the wild."

"I just want to understand this situation fully. You said this is a fish, am I right?"

"Correct."

"When I went to school, I was taught... or better yet, when I go fishing on the weekends with my buddies, we go to the water. A lake, pond, the crick behind my house, the ocean, but you know, someplace with water. Because Mrs. Watts, my second-grade teacher, taught me fish live in the mother-fuck-ing WATER! Yet you're telling me that a giant, dinosaur fish ate your friend in the middle of the playa, an alkali flat."

"But there's water on it now. And there's a species of fish in Africa and Australia that can..."

The sheriff bellowed over the top of Edward, "Lucille, please escort this fucking crackpot out of my office now before I have to arrest him!"

Lucille scurried into the office and linked her arm through Edward's before leading him out the door.

"But the BLM... Those guys know about it. They're feeding it. Talk to them!" Edward cried out as they reached the lobby.

"I'll get right on it, asshole!"

Lucille shut the door hard before Edward could say anything more.

Edward drove back out to the ranch owned by Bromwyn's friends. He had to prepare before Burning Man started. It might be impossible to find a way in once the festival was underway: They'd probably have someone sitting at the gate, watching for him. But he had to try. It was already Wednesday, and the gates would be opening on Sunday.

He looked up the weather, and it wasn't good news. An extended storm front was headed for the area. The Weather Service was predicting thunderstorms every day for the next two weeks, starting Saturday.

The gates opened at noon on Sunday to a partly sunny sky, and the line of cars stretched out for miles down the Burner Byway. The Black Rock City Dashboard on the Burning Man webpage listed the current wait time at the gate at over eight hours.

The playa had dried out between Wednesday and Saturday, but it wouldn't take much rain to change the situation—and fast. Rainfall was predicted to be light on Sunday, and Edward knew his only chance of sneaking into Black Rock City would be at night early in the event. He couldn't do it too soon, or he'd stand out like a sore thumb, but if he waited too long, the city would be full of people and someone was bound to notice him.

But the forecast was wrong. Instead of a light rain, the heavens opened up and sent down a deluge Sunday. The old lakebed filled up quickly, forcing organizers to close the gate. Campers were told to avoid driving around on the mucky ground and to stay in place because of the many lightning strikes in the area. Edward convinced Bromwyn's friend to give him a ride to the north side of the playa in the middle of the night Monday. It would be up to him to make it into Black Rock City from there.

Edward began the long slog through the muck, which was more akin to sticky maple and brown sugar oatmeal than normal mud. He hiked through the night, keeping to the edge as much as he could, always watching out for any sign of the fish.

When he arrived on the fringes of Black Rock City just as dawn broke, he looked like Arnold Schwarzenegger in the climactic scene from *Predator*. A small group camped on the edge of the city welcomed him in.

"Dude, what happened to you?" a young man with dreads asked Edward as he offered him a cup of coffee. "I'm Josh, by the way."

"I went out for a walk last night and lost my way. Perils of being a weak old man: I got stuck in all that mud and fell down."

Edward held out his arms, displaying his mud-streaked self from head to toe.

"That's harsh, man. No worries. We got some extra clothes around you can use. Molly, can you grab them?" Josh said, lighting up his bong with a smile.

"Thank you very much. I should probably just pack up and go though. I'm pretty sure my tent's toast after all that wind last night."

"No way, man. This your first time out here?"

"Yes."

"That makes more sense now. It's always hard your first time... not knowing what to bring or how to prepare for being out on the playa. Burning Man's all about sharing and surviving. We've got you, dude. You'll stay with us. We have plenty, right everybody?" Josh held out a bong to Edward.

Edward put his hand up to decline as the group cheered his addition to their ranks. Edward helped with the cooking and took advantage of their laidback mindset so he could keep watch for any sign of the creature.

As late afternoon approached, the dark clouds built up. It wasn't long before the lightning strikes began, and the rain started pouring down. Many of the Burners retired to their shelters during the deluge, but there were still far too many people out on the playa, putting themselves at risk.

Edward scanned the horizon for any sign of the fish's arrival. He could only hope its belly was still full from the large meals it had ingested over the past week. He moved toward the center of Black Rock City and worked to convince the revelers to join the many parties that had started up in the bigger encampments.

Heedless of the warnings not to drive on the playa during the rain, many of the burners had begun to operate mutant vehicles, along with other cars and bicycles adorned with lights. They were disturbing the water, which made it difficult for Edward to watch for any warning signs. On top of that, the vibrations and sound waves traveling through the water were likely to awaken the fish.

Edward watched a young woman climb aboard one of the art installations that looked like a vibrant multicolored ship on the water. She was straddling the bowsprit and using her hands to pull herself out to the end of it. Suddenly, movement in the sand underneath the ship caused it to dip, throwing her off onto the ground... hard, knocking the wind out of her.

The woman sat up and strained to catch her breath.

Just like Bromwyn, she failed to sense the danger.

Edward watched in horror as the head of the Playa Leviathan rose from underneath the woman and swallowed her whole.

"Oh my God! Run! Get out of here, everybody!" Edward screamed until he was out of breath. After a few moments, he realized that no one was moving. Instead, they were standing there staring at him as if he'd lost his mind.

"Geezer's on a bad trip," a young man dressed in a muddy furry costume snickered.

"Nothing magic about those mushrooms," a topless woman in her 50s replied.

"Didn't you see it? None of you... at all? It ate her. That giant fish swallowed her," Edward cried out in frustration.

"The only great white whale here is you, old man. Go sleep it off, man. You're ruining our fun." The man wearing a tight rainbow tie-dye jumpsuit pushed Edward toward the encampment.

Edward turned just in time to see several Burning Man officials approaching him from different directions. A burly man grabbed his arm, just before another one punched him, knocking him out cold.

Edward awoke several hours later in a tent. The noise of the festival was dim and far away. He sat up and grabbed his head as pain rolled through.

"Where am I?" he called out.

"It's 'bout time you woke up. You need to answer some questions." An official from the Burning Man Festival came into view.

"Who the fuck are you? I'm leaving. I don't owe you any explanations."

"You ain't going nowhere, asswipe. We've got a great thing going here, and you're sure as hell not going to ruin it."

Edward looked shocked. "You know about what's going on out there, and you aren't canceling the festival?"

"Of course, we do. Why would we cancel it?"

"People could die. That young woman just did. My colleague did a few days ago. You have a responsibility to keep your attendees safe."

"And we do... for the most part, anyway. You can never prevent all accidents. People will get electrocuted, fall off structures to their death, get hit by cars, hell... murdered even. And then there's the occasional partier who gets eaten by that fish out there. But we do the best we can."

"But..."

"But nothing. They all know it's risky. They come here anyway. They pay us thousands of dollars and sign their waivers acknowledging the risks. They leave the rest up to us. It's big business, and we aren't giving it up because of a few little deaths. Now it's your turn to give me some answers. Who did you tell about what you know?"

"The sheriff."

The official started snickering. "Barry was paid off a long time ago. Who else?"

"No one. We were trying to get the proof before we took it

to the world. We didn't want anyone thinking we were crazy."

"Who knows you're out here?"

"No one. I left in a hurry."

"What about this colleague of yours?"

"As far as I know, no one. She's single."

"Great. Just as we thought. Get up. You're coming with me."

Edward rose shakily to his feet. "Where are you taking me?"

"You're the dino fish guy, right? I've arranged a behind-the-scenes tour for you to meet your... damn. I can't remember what Barry said. Hmm... what did you call it again? Ancient wonder? Yes, that's it! Ain't that sweet of me?" The man dragged Edward by the arm out of the tent.

They reached a dark area on the playa a few minutes later. Then they climbed up on a temporary wood platform that had been erected there. Edward could see the hustle and bustle of Black Rock City in the distance. The man held a small metal whistle to his lips, one like the trainers use at Sea World to call the dolphins. He blew into it, and a short time later, Edward saw movement in the darkness in front of him.

The man gave Edward a brutal shove off the platform. He landed with a splash and looked up to see Phoenix only ten feet away.

"Hope you enjoyed your first, and last, experience at Burning Man," the man said with a laugh.

Then he turned and walked away.

"Ancient Wonder" by Sharon Marie Provost appears here for the first time.

Stephen H. Provost

Extinction Event

"Are we there yet?"

Little Lisa knew quite well that they weren't "there yet," because they weren't really going anywhere. But she was a fussy 3-year-old, which was like a Terrible 2 with a bigger vocabulary.

This was not a destination vacation for the Oswalds. Chuck and Clara had decided to do something different this summer and take their kids on what they called an "edu-cation" instead.

It had been Clara's idea. She'd seen a piece on *Sunday Morning* about a family who'd played a game with their kids called "Buffalo Bingo" on a road trip to Yellowstone. Unlike regular bingo, everyone's card was the same. The squares were marked with different animal symbols, with the buffalo in the center. The first one to call out a sighting got credit for that square, but others could still catch up if they spotted another squirrel, deer, or crow down the road.

"Isn't it brilliant?!" she had enthused.

Chuck had been less excited. He'd been planning a trip to Maui and had even booked a room at Napili Shores, where his parents had taken him as a kid. But they couldn't afford to do both trips, so he'd had to cancel.

"It's for the kids, Chucky," Clara had told him, laying a hand on his shoulder. He knew, when she did that, it was Game Over. Some wives used the gesture to comfort their husbands, but with Clara it meant "I ain't changin' my mind."

The kids hadn't been too happy about it either. The twins, 15-year-old Piper and Desmond, had wanted to spend the summer "hanging out," while 12-year-old Carl had complained he was too old for silly games. Not that he was, necessarily, but he was at the age where he needed to *believe* he was. Besides, he'd overheard his parents arguing about how they would spend the summer, and he would have much rather gone to Maui.

"How long *must* we keep doing this?" Piper whined.

"Until one of you gets a bingo," of course, Clara said, looking over her shoulder from the passenger's seat.

"C'mon, mom, that's never gonna happen." Piper leaned forward and thrust her bingo card in front of her mother's nose. Every space had an X on it except for the one in the center: the elk. Clara had changed the game because there weren't any buffalo in Nevada. But now it was starting to look like there weren't any elk here either.

"Yeah, mom," Desmond said. "All our cards look like that."

"If you keep on complaining, we'll have to send you back to

regular school," Clara said.

Piper sighed dramatically. Clara pulled this card whenever one of the kids started bitching about some homeschool lesson they didn't like. It always worked, partly because Clara had painted this picture of "regular school" as a military boot camp where the students were a bunch of potheads and bullies, the teachers were all pervs. Actually, just one of the teachers *had* been a perv, and none of the kids had ever been in the weirdo's classroom. He'd been fired, arrested, and was currently "enrolled" in the Lovelock Correctional Center. But none of that made any difference. Clara talked about public school the way some parents talked about hell, as a place reserved for delinquents and morons beyond any hope of redemption.

This time, though, Desmond didn't keep his mouth shut. "We've only got two years left," he said. "How bad can it be?"

"Desmond..." Chuck's voice was laced with warning. When it came to "good cop, bad cop," mom was the bad cop until things got bad. Then he became judge, jury, and probation officer.

"You know what *I* think?" Carl said, squirming in the backseat. "I think the elks are all extinct."

"Elk," his mother corrected. "The plural of elk is elk."

"Yeah," said Piper. "Elks live in lodges. They're a bunch of old guys, but they aren't extinct yet."

"I'm serious," Carl said, leaning forward. He was sitting in the third row of seats with Lisa, who was twirling her hair and pulling it around into her mouth. He ignored her. "Remember what mom taught us about megafauna. Slowths..."

"Sloths."

"And mastodons and mammoths and giant beavers."

Desmond snickered, and Piper punched him hard in the shoulder, then turned back to look at Carl. "Don't be silly."

But Carl persisted. "Elk are big like that," he said. "Besides, have *you* seen any on this trip?"

Piper rolled her eyes. "If I had, we'd be done with this stupid game."

Desmond sat up excited and pointed out the window. "Look!" he shouted. "I see one!"

Everyone looked where he was pointing.

"That's a *sign*, stupid."

"With an elk on it! That means they *have* to be around here somewhere."

"I've seen those signs before, and there's never been any elk," Piper said. "We didn't even see any in that city, Elk-o."

"See!" Carl said. "That's what I mean! They're extinct."

"You've convinced me," Piper snarked. "Now can we *please* just *go home*?"

"I have to go pee pee," Lisa whined. It was the voice she used when she *really* had to go. She was hugging her Bubu panda doll tight, as if doing so would help her hold it longer. Then, suddenly, she rolled down the window and declared, "Bubu has to go too!" In the same instant, she tossed the stuffed panda with the rosy red cheeks out the window.

"Daddy! Daddy! Stop! We can't leave Bubu behind!"

Chuck screeched to a halt and pulled off to the side of the road. They were in the middle of nowhere, without a restroom in sight. He ran around the side of the van and jogged back about fifty yards. The roadside was covered in sagebrush and rabbitbrush, so he had to do some hunting before he found the Bubu panda lodged halfway under a sagebrush plant, covered in dust. He pulled it free with some difficulty, cursing as the side of it snagged on the bush and tore. Some of the stuffing stayed behind in the brush, and he hastily pulled it free, pushing it back inside the bear.

"Pandas aren't bears," Clara always said. The kids always

called her a know-it-all behind her back. In the cartoon, Bubu had a boyfriend named Dudu, who actually *was* a bear. Was she aware when she bought the doll that she was advocating cross-species sexuality? Didn't she know that would confuse the kids? Carl had overheard that conversation, too. So had Lisa. She'd started to cry, and Carl had told her that Dad didn't know what he was talking about. Dudu was the best boyfriend in the world.

Chuck had a wet wipe for his glasses in his pocket, which he pulled out and started rubbing vigorously against the panda's once-white felt skin, but it only spread the smudge out.

"Dammit!"

He pulled more of the stuffing out and started throwing it around in a fit of rage, then hucked the poor disemboweled panda as far as he could throw it. Brushing off his pants, he stomped back to the car.

"Well?" Clara prompted, scrutinizing him.

"Couldn't find it," he huffed.

Lisa burst into tears. "Bubu! My Bubu! Waaaaaaaaah!"

Clara scowled, her face darkening. "You need to keep looking." Her tone brooked no argument.

"Fine!" Chuck said.

"Ohmygod!" Piper said. "Just buy her another one! They're, what, twenty bucks on Amazon?"

Clara tried to stay calm. "It's not the same. She's had Bubu since she was a baby."

"Ugh!" Piper replied, clenching her fists. "She said she had to go to the bathroom, remember?"

"Too late," Carl said. "She peed her pants."

"Well, we can't clean her up here," Chuck said. "*Someone* forgot to pack the baby wipes." He looked at Clara, raising his eyebrows, but Clara's scowl just deepened.

"Maybe because she ISN'T A BABY ANYMORE!" she nearly

shouted.

"Whatever," said Piper. "She's not the only one who has to pee."

"Had to," Desmond corrected, which earned him another punch in the arm.

"We aren't anywhere near a bathroom," Clara announced. They'd passed a blue sign a few miles back that announced the next rest area wouldn't appear for 128 miles.

"Then maybe we should stop arguing and get back on the road, hmmm?" Chuck suggested through gritted teeth.

"Wait," said Carl. "What's that up there?"

He pointed.

They all saw it then, a short distance up the road, although somehow no one had noticed it before.

Suddenly, everyone forgot about Bubu—except for Lisa, who was sitting there sobbing quietly. Carl started rubbing her back gently, trying to calm her, and she hiccupped, then curled up against the door and cried herself to sleep.

The building up ahead looked like a family farm, with a big aluminum barn, one of those old-fashioned water towers enclosed in a wooden frame, and a what looked like a silo or grain elevator. A small A-frame house that looked like it hadn't been painted in twenty years stood off to the side, a few yards from a stone chimney, a remnant of some pioneer settlement on the site. But the most remarkable—and disconcerting—feature of the property was its arched entrance, the kind often seen at the entrance to ranches. This one was different, though. It appeared, from a distance, to have been formed completely out of sheared and shattered bones. But as the Oswalds drew closer, they realized it was composed instead of antlers, which were strung along the barbed-wire fence enclosing the property as well. There were deer antlers, pronghorn antlers, even a couple of horns from bighorn rams. But by far the majority of the antlers belonged to a different species.

"What are those?" Carl asked.

"Elk horns," his mother said.

"See, dumbass?" Desmond needled him. "They're not extinct after all."

"They're not *alive*, are they?" Carl retorted.

Piper got out of the car and stood there, shifting uncomfortably from one foot to another. "As long as they have a bathroom, they can hang as many of those creepy horns as they want to. Come on. Let's go."

Chuck shook his head slowly. "I'm not sure I like the look of that place," he said. "It's private property, and I see a 'no trespassing' sign up there on the fencepost. Who knows what kind of people live there?"

"Well, there's only one way to find out," Desmond said. He got out of the car, slammed the door, and began power-walking up the road to the gateway. Piper followed, trying to keep up in her pumps and calling, "Wait for me!"

Chuck got back out of the car again and leaned back in through the window. "Stay here with Carl and Lisa," he told his wife. "I'm going to see what's up." Without waiting for an answer, he took off at a sprint and was able to overtake Piper, then Desmond, right as they got to the gate. He stepped in front of them, forcing them to stop, and the three of them stared up at the antler arch. It was even creepier up-close.

"Just stay here for a minute. I'll go in and see what kind of place this is—and if they even have a restroom."

He was using that "I'm the dad, so don't fuck with me" tone. Desmond looked skyward with an exaggerated eyeroll, and Piper was downright hopping back and forth on her feet, but neither one questioned it. They just watched as their father strode up the dirt driveway and veered off to the side, heading up to the dilapidated farmhouse. The door opened, and a man appeared.

They could barely make him out in the shadows of the entrance, but they saw him motion for their father to step inside.

Then he was gone.

Clara was on her third wet wipe, cleaning Lisa up. She'd peed all over herself, and Carl had been sent to the back to retrieve a change of clothing from the suitcase. Somehow, Piper had been able to hold it, but her bladder's biological clock was ticking. She and Desmond had given up on waiting at the gate and come back to the car.

"Dad's been in there almost ten minutes. Don't you think we should go in after him?" she whined.

Her eyes moved from her mother's face to Desmond's, but no one answered. Clara was too busy tending to Lisa, and Desmond was being his usual annoying self.

"Fuck it," she said finally. "Mom, let me know if anyone's coming." She ran around to the far side of the car, so it shielded her from the road, then she squatted, and pulled down her pants. The sound of fast-running liquid followed, along with a satisfied "Ah"... and then "Goddammit! I got it on my shoes!"

Desmond started laughing as Carl came around with Lisa's red dress with the white trim—the one that made her look like Little Red Riding Hood.

"I'll go," Carl said as his mother helped Lisa into the new outfit. She started smiling. It was her favorite.

"You'll go where?" his mother asked.

"Up to the house, to see why Dad's taking so long."

His mother gave him that look she always gave him whenever he volunteered to do something that she found utterly ridiculous. "You'll do no such thing. I'm going. And you two..." She looked at Desmond and Piper "...are coming with me. Carl, you stay here and look after your sister. Your dad's probably in there looking at old highway maps or something."

"Or maybe he's busy clogging up that poor guy's toilet." Piper laughed, and Desmond joined right in.

"Not funny, you two. Now that everyone's answered the call of nature, we need to get going so we can find that elk."

Piper threw back her head in frustration. "Like we'll *ever* find it," she said, overacting like she was auditioning for that part in *Romeo and Juliet* she didn't get last spring.

"We won't," Carl muttered, "'cause they're extinct."

Clara took both of them by the scruffs of their necks, like she had when they were young, and marched them away, up toward the weird cabin. When they got there, they knocked, and the same guy opened the door. Then they went inside.

"Where's mommy and daddy?" Lisa whined.

It had been twenty more minutes, and Carl was getting antsy too. "They're up in that house," he said.

"We should go find them," Lisa said, pounding her little fist on her knee the way she'd seen their mother do when she'd decided to do something. "Ow," she said. "That hurt."

Carl patted her on the head. "It's okay, sis. I think you're right. We should go up and find them."

They got out of the car, and a squirrel dashed out into the road.

"Sqwirl!" Lisa shouted, pointing and jumping up and down.

Carl turned at the sound of a Ram pickup barreling up the highway at 20 miles an hour over the speed limit. "Look out, Lisa," he said, grabbing her hand, but she pulled away.

"Sqwirl!" she squealed again and took a step toward the highway. They hadn't seen a single car out here in the past two hours, and now this guy was almost on top of them.

And he wasn't slowing down.

The driver didn't even try to swerve. The car just ploughed

on through, and there was a sickening thud. Carl winced as he lunged toward Lisa, pulling her back at the last second.

"Nooooooooo!" Lisa shrieked as she saw the squirrel reduced to a pancake of blood and bones and fur, unrecognizable as it lay there in the road. It'd had enough time to move, but the truck had startled it, and it froze in place, looking back and forth to both sides of the highway instead of running for its life. The poor animal had been in a state of shock. It didn't know what a pickup was. It just knew that something big was coming at it, and it didn't know what to do, so it had just stopped there, like it thought it could stand up to that big whatever-it-was that was racing toward it, either not knowing or not caring it was even there.

Lisa turned and buried her head in Carl's chest, sobbing.

"I'm sorry, sis," he said, stroking her hair. He was shaking himself, not so much from what had happened to the squirrel as from what would have happened to Lisa if he hadn't grabbed her hand. Lisa didn't even seem to know that she'd almost been run over. All she cared about was that poor little squirrel, which had gone out on a grand adventure that morning, never knowing that this day would be its last.

"C'mon," Carl said softly. "Let's go find Mom and Dad."

Carl had a bad feeling when he put his hand on the gargoyle door knocker, the same kind of feeling he'd had when the police showed up at the door, telling them Aunt Barbara had died. It was somewhere between not feeling hungry and feeling like he was going to throw up all over the place. He'd only seen Aunt Barbara a couple of times, but now...

He knocked on the door and waited, holding Lisa's hand tight.

At last, he heard footsteps coming toward them, followed by the sound of a latch being lifted. Then the door creaked as it was pulled backward by an invisible hand, and that same guy who had answered the door appeared in front of them. He looked bigger close up, especially his belly, which stuck out over his waistline. He was big all over, though. Broad shoulders, big hands, and big arms that looked like he'd spent a couple of decades working on the docks in New York.

"What can I do ya for?" he asked, crossing his arms over his chest.

"Our parents came in here," Carl said. "And our brother and sister."

"Oh, sure," the man said, uncrossing his arms and putting them on his hips.

"Can we see them?" Carl asked finally. Lisa was hiding behind him, holding on to his shirt.

The man smiled and stepped aside. "Well, of course you can," he said in a gravelly voice. "Come on in and make yourself at home." He stretched his arm out, inviting them in.

"Thanks," Carl said.

Lisa was still holding his hand as they stepped inside. The room was dark, because the shades had been pulled down over the front windows. An oil lamp in the corner cast more shadows than it did light: shadows that looked like spiderwebs as the yellow light bounced off the antlers of the animal heads that lined the walls. There were dozens of them: deer and pronghorn and more elk horns. Carl looked around for his parents and Desmond and Piper, but there was no sign of them.

"Like my collection?" their host said. "I'm Mac Bozeman, by the way. Pleased to meet you." He stuck out his hand, and Carl hesitated before taking it. "No need to be afraid, kid," the man said. "We're all friends here, right?"

"I... guess."

"And who might you be?"

"Carl. I'm Carl. Can we please see our parents, Mr.

Bossman?"

"Bozeman. The name's Bozeman with a Z. Got that?"

"Y-yes."

"Good. Now who's that hiding there behind ya?"

Lisa peeked out from behind Carl, then ducked back, quick as a flash.

"That's Lisa, Mr. Bozeman. Now can we...?"

The man held up his hand, cutting him off.

But Lisa spoke up instead. "Where are we?" she asked. "I see monsters."

Mr. Bozeman got down on his haunches and tried to speak in a higher voice, but it was still just as gravelly. "Those aren't monsters, sweetheart," he said. "They're some of my trophies."

"Did they die?"

"I'm afraid so, sweetie. You saw that big building out there?"

Lisa nodded.

"It's a slaughterhouse. I have to kill the animals so you can eat them."

"Ewwwww." Lisa made a face.

"Shhh," Carl said. "It's like the hamburgers at McDonald's. They used to be cows."

"Very good!" Mr. Bozeman enthused. "You earn a gold star, my friend."

"I'm not in school right now. It's summer, but my mom wants us to learn about all the animals in Nevada, so we're out here playing bingo trying to find them."

"Oh!" Mr. Bozeman said. "That's a very interesting game!"

"It's boring," Carl said. "We can't find an elk."

"Ooooh, that is a problem, isn't it?" Bozeman was talking down to him, which Carl didn't like, so he frowned and scuffed his heels on the floor. Bozeman didn't seem to notice, though. He just kept right on talking. "I'm afraid you won't find one, either," he said, pursing his lips together in a pout. "You see, I killed them all. Made them into jerky, like the kind you get at Maverik, except it's elk jerky instead of beef."

Lisa got on her tiptoes and cupped a hand to Carl's ear. "You were right!" she said. "They're stinked."

"EX-tinct," Carl corrected her. "Say, mister," he said, "if you killed all the elk, then how do you make any money?"

"Weeeellll," he said, drawing out the word. "I had to find something else to make jerky out of."

"Not deers," Lisa said, shaking her head fiercely. "They're so pretty."

"Oh, no," Bozeman said, wagging a finger in front of his face. "I wouldn't do that. I saw *Bambi* as a kid. It made me cry."

Lisa didn't know what he was talking about. She had never seen or heard of *Bambi*.

Seeing her blank expression, Bozeman said, "Come on. I think I should just show you."

"Mister," Carl said. "What about our parents, and...?"

"Don't worry," Bozeman said. "I'll have them meet us out there, and then you can all be on your way."

But the strange man didn't send word for anyone to fetch their parents and siblings, which made Carl hesitate.

"It'll be fine," Bozeman said, and grabbed both children by the hand.

"Ow!" Lisa squealed. "You're hurting me."

Bozeman ignored her and pulled the two of them out through a side door, then over a path of uneven stones to the big metal barn nearby. He pulled open a big door. It was dark and smelly inside, but he thrust them through the doorway and pulled the aluminum door shut again.

"Ew!" Lisa said. "It stinks! I can't see. I'm scared!"

"Don't worry, sweetheart," Bozeman said. "I'll turn on the lights, and you can see where I do all my dirty work."

He flipped a switch, and white, sterile light flooded the room.

"Now there," Bozeman said, pointing, "is where I hang my kills on meat hooks so they can bleed out before I process them. I cut their stomachs open so the intestines fall out onto the floor and they exsanguinate. Then I use a long knife to carve out their other organs. The heart, the lungs, the kidneys..."

Lisa screamed. It wasn't the kind of scream that a child makes when she's scared, but the kind anyone makes when they see something too horrific for human eyes to witness. There in front of them, dangling on four hooks, were Chuck and Claudia Oswald, and their two eldest children, Desmond and Piper. They looked out over the slaughterhouse with dead eyes, their heads bashed in and their stomachs gutted, bloody entrails spilling out along with feces and half-digested food. Piper's innards were still attached, dangling down to the floor like Rapunzel's bloody hair, so Bozeman strode over with a pair of shears and began hacking them apart. They fell with a splat on the floor.

Lisa had collapsed into a ball of tears, her body racked by waves as she sobbed and kept rocking back and forth on the floor, oblivious to the fact that she was sitting in her own family's blood.

Carl just stood there for a moment, frozen, unable to comprehend the sight before him.

"Well," Bozeman said, puffing out his chest, "what do you think?"

His disgusting, raspy voice snapped Carl out of his stupor, and he understood the danger. "C'mon, Lis," he hissed, "we gotta run!"

Without waiting for her to respond, he grabbed her hand and began dragging her toward the door. Somehow, she managed to get her little legs underneath her and started running with him, though he had to slow down to let her keep up. She was wailing and sobbing, her Red Riding Hood dress covered in blood that blended in, surreally, so that it almost looked clean.

"Come back!" Bozeman yelled. "We were having so much fun. Why don't we cut them down so you can see them up close?"

Carl nearly choked on the vomit that forced its way up from his stomach as he ran. He expelled it violently, then ran straight through it. And still he ran, holding on to Lisa's hand for dear life. He had to save her. Had to. She was his responsibility now. He couldn't let anything happen to her. He had to keep her safe...

Carl was heaving, shaking... or being shaken. What was happening? He opened his eyes and shot a crazed glance toward the driver, who was sitting beside him. She'd pulled off onto the shoulder and was leaning over him, shaking his shoulders like he'd been in a coma.

"Wha...?" he gasped.

Then the stench reached his nostrils.

"I'm afraid you lost your lunch, big brother. Big Macs smell a lot better before they go in than after they come out," she laughed. "There's a Flying J at the next exit." She pointed. "We can get you cleaned up in one of the showers."

"Wait? Where are we? We have to call the cops! Mom and Dad..."

"Slow down, there. You know we don't have a mom and dad. It's been just you and me since we were kids, getting passed around from one foster home to the next..." They pulled into the truck stop parking lot, and Lisa cut the engine. She turned and fixed him with a worried look. "You had one of those dreams again, didn't you?"

"Dreams? No... I... saw them. They were hanging from meat hooks in a slaughterhouse. It was..." His stomach started to convulse again.

"Okay, okay. Let's get you cleaned up so you can get your sea legs back."

He nodded and waited as she pulled a change of clothes out of a suitcase in the trunk. Then he let her hurry him toward the showers, feeling self-conscious about his soiled clothes and the smell that was wafting up from them. It seemed like everyone was watching him.

"Just trash what you're wearing. It's all old, anyway, and I sure as hell ain't driving around with that smell all the way to Colorado."

"Colorado?"

"Shhh. Just go get changed, bro. Get your head clear, then we'll talk when you get back."

Carl had to focus to stay upright in the shower. The warm water felt good, and he rubbed soap all over himself vigorously, trying to get rid of the smell and feel of vomit on his body. Through it all, he was having flashes of his parents hanging there, seeing blood and feces dripping from their bodies and those of Desmond and Piper. He felt dizzy, so he put his hands out and used them to brace himself against the wall, trying to expel those images from his mind. He didn't want to retch again.

By some miracle, he managed to make it through the shower without losing any more of that Big Mac—if there was any more of it to lose. Drying himself off, he changed into the clothes that Lisa had given him, then hurried outside. Tossing his soiled clothes in the trash can outside the front door, he hurried out to the nearest gas island, where his sister was putting the pump back in its holster.

"Now you smell like yourself again, stinky man," she teased him, but she could tell from his reaction that he still hadn't shaken his reverie. She opened the door for him. "Your ride awaits."

He flopped into the passenger's seat as though he'd just finished a marathon. Despite the shower, he was sweating like he was still running. He forced his eyes to focus on the dashboard in front of him, where he saw a small Bubu panda.

"Where did you get that?" His head was pounding.

"You gave it to me, silly goose."

"When?"

"Last week. Why?"

He pursed his lips and shut his eyes tight. "Mom and Dad bought it for you when you were little. You threw it out the car window, and Dad looked for it, but he couldn't find it."

"That's... impossible."

"I saw it happen!" Carl shouted.

"Carl." She placed a hand on his knee. "Aside from us not *having* a mother and father, Bubu is a Chinese cartoon that was created eight years ago. You're 39 years old, and I'm 30. I couldn't have owned a Bubu when we were kids." Her tone lightened. "And I would never have thrown Bubu out the window. She's too cute."

"Where are we going? I can't remember..."

"We're traveling from Glacier National Park in Montana to the Stanley Hotel, in Estes Park. Colorado. We went through Bozeman just before you fell asleep, and now we're in Billings."

"Bozeman," Carl murmured. "Mac Bozeman."

"Yeah, we had *Big Macs* in Bozeman. Are you starting to remember now?"

"No... The slaughterhouse..."

"Carl, you've got to stop beating yourself up over that. The vegan diet isn't for everyone. It's not like you killed the cows they put in those burgers."

"No..." Carl waved a hand. "It's not that. You don't understand."

"Look," Lisa said. "It's more than ten hours from Glacier to Estes, and this trip was *your* idea. The schedule you made up doesn't leave much time for stops. We have a reservation at the Stanley tonight, and I'm not about to blow 500 bucks on a room I don't even get to sleep in."

She pulled out of the parking lot and back onto I-90.

Carl turned to her. "Why are we on this trip? I can't remember..."

Lisa started laughing. "Because you wanted to see an elk," she said. "When we were kids in Nevada, they had all these signs posted. Our foster parents in Gardnerville, the Oswalds, took us on a summer vacation one year, and you kept telling them you wanted to see an elk, so we went out looking for one. But when we didn't find one, you started blaming them. You even said they were lying to you—that elk didn't exist. They called child placement and told them they wanted to keep me, but that you were too... unpredictable."

Carl looked straight ahead. "So it *was* real," he said.

"They had two kids of their own, Desmond and Piper. They always picked on you when their parents weren't watching. I told them I wouldn't stay if they took you away, so they took us both and placed us with that family in Battle Mountain. Don't you remember any of this...?"

"Not like... not like that."

"You felt so guilty after they placed us again, because the Oswalds were the nicest foster parents we ever had, even if their kids were a couple of assholes. She was a teacher, so she homeschooled us, and he made the best apple pie ever. But it wasn't your fault. I've been telling you that all these years, but you never want to listen to me." She punched him in the arm and called out, "Slug bug!" But Carl didn't react. He just kept staring straight ahead, like he'd stopped listening.

"Bro, I don't know what's going on. I don't think the hypnosis is helping. I think it's making you worse. Those dreams of yours... they're bleeding over into reality now. It's like you don't know the difference anymore."

"If I could just find that elk...," Carl muttered, "everything would make sense. But they're extinct. Why do they have to be extinct?"

"They're *not* extinct, Carl. I keep telling you... Hey!"

Carl's eyes were closed again, but he hadn't changed position. He was still sitting straight up, like he was looking out through his eyelids onto the road ahead.

"Carl!" Lisa shouted. "Don't you fucking go to sleep on me again! I'm not gonna clean up more of your puke. Do you hear me!? Do. You. Hear. Me?"

But he didn't.

It was twilight by the time they hit Loveland and turned north onto U.S. 34 toward Estes Park. Carl was still asleep as "Nights in White Satin" droned on over the radio. "You got that right," Lisa chuckled. "I'm never reaching the end of this drive." She took a sip of her energy drink and looked over at her brother. He hadn't moved a muscle since he'd fallen asleep. She wondered if he was having that same dream again, but it was impossible to tell. At least he wasn't convulsing and projectile vomiting into the windshield.

They rounded several curves and began climbing up the hill. She was looking forward to touring the Stanley in the morning, finding out why it was haunted and how Stephen King got inspired to write *The Shining*. But right now, she was too tired to think of anything except what she hoped would be $500 worth of a soft, welcoming mattress.

Without even realizing it, she closed her eyes thinking about it, then jerked the wheel as her eyelids popped open. She'd been close to drifting off the right shoulder. She slapped herself in the face and rolled down the window, turning up the music. Black

Sabbath's "Paranoid" blared out over the speakers. That would be enough to keep her awake... and, as it turned out, to wake up Carl.

He blinked and looked over at Lisa.

"Sleep well?"

"Like a baby. Thanks. How long was I out?"

"Most of the trip. Any dreams this time?"

He looked at her, puzzled. "What do you mean, 'this time'? I've been asleep since Bozeman."

"You mean you don't remember...?"

He raised his eyebrows, waiting for her to continue.

"You were having a waking dream!" Lisa was wide awake now. "You said our parents had been killed and I'd thrown away my Bubu panda, and..."

She clapped her hand over her mouth. His eyes were glazing over again. He shook his head vigorously, trying to keep the dream from returning to his consciousness. "I... don't...know..."

"What? You don't know what?" Lisa was growing frantic. She slapped him on the knee.

"...I don't know... what's... real... and what's... not."

It was like he was jumping back and forth between the dream and his waking state, struggling to stay in one or the other, but not knowing which side to choose. "I have to know...," he said. "I have to find... the elk... Then the game... will end..."

"Stop! Just stop!" Lisa screamed, trying to bring him to his senses. She grabbed a small bottle of water, unscrewed the plastic top, and threw its contents on his face.

He shook his head like a dog and sputtered. He seemed clear-headed again, but for how long?

"Sis!" he shouted. "The road!"

She'd only turned her eyes away for a second, but when she turned back, she saw a giant shadow looming just in front of her in the center of the road, like a monstrosity in the gloaming. It was too large to go around. To her left was a steep hillside, to her right a gorge that was even steeper. She slammed on the brakes, but it was too late to stop, so she veered sharply right toward the mountainside.

"ELK!" Carl shouted as they sideswiped the thing in the road, knocking it off its feet as the car spun, then hurtled into the mountain.

Paramedics arrived within about ten minutes, but both the driver and passenger of the car were dead at the scene. The elk though, was still alive. It had limped off the side of the road and disappeared into the forest.

At least for now, it was not extinct.

"Extinction Event" by Stephen H. Provost is based on his extensive travels in Nevada, during which he and Sharon happened upon occasional "Elk Crossing" signs but never set eyes on a single elk. They did, however, encounter several elk during their stay at the Stanley Hotel in Colorado. This story appears here for the first time.

Sharon Marie Provost

Hatchet Pass

"**H**ey boys, pardon my interruptin'. Have you ever heard of Hatchet Pass? Well, that's what us locals calls it, but you won't see that name on any of them maps you have there. They calls it Montgomery Pass, out west on Highway 6 headed towards Californy. It's now an abandoned stretch of land, dotted with the decaying ruins of a coupla of motels, a casino, and a gas station. Just a few miles down the road, not far from the border, there once stood a brothel, too, marked with orange letters on a large white barrel statin' "Janie's—Closed Beat it." The grizzled geezer chuckled and then coughed.

Carl and Anthony had been deep in conversation whilst drinking their Pabst Blue Ribbons when the tall, toothless, scraggly old miner interrupted them. They'd stopped at the small hole-in-the-wall Mina Club bar in Mina to discuss where to go ghost hunting next. They'd just left Goldfield earlier that afternoon after investigating down there.

"Is that country bumpkin talking to us?" Anthony said, with a smirk, before turning to address the man. "Excuse me. Are you talking to us?"

Carl chuckled and slapped Anthony on the back. "Classic, man. It's like we're in that movie *Deliverance*."

Anthony burst out laughing as Carl began to air-banjo as he screeched out the introductory notes.

The old miner laughed along heartily and waited for them to finish before resuming, as if he'd never been interrupted. "I heard you boys talking about needin' somewhere new and different to go ghost huntin'. I got just the place. Nobody ever goes there, of course, that's probably with good reason. But I'm sure two strappin' young boys like you will be just fine."

Carl had stopped laughing and started listening with rapt attention. "Why doesn't anybody go there? Is it dangerous? That sounds like just what we're looking for. Right, buddy?" He reached over and slugged Anthony's shoulder.

"Yeah, dude. So what's the story, Mr...?"

"Jed. Just call me Jed."

"Sorry about earlier," Carl said with a small shrug.

"No worries. All in good fun and all that. I 'member the good ole days of bein' young and havin' fun."

"Why do *you* call it Hatchet Pass? Was there a gruesome murder there?" Anthony asked, nearly salivating in eagerness.

"A hatchet murder to be exact. Back in late October of '86, years before you boys were born."

"Yesssss! Tell us the deets."

"Three men were workin' up at the Montgomery Pass Lodge, running the day-to-day stuff and fixin' the place up in exchange for room and board. One of the young men, Daryl Randolph Marshall, had been down on his luck for some time, owing to his love of booze, and he weren't never a hard worker. His job was already at risk because he kept leavin' all the work to his co-worker Lloyd. But then one night, he stole the money out of the till and used it to drink and gamble at the casino across the highway.

"When his supervisor, William Bennett, confronted him, there was a scuffle. Bennett had told him his continued employment would be up ta the boss who knew about his laziness already. Bennett woke up the next morning with his head throbbing and found he'd been beaten over the head. When he went to Lloyd's room, he found that Lloyd had been bludgeoned to death with the back side of a hatchet."

"Whoa, man. That's brutal. So what happened to Daryl? They fry him in the electric chair?" Anthony interjected.

"It took them cops six months to find him. He was found guilty in court and sentenced to life in prison."

"Well, then what's so dangerous about that?"

"I said he was sentenced to life. Ain't never said he was still there. He escaped 'round about five years ago, and hasn't been found. But there've been reports of people seeing him around that tumbledown hotel, hiding in the woods and carrying a hatchet."

"No way! That's fucking awesome. We got to go, dude. I ain't afraid of no old man running around the woods. No offense, Jed." Carl was giddy and ready to run out the door.

"None taken, my boy."

"Carl, let's go back into Tonopah and get some food. I think it's going to be a long night."

"Whoo!" Carl yelled as he ran out the door and jumped into

the Jeep.

Carl and Anthony pulled their Jeep Wrangler into the dirt just off the edge of the highway next to the remnants of the small motel. Most of the windows had been busted out, and the off-white paint was stained and peeling on the building. The faded white lettering on the once-red motel sign now appeared more of a dirty brown. The area was littered with old beer cans and other trash.

"This place has sure seen better days. Where's the casino he mentioned?" Carl asked, stretching as he climbed out of the driver's seat.

"When you went to the john, Jed said it burned down in 2010. It was somewhere over there though." Anthony pointed across the street to a dirt lot next to what looked like another old motel and the remnants of a tall sign.

"How about we walk around first and get the lay of the land?" Anthony asked as he unzipped his backpack, removing his camera and voice recorder.

"Sounds like a plan." Carl turned on his video recorder and narrated their findings as they skirted around the motel.

"To the right of the motel, there is a restaurant. As we round the corner behind the main building, there are several outbuildings as well as what appear to be multiple little cabins. I'm unsure if they were for guests or employees who lived onsite."

"Cut," Anthony yelled.

Carl paused the recording. "Let's check those cabins out and see if one of them belonged to that Lloyd guy who was killed. Maybe there's still a blood stain on the floor or blood spatter on the wall."

"Good ide... Wait! Did you just see that?" Anthony pointed into the tree line, lost in shadow. about a hundred feet away.

"What? I don't see nothing."

"Really? I'm sure I saw someone standing there watching us. When he saw me notice him, he ducked back, but I swear I can still see the outline of him."

"So, go check it out! What? Are you afraid?" Carl squawked like a chicken as he danced around Anthony, flapping his arms.

"Fuck you, dude! You go check it out, Mr. Brass Balls." Anthony held up both middle fingers in Carl's face.

Carl's face tensed as his anger began to boil over. He stomped over to the trees and disappeared into the shadows. Anthony chewed on his fingernails as he waited for Carl to return. Anthony turned to look as another car approached, coming up the highway from Tonopah.

Suddenly an ear-piercing shriek came from the woods and cut off abruptly. It was Carl. Anthony shifted back and forth in place, unsure what to do. They'd both left their phones in the car. He looked back toward the road, but the car was flying by without even taking notice of him.

Anthony heard the sound of someone approaching... fast. They'd be upon him any second. He held up his hands in a defensive posture as he turned back to face his aggressor. Carl barreled into him, knocking him to the ground.

"Did you shit your pants, dude? Oh God, are your pants wet?" Carl cackled wildly.

Anthony jumped up, ready to punch Carl. "I swear I will beat the fuck out of you if my video recorder is busted or the lens scratched!"

"Chill the fuck out, dude!" Carl held up the recorder in his hand. I grabbed it as I tackled you. "Didn't want you getting all butt hurt."

"Sometimes I really hate you, bro. Can we stop all this childish bullshit and get back to recording our show? This could be our big break. None of the other paranormal shows have been here. We have an exclusive."

"Fine! I'm not sure why we're friends. You don't know how to have fun."

The two young men walked back over to the motel and spent the next several hours documenting each of the rooms, the motel office, the restaurant, and then checked out the cabins. As darkness settled around them, they made their way back over to one of the cabins to hold an EVP session. Not having found any traces of blood, they choose one of the spookier ones at the back of the property.

It took them half an hour to film a quick intro segment and set up the full spectrum camera, lights, and set out an EMF meter.

"I'll be back in a couple, bro." Anthony said, as he hopped over the windowsill.

"You have to pee more than a girl, man."

"Whatever!" Anthony walked around the corner of the cabin and back to a small grove of trees. He unzipped his jeans and started to pee when he heard the crunch of pine needles behind him.

"Real funny, jackass!"

Anthony expected to hear Carl start laughing, but the night had become preternaturally silent. He held his breath and kept stock still so as not to make a noise. *I've gotta chill.* As he started to pee again, he felt like somebody was standing right behind him. He reached back tentatively. His fingertips touched a person, and he felt hot breath on the back of his neck.

A large man held a hatchet high above his head and brought it down on Anthony's head with a deafening crack. His skull caved in, and blood spurted from the wound as he collapsed onto the sandy soil with a weak "Ooommph!" The man hit him twice more with the back of the hatchet until his face had been obliterated. The macerated flesh soaked in a pool of blood and bits of bone and teeth. His eyeball had been pushed out of its socket and swung from a tiny filament of tissue.

Carl grew impatient as the minutes flew by. He'd thought he heard a small groan from Anthony shortly after he left. Anthony was always eating too much junk food so he'd probably had to shit as well.

"You better be shitting far away from this cabin! I don't want to be smelling that crap," Carl yelled out the window.

A few moments later he heard a scraping noise along the back wall of the cabin, followed by loud knocks.

"What are you doing, asswipe? Hurry up!"

The knocking sounds continued around the side of the cabin and then stopped by the front door. Carl waited for Anthony to jump in the cabin window, trying to scare him, but nothing happened. Carl stormed over to the front door, unlocked it and ripped it open. At first, his eyes couldn't understand what they were seeing.

Anthony was standing there. Well not actually standing but being held by someone in an upright position. His face was unrecognizable, but those were definitely his clothes and his steely-blue eye hanging on one cheek. Carl couldn't see who was holding him there, but he didn't pause to find out.

As he turned to run away, he heard Anthony's body hit the floor behind him, just before the blade of the hatchet buried itself into the side of his head, nearly slicing off his ear in the process. Carl fell to the ground and began to crawl away.

Carl heard large bootsteps tromping toward him, and then the hatchet was wrenched out his skull, slinging blood spatter on the front wall and door. He saw the shadow of the man holding the hatchet, swinging it down toward him again, and rolled to the side, narrowly dodging the blade.

The man's large foot stomped on his lower back, pinning him in place.

The blade of the hatchet came down on the back of his neck, severing his spine.

An old beat-up pickup pulled up behind the Jeep parked by the motel. Jed climbed out of the driver's seat with a leather satchel in hand, muttering to himself, as he walked up toward the lights glowing from one of the cabins.

"Them stupid young people nowadays. They don't have the sense God gave them. They thinks they is invincible. They take every word told to them as gospel. They've got that infernal internet at they fingertips, but can they be bothered to verify somethin' for themselves? No... they... can't. They didn't even notice my truck parked just up the road from them."

Jed entered the cabin and grabbed Carl's legs, pulling him out over the ledge, and laid him out on the tarp he'd brought in his bag. He then walked around the cabin to where Anthony's body lay.

"Everythin' I told them about that murder was true. But Daryl... I don't know shit about him. He was sentenced to life. That's the last I heard. For all I know, he's still rotting there or maybe he even died in the clink. But I sure as hell know he ain't runnin' around here. The only evil in those woods is me.

"My dad always said, 'If people make you sick, then you's probably not cooking them long enough.'" Jed laughed heartily until he started coughing again. He was stooped over, hands on his hips, trying to catch his breath. He snorted loudly and then hocked up a loogie on the ground. "I think them young'uns are tastier than Funyuns."

Jed dragged Anthony's body onto the tarp and then used it as a sled to get them back down to his truck. He picked up his cell phone and used his big sausage fingers to punch in a number.

"Got the fire going, darlin? I'll be back with dinner in an hour."

"Hatchet Pass" by Sharon Marie Provost was inspired by an actual violent attack that took place at the

NEVADA NIGHTMARE'S EVE

Montgomery Pass Motel in 1986. The motel, later renamed the Boundary Peak Lodge, is now closed and abandoned, along with the rest of the once-thriving stop along U.S. 6 just east of the California state line. It appears here for the first time.

SHARON MARIE and STEPHEN H. PROVOST

Stephen H. Provost

Curtain Call

The balding, middle-aged man stopped at the podium just outside the door to the saloon. He wore shorts and a KISS T-shirt, looking decidedly different from the cowboys and bikers who were regulars there.

The young woman standing there smiled at him, her black lipstick contrasting with her too-white teeth. "Are you interested in the tour?"

"What kind of tour? About the history of the place?" He'd seen a date painted on the front of the building: 1862. A lot of buildings in town were old, and a few offered tours: of mines, an old bank vault, a newspaper pressroom.

He'd been on a few of them and enjoyed them.

"It's a ghost tour. This is the most haunted saloon in all of Nevada. We've been featured on *Ghost Quest* five times."

The visitor chuckled. "That sounds fine," he said, straightening his back and puffing out his chest. "My wife and I have been to half the haunted hotels in Nevada. Ain't seen a ghost yet."

"So, you aren't interested?"

"On the contrary," the man said. "My wife *has* seen them, and me, I'm always up for a challenge. I'm a history professor. Name's Sid Stevens. I've read up on this place, and I'd like to see whether the local legends line up with the facts. Test the waters, if you will."

The woman looked mildly disconcerted. "You don't look much like a history professor."

Stevens shrugged. "It's a Saturday. No classes today. Why be uncomfortable if you don't have to be?"

The woman, who looked *very* uncomfortable in a black lace corset, nose and eyebrow piercings, and spiked heels, obviously didn't share that sentiment.

"How much are tickets?"

"Ten dollars."

"I'll take one." The professor reached into his wallet and pulled out a couple of fives and thrust them forward proudly.

The woman gave him the side eye as she took them, then handed him a ticket. "Next tour's in half an hour," she said. "You're welcome to hang out at the bar."

"Don't mind if I do," the professor said, walking over to claim a barstool as the woman left the podium and scurried into the bar behind him, disappearing through a door on the side.

"We'll have to watch that one. He looks like trouble,"

Maude whispered, pointing toward the bar.

"Him? He looks harmless," James said.

The professor's voice drifted across the cavernous, high-ceilinged room to reach them. The echo effect added to the spooky vibe of the saloon, which was good for business. "What's in a Blazing Orb?" he asked.

"Fireball and orange juice."

"Give me one of those," he said, and the bartender returned a moment later, glass in hand.

"Why do they call it a Blazing Orb, anyway? It's not round."

The bartender, who wore a ponytail and one of those long biker beards, laughed. "You know, orbs. Those white, blurry things that show up in photos sometimes. Folks think they're spirits."

"Or dust on the lens," Stevens scoffed.

The barkeep shrugged. "Maybe. But this place *is* haunted. We've been on TV, on…"

"I know. *Ghost Quest*. That show where they run around like chickens with their heads cut off, shouting about the devil and the boogieman. I've seen it. Talk about formula TV: Every episode's the same. Now the main guy's hosting a Halloween bake-off or something on The Cooking Network."

The guy shook his head. "Just take the tour," he said. "You'll see."

James turned to Maude and rolled his eyes. "I've seen his type before."

"Don't be so smug," Maude said. "We've got a lot of time and energy invested in this place. Do you want to see the tours tank because of some blowhard skeptic? Besides, this could work to our advantage if we play it right."

"The play's the thing," James cracked, then nodded sagely. "Who's the tour guide today?" He saw the flash of concern on her face and added, "Don't tell me it's..."

Maude mouthed the word "yep," then added aloud, "It's Oscar."

James groaned loudly, and the visitor must have heard him, because he pivoted on his barstool, drink in hand.

Maude glared at him, but with a twinkle in her eye. "That was good. You sounded just like a ghost!"

James smiled broadly. "I can use that," he said.

"Wherever you find your muse... but back to Oscar. I think we should keep an eye on him."

"Really, Maude? You know the guides don't like us micromanaging them."

"It's not their call. This is *our* place. It's just a summer job to them."

James sighed. "Okay. But if Oscar quits, I'm holding you responsible."

The bar began to fill up with customers, most of whom had the appearance of tourists. A slightly overweight middle-aged woman in a drab, olive green one-piece plopped herself down next to Professor Stevens at the bar. Her wavy hair was dyed blond, and she smelled like she'd been dipped in strawberry syrup.

"You believe in spirits?" she asked in a friendly voice.

Stevens, who was right-handed, deliberately picked up his drink with his left hand so she could see his wedding ring.

"I believe a lot of people like to make money off stories about them," he said.

"I like stories," she said, putting her chin on her hand as she turned toward him.

The strawberry stench was overpowering.

"So do I," he said. "Doesn't mean I think they're all true. My wife, on the other hand..."

"Oh. I see," she said, her voice suddenly cold. "Well, you might have said..." She got up and moved down the bar, finding a new seat next to another guy who was there by himself: a pudgy fellow with a five o'clock shadow in a green John Deere cap. He could hear her introducing herself to him, her voice suddenly friendly again.

Others filtered in. A graying couple who looked to be in their sixties, holding hands and gazing into each other's eyes like they'd just met. An elderly blind woman with a stooped back and wispy hair, accompanied by a service dog, a black Australian shepherd. A fellow in Old West cosplay, dressed up to look like Wyatt Earp and with a Derringer sidearm to match. It wasn't a prop. Nevada was an open-carry state.

By the time Stevens had been there half an hour, the place was full up. Some of the patrons weren't drinking; they were just sitting there. The tour was supposed to start now, but there wasn't any sign of a tour guide.

The professor was downing the last swallow of his second Blazing Orb when a gangly twenty-something kid came hurrying through the front door, nearly tripping over his own two feet. He could've been the boyfriend of the girl at the entrance, dressed all in black and tatted up with skulls and distorted faces of Mark Twain, Abe Lincoln, and Daryl Dixon from *The Walking Dead* that made them look like ghouls. Gathering his composure, he moved to the center of the room and asked, "Who has tickets for the 2 o'clock tour?"

Almost everyone in the bar raised a hand.

"Come forward! Gather around. There's safety in numbers... hehe. My name's Oscar Mercer, and you'll want to stay close to me. We're refurbishing the building, so some of the corridors have been sealed off. You'll see yellow tape across a few of the doors, too. For your own protection, please don't go beyond these barriers. Some of the floorboards are loose, and some of the fixtures have been found broken in those rooms. We want to preserve as much of the building's history as we can."

Stevens huffed under his breath. "Convenient," he whispered to no one in particular. "They can manipulate creaking floorboards behind the scenes to make the place seem haunted. Maybe they even have some sort of audio equipment that they keep behind closed doors."

"Shhh! Don't ruin it for everyone."

He turned to see the blond standing next to him, but she was already looking the other direction.

"Now, during our tour, you may recognize a number of exhibits that were featured in the *Ghost Quest* TV show. We'll be telling you some stories that you may find hard to believe, but which have been verified as *one-hundred percent*"—he said those words very slowly to let them sink in—"historically accurate by *Brian Baum* himself." He put an emphasis on the name, too, as though doing so lent additional authority to anything that was to follow.

"Who's Brian Baum?" Stevens piped up, and everyone turned to look at him. It had been impossible to miss the cardboard cutout of Baum and his fellow "questors," arms crossed and dead-serious expressions on their faces, that was on display just inside the door. "I assume he has a degree in history, and is qualified to 'verify' the stories you'll be telling."

"Brian Baum," the guide said, a little too loudly, as though he'd been personally offended. "The host of *Ghost Quest*." He pointed at the cutout. "He's investigated hundreds of paranormal sites, and he's been *here* more often than he's been anywhere else."

"Gave you some pointers, did he?" Stevens muttered, chuckling, but no one said anything.

"Follow me back outside," Oscar said, "and then come back in through the next door down and head up the stairs. Be sure to watch your step, and don't mind the creaks. It's perfectly safe."

The blind woman, whose name was Hilda McCoy, was the last person to reach the foot of the staircase. She stumbled over the second step and pitched forward, but someone caught her arm as she was about to fall. It was James.

Her dog, whose name was Missy, sniffed his hand, then nuzzled it.

"Why, thank you, young man."

"You're most welcome, ma'am. Here, let me help you up the rest of the way."

The woman shook her head. "If you don't mind, I think I'll let the others go on ahead and rest down here for a while. Do you know of a good place to sit—other than the bar? Maybe someplace quiet? I know that nice young man Oscar wanted us to keep up, but..."

"It's okay," James said. "Maude and I make the rules; he just tries to follow them—not very successfully sometimes."

"Is Maude your wife?"

James laughed. "Oh, no. Just my partner. I'm old enough to be her grandfather."

"Oh..., I see. Well, thank you..."

"James. You may have seen me in *Othello* or *Cardinal Richelieu* on Broadway."

"No, I'm afraid I've never been farther east than Ely. But thank you, James. I just need to catch my breath a minute."

"I've got just the place. There's a bench right back beyond the bar, in the crypt. We can wait there until the rest of the tour makes its way here. You'll miss a few attractions upstairs, but the crypt is the best of all."

Hilda's breathing was labored as she made her way back through the bar, exhaling with relief when they finally reached the bench.

"Did you say this is a crypt? Why would they have a crypt in a saloon?"

"It's not a crypt anymore," James said, patting her hand reassuringly. "But I'll let Oscar tell you all about it when he comes back. That's his favorite part of the tour."

"All right, then." Hilda patted his hand back. "Do you mind if I just lean on you and rest a while? Wake me up when the tour comes around?"

"Of course," James said. "I'll be sure to wake you the moment they arrive."

Oscar descended the stairs and led the tour back into the saloon, passing the bar and coming to a halt inside a dark, narrow, high-ceilinged room encircled with unfinished stonework. Water oozed and dripped down from somewhere high above, and there was a distinct draft filtering in from some invisible opening; everyone said it felt twenty degrees colder here than the rest of the building.

Hilda's head still rested on James's shoulder.

He didn't rouse her.

She didn't stir at the clattering of shoes on the floor as the tour entered the room, or when Oscar started telling them all about it.

"This," he said proudly, "is the crypt. You may be asking why we call it that. Many people have experienced a paranormal presence here, and do you know why?"

"Why?" the blonde in the olive-green dress said on cue.

"Because one particularly harsh winter, the entire city was besieged by a plague of bitter cold and crippling disease. Between frostbite and pneumonia, many of the men who worked in the mines lost their lives. But the ground was frozen solid, and there was no place to bury them, so the owners of this saloon graciously offered the room where you're standing as a temporary crypt. The townspeople brought the bodies in here and stacked them all the way to the ceiling until the freeze had passed in spring."

"Whooee!" the guy in the sheriff's outfit exclaimed, "it musta smelled somethin' fierce in here by the time them bodies thawed out."

"Wait a minute. Wait a minute," Stevens interrupted. "Are you telling me they couldn't bury the bodies because the ground was too hard?"

"That's right," said Oscar.

"And these were *miners*, right? Men who earned their living digging in the ground?"

Oscar scowled. "Yeah..."

Stevens turned to the people around him. "Don't you get it? None of this ever happened. It's all Grade-A bullpucky. Miners dig shafts a thousand feet into the earth. And this guy is telling you they couldn't dig *graves* to put a few corpses six feet under, just because the ground was a little hard? How gullible does he think we are?"

The other people on the tour just looked at the professor, then at Oscar, then back at the professor.

"You would think," Stevens said, "that such a horrific event would have made the news. The entire town's economy would have been destroyed by such a catastrophic winter! And what about the desperate act of storing all those bodies in the back of a saloon? Don't you think one of those sagebrush journalists, with their penchant for writing bizarre stories about bizarre things, would have written about *this*? It doesn't get much stranger than a crypt in a saloon. But they didn't say a word about it. I looked it up, and I couldn't find it anywhere. Not a single reference to it in any newspaper. The owners just dreamed it up to make money off people like us, who take these tours."

Oscar just stood there, dumbfounded. Nothing in his script had prepared him for anything like this. He looked like a stand-up comedian who'd just frozen as some heckler started booing and pelting him with tomatoes.

It was cosplay Wyatt Earp who finally broke the silence. "So what if they *did* make it up?" he said, pointing at Stevens. "It's ten fucking dollars!"

The professor stared back and opened his mouth, but old Wyatt was just getting started. "How much did you pay to see those clowns on that T-shirt of yours in concert? A couple of hundred smackers? More? You *know* they're just four regular guys behind that makeup, but you don't want them to take off that makeup and spoil the illusion, do you? Well, we don't want *you* to spoil *our* illusion, either. So why don't you just *shut the fuck up!*"

"Well," said the gray-haired woman in her sixties, "there's no call for that kind of language, is there, Anders?"

"No, darlin'," her husband said. "There's not."

The sheriff turned around and stomped out. "They can keep their damn ten bucks. I'm out of here."

The people on the tour kept looking around, unsure what they had just witnessed or what to do next.

Finally, Oscar broke the silence. "I have one more thing to show you before we conclude our tour," he said stoically, clearly reading from a script he'd memorized. "I'm sure you've all heard of the woman in blue, our most famous ghost. If you look very carefully as you exit the crypt, you'll see some stairs, and at the top of those stairs, you just might see our most famous spirit. One of our guests snapped this photograph of her several years ago."

The tour members, relaxed a bit by this new distraction, huddled around to look at the photo. The hazy figure of a woman in a blue dress stood at the top of a spiral staircase.

"Now, if you'll just follow me around the corner..."

The people on the tour let out a collective gasp as they followed Oscar and raised their eyes to look at the top of a very narrow spiral staircase—the same one they'd just seen in the picture. There at the top stood a woman in a long, formal blue dress, billowing out and loosely pleated into waves of fabric that swirled around her ankles. She wasn't entirely corporeal, but she was definitely visible; her translucent form seemed to flicker in and out of existence, disappearing whenever one tried to look directly at her.

Stevens grabbed his cellphone along with the others and started taking pictures.

"Hello, Lena," Oscar said nonchalantly.

She didn't answer, but waved, then stepped backward... and simply disappeared.

Stevens gaped up at the top of the staircase. "How did they do that?" he whispered under his breath.

"*They* didn't do anything," the blonde sniped. "It was Lena, the ghost Oscar was telling us about, wasn't it Oscar?"

"Yes! Yes, it was." The tour guide's voice, suddenly louder and more resonant, left no doubt that he felt vindicated.

The professor's tone was the opposite: mystified. He looked at the series of photos he had taken, and saw that they looked almost exactly like the photo Oscar had shown them. It was the same person. The same ghost. The same... something. "There must be some rational explanation...," he muttered.

He was still looking at his phone when a disembodied groan issued forth from behind him, a groan that made all the visitors—including the professor—jump in unison... and sent most of them running. But not Sid Stevens. He was determined to find the source of it, to reassure himself that there was some reasonable way to explain what he'd just heard and witnessed . He expected to find someone with a tape recorder or somebody cupping their hands over their mouth; maybe even a hidden projection device pointed at the top of the staircase.

What he found there instead was a woman, lying motionless on the floor, as though she'd slumped to the side and fallen there. A black Australian shepherd with a bit of white on its chest was sitting beside her, whining and licking her face. But she wouldn't wake up. No matter how much the dog wagged its tail and nuzzled her, she just wouldn't wake up.

James stroked the side of Hilda's face, and she awoke.

"Oh dear," she said. "I must have nodded off. How long until the tour reaches us?"

James shook his head. "I'm afraid they've come and gone."

Hilda's face fell. "What did I miss?"

"Just Maude's grand entrance," James chuckled. "But here, let me introduce you properly."

A woman stepped around the corner. She wore a fancy blue dress and a smile that was equal parts mischief and satisfaction.

"Or Lena," she said. "Just another role for me to play."

"Then what you said about Broadway," Hilda gasped. "So you really *are* actors, then!" Hilda said.

James smiled and suppressed a laugh. "Not just actors, but two of the finest actors ever to grace the opera house stage."

"Such modesty!" Maude chided.

"But," Hilda stammered, "that must mean the professor was right, and this entire tour was just an elaborate charade."

"No," James said firmly, "you're wrong about that."

He helped Hilda to her feet, and she stood taller and more steadily than she had in a very long time. Then she noticed Missy whining at her feet, clearly distressed. "Oh my," she said, "what has her so in a tizzy?"

Maude fixed her with a sympathetic smile. "She misses you."

"But I'm right here! Missy, it's okay, come here."

The dog started spinning in circles, and her whining grew louder. Then Oscar and the woman from the front door came to take her out, snapping a leash on her and leading her away. She pulled against them, but eventually disappeared around the corner.

"Why are they taking her away?" Hilda said. "What's happened?"

"Should you tell her, or shall I?" Maude asked.

James didn't answer her. He just came right out with it. "I'm afraid you're dead," he said to Hilda. "Sorry."

Maude frowned at him. "Sorry? Is that the best you can do? Just like a man. You can bring the house down playing Richelieu, but you can't even muster a little sympathy to welcome our new friend. And while I'm at it, that ridiculous groan you made was so over the top! It sounded like you were struggling to pass gas. You're definitely out of practice, my dear."

James gave her a sheepish look. "Maybe we should go back to the opera house."

"Don't be silly," Maude said. "That place has burned down three times! With our luck, the minute we went back there, it would go up in flames again."

"Just like a Blazing Orb," James joked.

"Stop," said Maude. "Just stop. You know we have the audience we need here. The acclaim. The fanfare. We may be pretending to be *other* ghosts, but that's what we do as actors. And they still love us. This is our home now. This is our stage! And you," she said, turning to Hilda, "are welcome to join our little company. That Stevens fool will go out there and swear to everyone that he really *did* see a ghost, which, of course, he did. And we'll be more popular than ever. There's no better publicity than a converted skeptic... even if he was right about the crypt."

"Well, I did die there, so, I suppose it really is a crypt now," said Hilda.

She laughed.

James laughed.

Maude laughed.

And they all got ready for their next performance. The nighttime tour was just a few hours away.

James Stark and Maude Adams were two of the most famous actors to grace the stage at Piper's Opera House. Stark was known for his portrayal of Cardinal Richelieu and had, in fact, appeared on Broadway. A photo of Adams hangs in the opera house. It served as the inspiration for Richard Matheson's novel "Bid Time Return," later adapted for the screen as "Somewhere in Time." "Curtain Call" by Stephen H. Provost appears here for the first time.

Sharon Marie Provost

With a Little Help From My Friends

T he long, boring drive through the Nevada desert was finally over. Unfortunately, it didn't look any more exciting now that they had reached their destination. Goldfield, Nevada.

Whoop-de-freaking-doo! What's so goddamn special about this place? A few supposed ghosts? Why did Caroline have to drag me along? I'm not her dog or her dolly.

Everyone in the van could feel Dennis' frustration. Caroline's friends didn't want him along on this trip any more than he wanted to be here. But she had insisted, and nobody dared argue with Caroline. She'd been the unofficial boss of the group since grade school.

They were all just trying to make the best of a difficult situation. It wasn't like they didn't all feel bad for Dennis, who had no *real* friends. Covered in acne, he'd used a wheelchair since he was 14, when he'd been in a bad accident. Caroline had been behind the wheel: a newly licensed driver who'd had a few too many swigs of Daddy's bourbon. But he just had such a bad attitude. He seemed to live in a constant state of depression and anger.

Ever since that accident, he'd become part of Caroline's friend group, even though he didn't belong. Two years younger than the rest of them and ill-suited to be a part of the in-crowd, she forced him to accompany them, in an ill-conceived attempt to make amends. She'd never accepted that you couldn't force a square peg into a round hole, no matter how many times you tried.

The group had decided to spend spring break of their third year in college down in Las Vegas. They were all finally 21, so booze, clubs and gambling on The Strip sounded like fun to all of them. Except for Dennis, too young to participate in any of the fun, but still forced to tag along.

"You going to sign me into the kiddie room at the casino, Sis? Give me a couple of rolls of quarters to play video games like a loser?" Dennis had asked the day she told him, his anger boiling over in his voice.

"There's lots of activities you can do in the different casinos. Go to a Cirque du Soleil or comedy show, visit the aquarium, ride in the gondola, go to the top of the Eiffel Tower; there's a roller coaster at the New York... well maybe not that, but I'm sure you'll be entertained. And we have a really fun activity planned for the ride down from Reno..."

"Oooohhh, let me guess. Visit a ghost town... in a wheelchair? Get candy in Beatty? I'm not fucking 5 anymore, Caroline!"

"You don't have to be such an ass, you know, Dennis! We're stopping in Goldfield."

"No fucking way! You and that goddamn ghost hunting show. We're not going into that stupid Goldfield Hotel with that fake story about Elizabeth, are we?"

"No, but..."

"But what?"

"We're going to the Goldfield High School."

"High school? I just graduated from one. I don't need to see one of those hellholes ever again. But thanks for the offer!"

"No, it's haunted. Really! I know someone who went there. We have the whole place to ourselves. It will be fun."

"Whatever! It's not like you'll leave me alone until I agree to go. Just leave me alone for now. Okay?"

"You're such a dickwad, Dennis. I'm trying to be nice. You need to get out and have fun. I just wanted to help."

"Who asked you to?"

"Find some friends and get a life. Then I'll leave you alone."

Caroline had walked out and slammed the door. Dennis kept hoping that she'd finally gotten pissed off enough to leave him behind, but she'd been on his ass yesterday to pack so they could hit the road the next morning.

The group drove down to the Santa Fe Saloon first to check into their motel rooms. They were scheduled to meet the tour operator at 4 p.m. to learn the layout of the high school, and then the investigation would run until 9.

When they pulled up in front of Goldfield High School, Dennis' anger only grew. "How the hell am I supposed to get in that place? You can't get over your guilt about me being in a wheelchair, but you can't seem to remember that buildings in Old West towns are not wheelchair-accessible."

"I'm sorry, Dennis. We'll figure it out."

"We'll carry you up," Rodney said, gesturing to himself and Gage.

Valerie and Cassandra smiled. "We'll bring up your chair," Cassandra chirped.

"And who the fuck are all those people?" Dennis growled, pointing over to a group of fifteen people standing over by the flagpole in front of the school."

"Oh, did I forget to mention them?" Caroline asked, feigning innocence.

"I told you he'd be pissed. You owe me five," Rodney whispered to Gage.

"You see, the Goldfield Paracon is this weekend, and we're going to be part of it. We're all doing the investigation together. It'll be fun. They have lots of experience." Caroline looked so proud of herself.

"I told you I wasn't interested in all this ghost bullshit."

"Hold your tongue. There's a little girl over there," Caroline scolded.

"Fine... ghost nonsense. Just take me back to the room at the motel."

"You're already here. Just be a sport for once. Do it for your sister," Cassandra coaxed.

"I'm not the one who *owes* her. I didn't paralyze her... it was the other way around."

Caroline turned around, and Dennis heard the sniffles start.

Here we go again. Now I'm the bad guy.

"Low blow, dude," Gage mumbled.

"I've told her a million times, she don't need to do this shit. I don't blame her. I'm not mad. It's fucking life. Bad shit happens all the time, especially to me. I just want to be left alone."

"You're so ungrateful. You don't know how much she worries about you and how hard she tries. Is it that hard to accept a little help and kindness from your sister?" Valerie was ramping it up into a full-blown lecture.

"Fine. Fuck it! I give! Let's go have some fun. Woohoo! Yes!" Dennis bellowed another couple of whoops and howls. The others who were there for the tour turned toward him, then quickly looked away.

The tour guide and leader of the Paracon waved them over and introduced himself as Tom, then began covering all the usual rules:

Don't remove any objects.

Don't deface the property.

No running in the building.

Ouija boards and seances are strictly forbidden.

Be respectful of the spirits in the building.

Tom then split the crowd up into four groups of five, each one assigned a paranormal investigator from his team. Dennis was pleased when he was separated from his sister and her friends.

"Welcome to Goldfield High School. We are so happy you joined us here today to learn a little history about this school, and experience the fascinating world of the paranormal. Goldfield has a rich and sometimes tragic history. Many men, women and children of all ages have died here in barroom brawls, mining disputes and disasters, and of course, from disease.

"I'm sure you've all heard about the ghost stories connected with the Goldfield Hotel and other locations in town, but today our focus is on the high school. You will primarily be dealing with spirits of children that have been drawn to stay here because of the fun they had here, since the school provided them luxuries

SHARON MARIE and STEPHEN H. PROVOST

that weren't available to them in their mining encampments. Contrary to popular belief, ghosts are not always tied to the location where they perished, so we may even encounter a miner or someone else who lived in Goldfield during its heyday.

"Each group will start by investigating a different room on the second floor, where the main school entrance is located. This will allow everyone the ability to ask questions of their investigator as well as actively participate in the investigation. Also, it is important to be quiet when we are running EVP sessions, which is much easier to do in a small group. When we all have rotated through each room on this floor, we will all conduct a fun experiment together as one group in the auditorium on the third floor—one we've had great success with in the past. It's sure to convince even the staunchest skeptic or disbeliever."

Caroline and her friends helped Dennis get to the top of the stairs as promised and settled him in his chair before joining their respective groups.

Dennis was bored out of his mind as they investigated the classrooms. EVPs were a total bust. He had been assigned to a rowdy group that didn't understand being quiet any more than he understood why all these people wanted to be here.

Dennis was unconvinced by the spikes in the readings on the EMF. The dowsing rods they used seemed like the perfect ghost hunting tool for an "investigator" to pretend they were receiving a response with a tiny, imperceptible tip of their hands.

But all of that changed when the entire group reassembled in the auditorium.

Tom once again addressed the crowd, "I hope you've all had fun tonight and seen something you can't explain. But no worries if you haven't; that's all about to change in just a moment. I need all of you to spread out around the room in a large circle, with everyone roughly spaced out evenly apart. Pretend you're back in grade school."

Then he began to point at certain people, asking them to scoot over and create five unoccupied spots around the circle.

"I'm sure you're all wondering why I did that."

A chorus of "yeses" and "yeahs" echoed around the room, accompanied by nods.

"Those spots are for our special guests. If we're lucky, knock on wood," Tom said as he reached over and knocked on a wooden column, "...and we always have been, they are going to play some games with us. Let's start with a simple one: a counting game.

"I'll start and say 'one' and then, one-by-one, we will go around the room clockwise and have each of you count off. When we reach you..." Tom pointed at the fourth person, "... you will say 'four,' and then we will wait ten seconds for a response from one of our ghostly guests, and then you'll say 'six,'" he said, pointing to the fifth living person but sixth spot around the ring.

"Everybody got that?" Tom asked with a smile.

A few people looked puzzled, but most were excited.

Dennis rolled his eyes.

More stupid EVP sessions. This is destined for failure. These people are idiots.

Tom loudly stated "one" and then looked to his left. That was followed by two, three, four, silence, six... and so on until the circle had been completed.

"Ready for this, folks?" Tom asked with an impish grin as he pressed a button on his digital voice recorder to play back the recording.

Dennis heard the gruff voice of the fourth man say "four" and then two seconds of silence before there was a tiny voice that said "five." The assembled group gasped and laughed when they heard something they hadn't expected.

"Want more?"

"Yes!" Dennis called out, unintended excitement in his voice. He fought to regain the stoic expression he'd worn all night.

Tom restarted the playback, and Dennis was shocked to hear four different voices of children fill in the four remaining gaps in the circle as their turns came up.

"What's next?" Dennis called out when the cheering and animated chatter amongst the participants died out.

Tom laughed. "Now that's more like it. I told you we'd have some fun tonight. Everybody remember Duck, Duck, Goose?"

One of the children in attendance called out in an excited voice, "Yes! I love that game!"

"Wonderful! This game will be a little more interactive, and the rules will be a bit different. For the first round, I'm going to point to one of you, designating you as the goose. I want each one of you to say 'duck' as we go around the circle until we get to the 'goose' who will announce himself at that point.

"For the next round, the goose will become the new picker and will walk around the circle, stopping to touch the arm of the person they choose as the goose without saying anything out loud. It's up to the picker to decide which special guest will be the next goose."

"How do we know where a ghost child's arm is located?" Gage called out, snickering.

"I trust you'll figure it out. Precision is not important. It's a children's game. The final round will be lots of fun, as one of our ghostly pupils will announce a designation for each one of us."

Dennis sat there, his muscles in knots, as he waited for the group to finish making the first recording. Tom began the playback, and Dennis heard "duck" repeated eight times by different members of the group, including two of the spots inhabited by the ghosts. Then Rodney announced himself as the "goose."

Then, Rodney walked around the circle and chose the fourth child spirit. They all heard a darling little girl announce "goose." Finally, the moment came that Dennis had been most excited about. The little girl would be responsible for saying what each of them were.

Her sweet voice kept saying "duck," and the circle was nearly complete. As his turn came up, Dennis twitched with excitement. He heard her giggly voice call out a resounding "goose" when she reached him. Dennis broke out in the first smile that Caroline and her friends had seen in years.

Tom clapped and joined the laughter of the group. "Well, I hope you've had as good a time as we've all had today. A few of us are going down to the first floor, which housed the classrooms for the small children. When we're done, we'll exit by going up the three stone steps underneath the grand wooden staircase where you entered the school. Anybody who'd like to is welcome to join us."

Dennis rolled his wheelchair over to Caroline and her friends.

"Are you guys going down?" Dennis asked.

"No way, man. I think it's time we hit the Santa Fe Saloon for drinks rather than just going to our room," Rodney declared.

"No such luck. Santa Fe closes at 9," one of the Paracon attendees said.

Caroline nodded. "This was fun and all, but I think we're done ghost hunting for now. We can break out the tequila we brought and party back at the room."

Valerie and Cassandra agreed.

"Let's blow this joint, dude. Ready for us to carry you down, Dennis?" Gage asked as he leaned over and slid his arm under Dennis' legs.

"Take me down to the first floor. I'll find my own way back up," Dennis interjected.

"That would be a first. How exactly you going to do that, bud? Super powers you haven't told us about?"

Tom approached with two of his investigators. "We'll be happy to help him get out of the building later. Did I hear you're staying at the Santa Fe? We can even give him a ride over afterwards."

"Cool. See you later, Dennis." Gage turned and exited the room with Rodney, Valerie and Cassandra in tow. Caroline looked back, reluctant to leave at first, but then followed her friends out with a small shrug.

"Guys? I thought you were going to carry me down," Dennis called out after them.

"Don't worry about it, man. We've got ya. We were hoping you would want to come down. We get more interaction with the littlest kids when we go down to their floor. Ruth is usually very shy and selective about who she interacts with, and she clearly liked you," the man to Tom's right said. "I'm Gus, by the way."

"So that's her name? The girl who chose me as goose?"

"Sure is," Tom interjected. "I could see from the first moment you got here, you were a disbeliever. Our little ones here are usually quite persistent about changing the minds of those who don't believe in them. I'm glad you enjoyed the experience."

"I really did. Thanks for helping me out."

"You ready for Alex and me to carry you down now, Dennis?" Gus asked.

"Let's do it."

The team spent the first hour with Dennis teaching him more about the different kinds of equipment they used, then let him spend the next hour doing his own investigation on the first floor using a digital recorder.

Every time one of them came by to check on him, they found him deep in an EVP session. It was like he was having a full-blown conversation. Tom was excited to review what Dennis had received.

"Hey there, Dennis. We've got to get back to our room at The Stop and Stop Inn. We're heading back to Vegas early in the morning. If you give me your email address, I'll send you any recordings with good evidence."

"Thanks, man. That would be great."

The team carried Dennis out of the school and set him down in his wheelchair.

"I think I'll enjoy the fresh air and make my own way back over to the motel. Thanks again for your hospitality."

Dennis took his time exploring the town while he pondered the night's events. Those spirits had made him feel more comfortable and accepted than anyone had in years, even his own sister. He knew it sounded crazy, but he wanted to stay there.

Finally, he made his way back over to motel, knowing that Caroline would send out the National Guard before long if he didn't make an appearance.

Except he was wrong.

All five of them were passed out on the floor, too drunk to care or even know he had arrived safely. He tried to wake Caroline and let her know.

"Leave me the fuck alone, Dennis. You're back. Good for you."

"Screw you!" Dennis yelled out as he slammed the motel room door and rolled away.

I have to go back and see if I can get back in. They'll want to see me again.

The next morning, Caroline awoke to Cassandra shaking her and calling her name. "Damn it, Caroline! Wake up! Dennis isn't here. He never came back last night."

"What are you talking about? Yes, he did."

"He isn't here. He never slept in his bed. None of us ever saw him."

"He was here. He woke me up, and I told him to buzz off. Has anyone checked the van? Maybe he slept there."

"He isn't there."

"The saloon. That diner up the road... what was it called? Dinky Diner?"

"Nowhere. That's what I'm trying to tell you."

"Did anyone check that stupid high school? He sure had a man crush on it last night."

"No. Let's go."

"I wanna sleep a little longer."

Valerie cut in as she came to the open motel room door, "Too bad, Caroline. He's your brother. You have to help us. The boys are waiting out in the van. We've packed up everything, including your stuff. Let's go."

"Fine. I swear I'm going to kill him when we find him."

"Only if we don't first," Valerie agreed as they walked out.

A man from the next room over shook his head in frustration. "Kill him somewhere else, and keep it quiet. My kids are trying to sleep."

When the van pulled up in front of the high school, the friends were shocked at what they saw. The barbed wire-covered chain-link fence was open, as was the front door to the school.

Like it had been *left* open, rather than broken into.

Dennis' wheelchair lay on the ground at the foot of the stairs, but he was nowhere to be found.

Rodney threw up his hands. "What the fuck do we do now? I don't want to go in and get picked up for trespassing. The police are parked across the street behind the courthouse there, just up the road a couple hundred feet."

"Why aren't they here already?" Cassandra asked.

"It's 6 a.m. on a Sunday in a tiny ass town. Probably no one on duty, except on call for emergencies," Caroline said as she pulled out her phone.

When the call was answered, the police told her to wait outside; someone would be there in a moment.

The officer who walked across the street had them relate the events of the previous night and then started asking questions. "You say your brother is a paraplegic... so he uses a wheelchair?"

"Yes, officer."

"Well if you don't mind my candor, how in the Sam Hill do you propose he got in the building?"

"I don't know, officer. I don't even know for sure he is, but that's his wheelchair." She pointed toward where it lay, near the stairs.

"I'm going to go look around now. I want you all to stay right here. That clear? We don't appreciate a bunch of drunk co-eds causing trouble in our town."

"Yes, officer," they all agreed.

They heard the sirens from the approaching ambulance before the officer emerged.

"Do you know of someone who might have wanted to hurt your brother? Or was your brother suicidal?"

"Oh my God! What are you saying, officer? Is he dead?"

"Excuse me, ma'am. I'm the one asking questions here."

"No, sir, he wasn't. Actually, he had the time of his life last night. I haven't seen him that happy in years... ever since the accident."

"Is that so?"

"And the five of you are you the only ones who came here with him?"

"Yes, sir. I'm his sister, and these are our friends. We all go everywhere together."

"Yes," the others agreed.

"What happened, officer?" Cassandra asked, tears in her eyes.

"I don't know what to think about what all of you have said. I can't imagine how he could have done what he did without help or it being outright murder."

"Murder?" Caroline gulped.

"Your brother is lying on the second floor. You want me to believe that, somehow, he got up to the third floor and flung himself over the railing to his death *alone*, with a note clutched in his hand?"

"Dear God!" Caroline broke down into sobs.

"What... did... it say?" she asked through her tears.

The officer had placed the note in a plastic bag and held it up for her to read it.

You don't have to worry about me anymore. I feel like I finally belong now. I've gone on to a better place with a little help from my friends.

"I think we all need to head over to the station and do a *lot* more talking. None of you are leaving here anytime soon," the officer said as another officer pulled up behind the group.

"With a Little Help from My Friends" by Sharon Marie Provost was inspired in part by a paranormal exercise the author took part in at the Goldfield High School. It appears here for the first time.

Stephen H. Provost

The Ballad of Miles and Lizzie

Miles

She done me dirty. Ain't no two ways about it. The woman is a witch, the kind that casts a spell over an innocent man so he can't resist her. Then she tires of him, so she up and runs away. That's what Lizzie done. She took off for Wyoming with her "husband"... who wasn't her true husband, because that's *me*.

She won't admit it, though. She'd go to her grave with our

marriage still a secret—that's what she told me, and I've got no doubt that's exactly what she'll do. That's just the kind of woman she is: stubborn as a mule—and built tough like one too.

Don't get me wrong. She's an ample woman, and that's just to my taste. I like a challenge, too. But I never wanted *that* kind of challenge. I didn't know she was already married to that poor excuse for a man, and with eight kids by him to boot. Josiah didn't deserve her. That's what I told myself when I finally met him. But it turns out *I* was the one who didn't deserve her—or rather, what she done to me.

They call me "Old Man Fawcett" because I'm pushing 60, but I have needs like any man. I suppose the Almighty must've frowned on that. That's the only reason he would set me up with *her*.

I was in San Francisco when I decided to procure the services of a marriage broker named Lizzie Thomas. She took $105 out of my pocket and set me up with *my* Lizzie. And she was mine, no matter what anyone else might say.

She still is, too.

Elizabeth

I thought it was a harmless amusement at first. I was in San Francisco when I saw a sign for someone calling herself a marriage broker and, being curious, wandered in to find out the nature of her services.

The next thing I knew, she was telling me about a gentleman who had been in to see her just recently. He was from Manchester, just like I was, and she believed he might very much like to meet me. Being curious about this as well, I decided there would be no harm in allowing her to place me in contact with the man.

That's how we met. It was the biggest mistake of my life.

Miles

When I met my Elizabeth Atherton, it was love at first sight. Fifteen years my junior, she was, to my eyes, the most beautiful creature ever to grace God's green earth. This was, I told myself, exactly what I had been waiting for, and spent lavishly to win her affections, decking her out in jewels and fine clothing. Seeing her receptive to my overtures, I lost no time in asking her for her hand in marriage.

I was nervous that she might not accept a proposal offered so hastily and with such eagerness, yet she accepted with an eagerness that matched my own.

Our bond made legal (or so I thought), I took her with me to my home in the central part of California, down by Fresno, and there we spent the next few months. We were happy, or so I dared to assume, yet I was so beguiled by Lizzie that I took no account of her dark moods or the troubled looks that crossed her face from time to time. Then, one evening, I found her weeping on the sofa, head in her hands.

"It was... all a mistake," she was sobbing. "All... a mistake. I never meant..."

"What?" I asked her, but she wouldn't answer.

I tried to calm her by rubbing her back, but she pulled away from me and refused to say a single word to me the rest of the night. When she fell asleep there on the sofa, I hadn't the heart to rouse her, so I retired to our room and fell into a fitful sleep. When I woke the next morning, she was gone. A note left on the table, which I opened and read through bleary eyes.

My dearest Miles,

It breaks my heart to leave you, but leave you I must. I have a family in Nevada I must attend to. I know you meant well bringing me here, but I cannot tolerate this place. Had we remained in San Francisco, perhaps things might have turned out differently. But here I know not a single person and am in constant mourning for the life I once had.

I am leaving this morning on the stage to Sacramento, and thence will cross the mountains and proceed to Carlin, where I will be reunited with my loved ones. Do not attempt to follow me. If you do, I fear it will not end well for either of us.

—Forever yours,
Elizabeth

A family? What could she mean by that? She had told me she was widowed. Did she have children who needed looking after? In this I could help her, I told myself, if only she had confided in me.

But she had said nothing of it.

I engaged the services of an attorney to see whether I could find out any more about Lizzie's background. I was stunned and chagrined when he told me that my beloved wife was, unbeknownst to me, already married to another man—and that this man was living in the very town she had mentioned in her farewell note.

I was livid at first, yet part of me could not be angry with her. She had revealed to me her destination. What was that if not an invitation to follow her?

I made up my mind to do exactly that. I sold my land in Fresno, collected my belongings, and boarded the stage for Sacramento. I had never heard a whisper of this place called Carlin, but I'd be damned if I didn't find it.

Lizzie needed me. I knew it.

I would not let her down.

Elizabeth

I don't know whether I intended to have Miles follow me. I was wrought with guilt over how I had treated him and truly missed him, but I was uneasy about what would happen should he find his way to Carlin. I felt remorse, too, for how I had treated Josiah. Our marriage had become less fulfilling over time, but I had taken vows to him, and I had broken those vows in marrying Miles.

It wasn't as though I still had feelings for Josiah. The fire that once burned between us had long ago been extinguished by the trials of raising eight children and the rigors of life in the West. Through it all, I had molded him into the sort of person I thought he should be: a docile, obedient husband. In the process of so transforming him, however, I had lost any attraction to him. Rather than being married to him, it was as though I owned him, much as a master owns a fawning puppy.

Being so cowed, Josiah was naturally indifferent to my comings and goings—he seemed unsurprised to see me return now, having left him several months prior. He had never been taken by fits by jealousy, and told me he had become absorbed in his job working for the Central Pacific Railroad.

He had no illusions that he would ever receive any sort of affection from me, and he offered me none now. He merely placated me to avoid the fits of anger he knew would follow if he failed to meet my needs.

Our relationship had become odious, but also comfortable. I had been drawn to Miles because I saw in him the fire, the desperate need for me, that Josiah lacked. But that same need, I feared, would turn to rage once he realized my deception. I had told him willingly, and I had let him know where to find me.

What might happen if he came after me?

Miles

My mind was conflicted as the train pulled into Carlin. I loved Lizzie as fiercely as ever, but she had lied to me about so much. I knew not what awaited me at our reunion.

When first I saw her, I was overcome by feelings of excitement and relief. She *had* told me exactly where to find her; I was sure that meant she intended to leave her husband and reconcile with me. All was forgiven, I told her, assuring her that if she divorced her husband and returned to California with me, it would be as though this sordid mess had never happened.

She wanted to know if I was still living in Fresno, and she brightened a little when I told her I had sold that property.

"Why don't you settle here in Carlin?" she suggested.

Did this mean she was going to leave her husband?

No, she said. That would cause a scandal, and she still had a responsibility to care for her children.

At first, I was so overjoyed simply to be in her presence again that I agreed, bought a neighboring ranch there in Carlin, just to be close to her.

I was encouraged by the coldness I witnessed between her and her husband, to whom she introduced me as "an old acquaintance." He did not question this in the least, accepting it as though it was the Gospel truth. Whenever I saw him after that, he said a polite "hello" but did not engage me in further conversation—not out of any malice, or so it seemed, but out of extreme disinterest. He stayed quiet most of the time, just mumbling to himself and keeping his distance. He was a beanpole, forty pounds lighter than Lizzie. Though half a foot taller, he seemed to cower in her shadow, bowing his head and saying "yes, mama" when she spoke to him, like a child who feared being chastened.

This went on for some time, and it became apparent that Elizabeth was content in the distant relationship she had with Potts. She had a hold over him, as she did over me, but of a different sort: the kind of spell that is cast over a toad to keep him in the cauldron as he boils. Perhaps she had seen in me a toad, as well, but upon transforming me into a prince, decided she preferred the other form.

A toad I would never be, much less the toady as Potts had become. And so she had discarded me, making it clear one day that she was not inclined to rekindle our former relationship.

"I am happy with my husband," she said. "Leave me be."

Now it was I with whom she was distant. Perhaps, I considered, she had placed the same sort of enchantment on Potts long ago, winning him with her wiles and then rejecting him... that he might desire her all the more.

"You owe me a debt," I reminded her, my tone hardening.

"I owe you nothing. You were generous with your gifts, but gifts they were. No condition was placed upon them then, or did you think me a common harlot?"

"They were given... under false pretenses," I stammered.

"Had my 'pretenses' been true, would the condition you placed upon them have been any less?"

I could see, in the way she was speaking, how she had brought Josiah Potts to heel and placed him in his present condition. It was exactly by the means she was using against me now. She had, I was now sure, always been the same conniving woman who stood before me. The spell she had placed on me was broken, and the anger I had quelled in hopes of winning her back was fast returning.

"You owe me at least the money I paid that marriage broker," I snarled. "I was promised a lawful wife, not a bigamist!"

She opened her mouth to protest, but I would not let her speak: "Remember," I said in a low and menacing tone, "bigamy is a crime. If this were brought to light..."

For the first time, I saw her shrink back. She had not considered this. "What would you have me do?"

"First of all, I would see the $105 I paid the San Francisco woman returned to me. Secondly, as I believed I was getting a wife, the least you could do is behave as one in ways that will not offend your chastity. As I am here in this desert by myself because of you, I would ask merely that you bake bread for me and do my laundry as I need it. If you do these things, I will keep quiet about your deceit."

She nodded her head once. "I can do that." She was clearly shaken.

Her assent did nothing to assuage my bitterness, but at least it was something. I pulled back, for the moment, on my threat to expose her. But I vowed that I would hold it in reserve should I have need of it in the future.

Elizabeth

My worst fears had come to pass: Miles had threatened not only me, but my very world. I had only myself to blame. I had surrendered that world to him willingly, only to realize that I wanted it back. Now that I had reclaimed it, he was threatening to snatch it away from me again. I had agreed to his demands, but I was no fool. I knew full well that he could expose me as a bigamist on a whim, should he decide to do so. I was used to being the one in control.

I was not in control here.

I knew I had to be rid of him once and for all. A new year was approaching, and it was time for new beginnings. I discussed the matter with Josiah, and he agreed that we should sell the ranch in Carlin and move to Wyoming, far away from Miles Fawcett.

I decided it was only right that I bid Miles a formal farewell, so on New Year's Day of 1888, I invited him and a friend of his, J.D. Linebarger, to our ranch for a celebration. Mr. Linebarger arrived around 4 in the afternoon and brought with him a bottle of whiskey, which he insisted that we all sample. Miles took one drink, while Josiah and I drank more liberally, our eagerness fueled by our discomfort at having Miles there. He had brought up the subject of further debts he believed we owed him, which only added to my anxiety.

Once the drinking was done, Miles rose abruptly and announced it was time to take his leave. But a storm had blown in, and it was snowing heavily. Mr. Linebarger offered to take him home, but I insisted that he spend one last night in our home. If I could dissuade him from pushing the matter of the debt further, I could say farewell to him and be assured he would be out of our lives forever.

"Do not go out tonight, Miles," I said, speaking more warmly to him than I had in months. "Come and stay with me." (I used "me" rather than "us" intentionally, but was both relieved and perturbed when Josiah chimed in to agree with me.)

Miles

When Elizabeth asked me to stay the night, I was at first taken aback, then began to sense that she was up to something. I agreed on the condition that I have something to feed my horses. Linebarger offered me the feed and went out with me to retrieve it, using the opportunity to repay him a debt of $5 that I had owed him for some time.

When I withdrew the money from my purse, Linebarger noticed it also contained a sum of money in $20 pieces and small change.

"Don't go back to that house," he warned me. "Elizabeth is in one of her moods. It ain't safe."

I knew all about Elizabeth's moods. I had dealt with them many times, and had often placated them by buying her gifts. It occurred to me that if I did not get the money she owed me that night, I might never get it. Her husband had just received his pay, and the woman would likely spend it all before I had a chance to collect it.

"That's the very reason I'm going back to the house," I told him. "I'm not afraid of her. If anything, she should be scared of me exposing her."

"For what?" he asked.

I told him I would keep my mouth shut about it if she gave me the money, but if she refused, he would be the first to know.

I need not have been concerned. That night, when I returned to her home, Elizabeth apologized for her rudeness, and Potts handed me the money they owed me. We shook on it, and I said we were all square. Then I went upstairs to enjoy a restful night's sleep.

When I awoke, I was surprised to find myself the only person in the home. I began searching the rooms, but there was no sign of either Elizabeth, Potts, or their children. They appeared to have taken their belongings with them. Then I remembered her saying they had decided to leave town; I just hadn't realized it would be so soon.

I wasn't happy about the prospect of doing my own laundry with Elizabeth gone, but on the other hand, I was glad the entire affair was concluded. At least they had given me the money they owed me...

Then I noticed it: The money was gone.

I looked around frantically, but it was nowhere to be found.

Running outside, I began searching the ranch for any sign of the Pottses, but there was no sound save the mournful rush of wind over the snowdrifts that had been left the night before. I decided to return to my own ranch, but noticed the sleigh I had driven the previous day was gone as well.

By the time I finally got back to my ranch, I was stunned to learn that the Pottses had taken possession of the property—and had already sold it. Some men there had taken possession of it and were waving around the bill of sale gleefully, saying they were grateful I had sold it to the Pottses. They had another document with them as well: a contract with my signature deeding the ranch to Josiah Potts.

But I had never signed any such document.

How long had I been sleeping? Had the woman drugged me and left me there so I wouldn't awaken until they had forged my signature and hurried off to sell the property? My property?

Unwilling to confront the men who believed the ranch was now theirs, I decided to return to the Pottses' ranch and take possession of *it* myself! If they could steal my home from me, turning the tables on them was only fair. At least it would provide me with a place to stay while I considered my next move. I kicked at the snow as I trudged back the way I had come, cursing the day I met Elizabeth Atherton, real name Elizabeth Potts.

Miles

When I realized the Pottses were not coming back from wherever it is that they'd gotten to, I knew I had to lure them back to Carlin. They had my money, and they had sold my ranch out from under me. Yes, I had their ranch now, but it wasn't enough. Elizabeth Potts had done me wrong for the last time. I was determined now to make her pay—not in cash, but in blood. The next time I saw her, I vowed, she would be hanging from a garrot.

The only question was, how would I get her back here? The

obvious answer was that I would accuse her of a crime. Bigamy wasn't enough. It had to be something else. Fortunately, down in the cellar of the Pottses home lay just the sort of incriminating evidence I'd been looking for.

George

The ranch house in Carlin had been a steal. Whoever had owned it had obviously been eager to get rid of it, and the terms of the deal were too good to pass up.

But upon taking possession of our new home, there was something about the place that just didn't sit right—at least to the missus. She claimed to hear noises coming up from the cellar. At first, I didn't pay it any mind, but when I apparently didn't give her reports the credence they deserved, she decided to go over my head.

She'd been sending letters to the editor of the *Carlin Free Press* under the name Busy Bee for some time, and she decided the latest would address the topic of the ghost under the stairs:

Editor, Press:

I have been intending to write to you for several weeks, but you know when one moves into a new place, one naturally is kept very busy for a while. And in addition to other matters of interest, it is a little exciting when one has the good luck to move into a veritable haunted house. Not many persons have such a thing happen to them these days. So far, the ghost hasn't scared any of us, but he is here just the same. Sometimes he taps on the headboard of the bed; other times he stalks across the kitchen floor, and then he hammers away at the door, but nobody's there. But the gayest capers of all are cut up in the cellar. There he holds high revels, upsets the pickles, and carries on generally.

—Busy Bee

Elizabeth

We'd made a clean getaway—or so I thought. That meddling J.D. Linebarger had only fired up Miles Fawcett. But the snowy New Year's night had been our ally, concealing what had to be done.

We'd resettled in Rock Springs, Wyoming, and life was... predictable once again. I swore never again to step outside my marriage, not for Josiah's sake, but for the trouble it had caused me. I wanted a stable life. A secure life. I just couldn't help it if I had expensive tastes.

But that stable life was not to be. To our shock, we were visited by lawmen who invaded our home and placed us both under arrest for the act of murder. A man's body had been found by a man named George Brewer, who we knew had leased our former house from us. It was there, in the cellar, that the corpse had been discovered. The man's head had been caved in by a blow from an axe; the corpse mutilated and buried under a layer of dirt.

We denied everything. Josiah swore that he didn't know anything about it, but when the lawmen told them the body had been identified, we had to change our story. Yes, we knew about the dead man. But he had committed suicide in our home, and we had cut up the body ourselves and buried it. Josiah had been thorough. He tried to burn the body, then severed it at the knees and the middle of the backbone, wrapping the remains in a pair of blankets. He removed the head and buried it separately under three feet of dirt and some straw.

He did all this for fear that we would be blamed.

Now that blame had come back to us in any case.

It had also been discovered, they said, that we had forged the bill of sale for a neighboring ranch, and thus were suspected of grand theft in addition to murder.

I went white when he told me that. I knew then that Miles Fawcett had made good on his threats of making me pay if I ever crossed him.

We were taken to the jail in Elko to await trial for homicide.

Miles

After Elizabeth was brought back to Elko, I took satisfaction in her new predicament. Now she was in jail, just as she'd confined my heart to a jail of its own by way of her witchcraft and deceit.

I kept up with the trial in the press, and was gratified when both she and Potts were found guilty. The penalty was the gallows. Elizabeth would become the first woman in the history of Nevada to be hanged.

One report, from the *San Francisco Examiner*, exposed her as every bit the shrew I knew her to be. It ran thus:

During the time that she spent at the Elko County Jail, Mrs. Potts gave ample proof of her fearful temper and terrible tongue. The slightest command that she did not care to obey would start her into a fury.

She was a large, powerful woman, and as stubborn as she was strong, as vicious as she was passionate...

Last night, Mrs. Potts had her last tantrum. She upbraided her husband in the next cell, called him a coward and a sneak, and when the officers sought to pacify her, she turned on them and berated them fiercely. Then she took to striding up and down the corridor. She seemed at last to have walked her temper down and

126

wanted to go to bed, not, however without a parting curse at her husband, who by this time was asleep in his cot.

I congratulated myself. I'd gotten inside Elizabeth's head, and I'd made her turn on Josiah. They both deserved that and more.

The best was still to come.

Elizabeth

My fate was sealed.

Accused. Tried. Convicted. Now nothing was left but the execution. Would they really hang a *woman* for a murder based on circumstantial evidence? The town was demanding it, so I knew they would. Miles had turned them all against us, even though we'd been there long before he arrived.

But I would be damned if they were going to put me up on the gallows. I'd always been in control of my life, and I wasn't about to give anyone the satisfaction of taking it away from me. If it was forfeit, I would die by my own hand. I had a pen-knife hidden in my hair, and Josiah had sharpened a piece of slate: He had pledged to join me in departing this world. But his belly was as yellow as ever, and he chickened out at the last minute. Cowardice was his way, and he held to it right up to the end.

He just fell asleep, as though he had not a care in the world, and I cursed him loudly in front of the guard. He paid it no mind and slept on.

No matter. I didn't need him. I never had. I would do the deed myself. I lay down in my cot and pulled the covers up over me. Then, in the safety of my cocoon, I withdrew the pen-knife from my hair and jammed the blade up into my wrists. I failed to hit an artery, so I tried again, this time with more force, but again my aim was not true. It didn't matter how hard I thrust the knife up into me, it was the placement that mattered.

Finally, in a final attempt, I hit home and blood began to pour out. The smell of it intoxicated me, like some vampire in the birthing. I moaned in agony and ecstasy as it washed over me, my baptism into impending death. But one of the guards must have heard me, because he came in and threw back the covers, sending blood spouting into the air.

I laughed as he restrained me and howled as I tried to fight him off, but in the end, the loss of blood had weakened me, and I was unable to resist him. The guards, alas, were able to stem the flow of blood and bandage me up... that I might face death at their hands instead of my own. They loathed me so greatly that they would not even allow me the privilege of dying at my own hands; it was they who would separate me from this life—in *their* time and on *their* terms.

I awoke the next day, composed and determined to remain so. I laid out a white dress that I had sewn especially to wear on the day of my demise. I'd been married in black, I told them, and it was a hoodoo, a kind of dark curse. Now I would die in white and see what sort of luck that would bring me.

The thought of this, and of my treatment by those guards the night before, darkened my mood even further. So when a reporter from the *Examiner* asked to interview me later that day, I held my tongue and stared her down wildly. "If I go out of that door to be hanged and find this woman in the yard, I will strangle her," I spat.

I told her what I'd been saying from the beginning: That I had killed no one, that it had all been a set-up, and they were about to kill an innocent woman.

Miles

Of course I attended the execution. I wouldn't have missed it.

A gallows had been erected in the southwest corner of the prison yard: It had been specially made in Placerville to accommodate two hangings. It was a few minutes past 10 in the morning on June 20, 1890.

I saw Linebarger there and whispered in his ear. "She's about to get what's coming."

He didn't turn to face me but merely said, "It's about goddamn time."

The warrant had been read to the condemned before they emerged. I learned from a murmur in the crowd that Potts had proclaimed his innocence, and that Elizabeth had done likewise, raising her hand and declaring, "I am innocent, so help me God."

It was a lie: She had never been innocent for a single moment in her life.

A few minutes later, the two of them came out into the courtyard and ascended the scaffold. There they shook hands with the officers and ministers. I could barely hear it, but I could see Potts mouth the word "goodbye" as he looked at Elizabeth. Then they leaned forward and shared a kiss, but Elizabeth wasn't looking into his eyes, she was looking in my direction. She wanted me to know she knew I was there, and that she knew what I had done to her.

Their shoes were removed, and their arms and legs strapped. Neither of them flinched.

"Lord have mercy on me," Elizabeth kept saying. "Lord have mercy on my soul."

He'd had no mercy on me—if, in fact, he even existed. And if so, why was she deserving?

Then, at 10:44 and 30 seconds, the floor dropped away

beneath them, and Elizabeth fell, her hands and feet quivering in a final, futile dance with life.

She was still looking at me when she mouthed the words, "See you in hell, Miles."

Miles

The plan had gone perfectly. I had remained there in the Pottses' house, living quietly in the cellar and emerging only for a breath of fresh air, until the new tenants took possession of the home.

The Pottses hadn't left much there, but there was some food—including a few jars of pickles. It was enough.

When the tenants arrived, I bustled around a little down there so they'd notice me and wonder what was going on.

When I could tell their interest had been piqued enough to investigate, I snuck out and let the rest of the plan fall into place. In due course, they discovered the body, which the Pottses had dismembered beyond recognition. I, of course, had put it there. Having disappeared, the entire town assumed that the body was mine, and the case was easy enough to prove when one took into account the town's bias against them and the circumstantial evidence they'd been foolish enough to leave behind.

They *had* robbed me of my home, my sleigh, and my belongings, after all.

I never bothered anyone again after that.

Yes, most think that the body they found down there was mine. But a few friends of the Pottses clung to the idea that someone else had put it there—someone who had a vendetta against them.

Of course, I was that someone. Whether the body was mine or not is another matter.

Either way, I'll never tell.

NEVADA NIGHTMARE'S EVE

The above is closely based on a true story. Elizabeth Potts was hanged with her husband Josiah on June 20, 1890, at Elko. She thus became the first woman to be executed in Nevada. The charge was the death of Miles Fawcett, with whom she had entered into a bigamous marriage in San Francisco and lived for a brief time in Fresno. He did, in fact, follow her to Carlin, and he did disappear after spending a snowy New Year's Night at the Pottses home. Mrs. Brewer's actual letter alleging that a ghost was in her cellar is included, as is a piece of reporting from the San Francisco Examiner. *Other details were gleaned from various press accounts as well. "The Ballad of Miles and Lizzie" by Stephen H. Provost appears here for the first time.*

Sharon Marie Provost

Road Hazard

A news flash ran across the screen on the television behind the counter at the convenience store.

"Police are warning travelers in Nevada along Highway 50, 'America's Loneliest Road,' not to pick up hitchhikers. Two travelers have been murdered, and several have been reported missing over the past month. It is unknown if the disappearances and murders are connected at this time.

"In several of these cases, the victims were seen picking up an unknown man seeking a ride. We have an artist's rendering of the man wanted for questioning in regards to this ongoing investigation. If you have any information, please call the Nevada

Highway Patrol or local police."

Bobby looked up at the screen intently, taking note of the man's appearance. There wasn't much to go on. The man wore a hoodie pulled forward to obscure his face. The only features of note were his prominent cheekbones and a classic "pornstache."

"Better be careful out there, buddy," the clerk said as she handed him his change.

"Yeah. Thanks. I do a lot of traveling, so it's good to know what's going on. Have a good day, ma'am!"

He walked out with his purchases and climbed into the car, tossing the bag on the passenger's seat. He pulled out a cold bottle of water and downed it in one long chug.

Time to hit the road. It's getting late, and I need to reach my destination before dark.

Jamie had offered to take over driving when Gary became tired. They'd stopped off at Middlegate Station first to share one of its famous Monster Burgers. On the way in, they stopped on the porch for the obligatory tourist photo in front of the "Middlegate—Middle of Nowhere" sign. Gary, grumpy from lack of sleep, didn't have much patience trying to line up the camera right for a good selfie.

"Hey, folks. Would you like me to take that for you?" said a man with a thick, ridiculous-looking mustache, sitting nearby in a plastic chair.

"Oh, thank you so much!" Jamie snatched the phone from Gary and held it out to the man.

The man snapped a couple of photos and gave her the phone back. "Tourists, I presume?"

Gary turned away and went inside without saying a word.

"Yes, we're from San Francisco and traveling to Salt Lake for a vacation, and we decided we had to see the famous 'America's

134

Loneliest Road.'"

"Might I make a suggestion?"

"Sure."

"Just up the road a piece, you'll see a sign for State Route 722. That's the old Carroll Summit Route. It's an old section of Highway 50—and the Lincoln Highway too, for that matter, before they moved it to the current alignment.

"It's a lot prettier than more of the same old desert. You'll see Gibraltar Canyon—like a little Grand Canyon—and some of the steepest, tightest hairpin curves you'll ever experience as you head to the top of Carroll Summit. It'll lead you right to Austin, the next place of interest on the highway."

"That sounds amazing. We might just do that."

"I hope you enjoy it. I should be going," the man said as he stepped off the porch and headed out to the parking lot.

"Have a great day." Jamie, a smile on her face, headed inside to find her wayward husband.

Gary, who wasn't up for much talking, devoured the food while she chattered away to him.

"I'm just going to sleep anyway, babe. I don't care what you do."

"You don't even want to see the pretty scenery?"

"I've seen the real Grand Canyon. You've seen one, you've seen 'em all. Do what you want."

"Whatever," Jamie mumbled, munching on a fry.

When Jamie went up to pay, she asked the girl behind the bar about the route, and she'd received another glowing recommendation. Gary had dropped off to sleep before they even returned to Highway 50.

Feeling a little weary herself, she decided the scenic route might be just what she needed. She turned off on State Route 722, just after the Shoe Tree, as she had been directed. The twisty turning, steep mountain roads over Carroll Summit sounded a lot more interesting than more flat, desert scenery.

Jamie had just passed Eastgate Station, a former waystation for the Central Overland Route in the 1800s and a stop along the old Lincoln Highway, when she came across a craggy outcropping on both sides of the road.

Her eyes traveled up the rocks, and she realized a young bighorn sheep was looking down at her. She pulled over to the side a short time later, debating whether to awaken Gary, when a small group of young bighorns needed to cross the road. Just a mile farther up the road, she saw Gibraltar Canyon off to the right side of the road.

Jamie, distracted by the river flowing through the canyon, didn't notice the three metal tire spikes in the road.

Until the car shook as it rolled over them, and she heard the sharp hiss of air. The wheel jerked to the right, so Jamie eased on the brakes.

"Fuck!"

The car thumped, rolling to a stop, on the rapidly deflating tire. Gary's gentle snoring ended with a snort, jarred awake by the rough ride.

"What the fuck?" Gary groused.

"Flat tire. I ran over something in the road. I didn't see it until too late."

"Goddammit, Jamie! That's the last thing I needed right now," Gary jumped out of the car, slamming the door shut. He ripped open the trunk and began throwing their luggage on the ground around them.

Jamie piled it up off to the side of the blacktop and helped him pull out the spare tire, returning the items once it was out. Gary bitched to himself as he wrenched the tire iron, loosening the lug nuts.

"Need help?"

"I think you've done enough, don't you?"

Jamie blinked away tears. "I'm just gonna go look around a bit then. Get out of your hair."

"Sorry," Gary mumbled, under his breath. He could see the dejected hunch of her posture as she walked away. "Forgive me for being a grumpy ass," he called out.

Jamie lifted her hand and gave a small wave over her back. She walked up the road about a half of a mile to get a better view down into the canyon. The surrounding hillside was all rocky and desert brush, but in the floor of the canyon was a lush oasis.

Grass and trees grew alongside a wide creek that wound through the canyon. A herd of cattle grazed along the creekside and lounged in the shade. She looked up into the sky, drawn by the screech of a hawk gliding down to catch a kangaroo mouse running through the sagebrush.

"Babe, this is amazing! You really should come check it out when you're done," she called out.

She looked back when she didn't get a response, but she couldn't see him by the car. It was still sitting propped up on the jack.

She started back to see if he needed help.

"Gar, where are you?" He hated when she shortened his name, but maybe he would at least respond.

But she was met with silence.

When she reached the car, he was nowhere to be found. She'd hoped he'd been crouched by the trunk, just out of sight. As she turned around, searching the area, she noticed another vehicle parked about a quarter-mile up the road on the other side, about fifty feet down a dirt road. A man standing by the Jeep raised a hand when her gaze met his.

Gary must be over there getting help or talking.

Nearing the Jeep, the man turned to face her, and she recognized him, or more so, that mustache. It was the man from Middlegate Station.

"Hey, you! You took my suggestion."

"Yes, we did," Jamie said, unease building up in her gut. It didn't feel right that he was just sitting out here after he'd suggested that they take this route.

Had he already been parked there when they got the flat or arrived while she was distracted?

She looked around the area nervously, not seeing any sign of Gary. As her eyes scanned farther to the right, she caught sight of sharp, triangular spikes—they almost looked like jacks from that old game... except these were perfect for puncturing a tire.

Their tire.

She backed away, trying to act nonchalant. "You seen my husband, Gary?"

"Nope. I just drove up a moment ago, and I only saw a disabled car, and a woman standing by the canyon. You, I presume?"

"Yep. I guess I'll have to go find him." She turned away slowly, keeping one eye out on her periphery for signs of movement from behind. She took a few steps and flicked her head back on the pretense of saying goodbye, and that was when she saw it.

An expanding pool of blood flowing across the ground, just behind his Jeep.

Gary! What do I do now?

Jamie took off on a dead run toward the car. She had to find something to defend herself. And Gary.

The tire iron!

Just then, she was ripped backward off her feet when a hand grabbed her hair, up by the roots, and yanked. She fell back on her ass and reached up to grab his hand, trying to wrest his grip on her hair. He dragged her across the blacktop, tearing the flesh from the backs of her bare thighs and calves.

"Not so fast, scared little rabbit!"

Jamie screamed for all she was worth... although, she hadn't seen another living person since she turned down this road—except for this bastard. All she managed to do was send a murder of crows squawking and flying into the air, headed in the opposite direction.

"No one's going to hear you. There's a reason I sent you down this road, other than the natural beauty."

When her butt bounced down from the lip of the blacktop, Jamie planted her palms into the dirt and pulled her knees up, digging her heels in against the edge of the macadam. Her body arched up backward, and she was able to regain her footing. Those hours of yoga each week were coming in handy.

She locked her hand around the hand that was gripping her hair as she dipped and turned swiftly.

Now she was facing him. It was her only chance to get the upper hand.

In one swift motion, she kicked out with her right foot, connecting solidly in his groin.

"Oooomphh!" He doubled over, loosening his grip on her hair.

Jamie broke free. She didn't pause or look back this time. She just took off toward the front door of the car. She'd lost track of her own cell phone. With any luck, Gary had left his charging in the car, and she'd be able to get a signal and call 911.

"Uhhh!" Jamie stumbled, and her pace slowed to a few lumbering steps. There was a gurgling sound as she took a breath, and then a spray of fine blood droplets when she expelled the air. She reached behind her, fumbling around her back.

A blade was sticking out of it.

She turned around to find her attacker and saw him standing at the edge of the road, a devilish grin on his face and another large hunting knife in hand.

"Didn't expect that one, did you?" he asked with a cackle.

He walked across the road and yanked her arm, pulling her along. A couple of lurching steps later, Jamie fell face-first to the ground, weak and light-headed.

The skin on her nose was ripped off when her face bounced off the pavement. The next bump knocked her front teeth out. He dragged her body back behind the Jeep to where Gary lay, his lifeless eyes staring up into the sky.

The man was talking to her, but it was hard to concentrate—she couldn't take her eyes off Gary.

"Guess you guys weren't listening to the radio. Those warnings about the 'Lonely Road Hazard Ripper' have been all over the media the past few days. If you had, you might not have listened to a recommendation from a man fitting my description."

Jamie didn't respond—fixated on Gary's throat, which had been slit from ear to ear.

Seconds later, her throat was as well.

The man loaded the bodies into his Jeep and drove up the winding curves, stopping near the top of Carroll Summit. He looked down the snaky road: He didn't see anybody making their way up from below, and he'd hear someone who might be coming from above. He opened the back of the Jeep and unloaded the bodies, pushing them over the edge to tumble down the hill into a secluded ravine down below.

It would be a long time, if ever, before they'd be found.

The heavyset, mustachioed man wearing a cowboy hat stepped down out of the white Chevy Express van that he'd had overhauled with a Sportsmobile 4x4 conversion. People gave him wary, sidelong glances. It looked like those old "kidnapper" vans from the '70s and '80s, but built for off-roading and camping. He tipped his hat at a woman who'd pulled her daughter closer to her while ushering the child out to their car.

He'd just finished filling his tank at the Champ's Station in

Eureka, and he went inside the little store to get a few snacks. He had a long day of driving ahead of him. He'd recently retired, and now he'd been tasked with a special mission by his daughter. He'd always wanted to travel, so this had worked out great.

When he exited the store, a young man with a backpack was standing at the edge of the parking lot, looking up and down the street. The young man wore jeans and a polo shirt. He looked to be in his mid-to-late twenties and had sandy blond hair.

"You lost, kid?"

The young man looked over at the man. "No. Just hoping to find a ride."

"Where you headed?"

"Fallon, but I'd be happy with however far you can go."

"I'm going that way. Hop in!"

The young man's face broke out in a wide smile. He climbed into the passenger seat and set the bag between his feet.

"You can set that in back. It's no problem."

"That's alright. I have all my stuff in here… you know, snacks."

"Okay."

"Hi! I'm Tom. Nice to meet ya."

"Bobby. Thanks for picking me up. My car broke down here, and it's going to be a week before they get it fixed. I've got to get back home for work this week. My friend said he'd bring me back to pick it up, but no one was available to come get me. I was starting to get worried. My boss is a tight-ass and woulda fired me if I missed work."

"Happy to do it. I'm not on a tight schedule—the world's my oyster as they say—so I got time to help out my fellow man and all that bullshit."

The two men sat in silence for a while, listening to the radio. Then a news bulletin cut into the middle of "You Really Got Me" by The Kinks.

"Police are once again urging motorists along Highway 50, 'America's Loneliest Road,' to be careful about picking up hitchhikers. They are also asking drivers to be watchful for potential road hazards that may have been set out to disable motorists, putting them at risk of an attack. The man dubbed the 'Lonely Road Hazard Ripper' by the press is still active in the area. He has been tentatively linked to a string of seven missing persons cases and six murders along the stretch of highway between the Fallon Flats and Baker, Nevada.

"The police have released a rendering of the suspect done by a sketch artist. He is believed to be between 25 and 45 years old with black hair and a thick mustache. You can view the sketch on our website or the Nevada Highway Patrol's site. If you have any information, please contact Secret Witness, your local police, or the Highway Patrol."

Bobby shook his head and said, "Sheesh! That guy scares me. I drive this road all the time, and it's had me a bit nervous the past few months. Then here I am stuck hitchhiking myself. I didn't know what to do though. That's why I was so relieved you picked me up. And surprised."

"Surprised? Why?"

"That you picked me up with all the warnings."

"'Spose that's true, but I ain't no shrinking violet. Besides, you don't exactly look like a serial killer. Am I right?" Tom slugged Bobby in the shoulder and guffawed.

Bobby smiled awkwardly, trying to be a good sport.

"What does a serial killer look like though? They mentioned people's cars being disabled, so he might be taking them by surprise. Or maybe he's 'got a special set of skills.'" Bobby laughed at his own joke.

"So, Liam Neeson's out here murdering people?"

"You never know."

"You'd probably never guess by looking at me that I'm really good at throwing knives."

"That so? Guess we all have our talents. I'm sure someone will catch up with that bastard before long. He's gotten cocky, and he's not nearly as smart as he thinks he is. They never are."

"Maybe. I guess we'll see. He's convinced quite a few people to pick him up and give him a ride, only to somehow get the jump on them somewhere along the road. Even after all the warnings started, people still picked him up and nobody ever reported a suspicious man. I mean… who wears a pornstache these days, except maybe Sam Elliott? And who trusts someone sporting one?"

"You have a point there," Tom said in a wry tone, twiddling the hair of his thick mustache.

Bobby grimaced. "Sorry, I didn't mean anything by that. Yours is much more fashionable. Anyhow, there's never any witnesses of the attacks themselves. He's disabled people's brakes and caused slow leaks in tires and even left a large object in the road causing a guy to crash. Did you hear about that first girl he killed, on Pancake Summit?"

"Oh?"

"She's one of the cases they mentioned with those road hazards. They found a car parked on the side of the road with a punctured tire and had it towed away after 48 hours because it was considered abandoned. When the plate was run, it was linked to a missing person's case.

"The story was reported on the news, and a driver came forward to report seeing some woman pulled over with a flat tire. But the guy saw a man standing there talking to her, so he didn't bother to stop. Later on, police working the scene found one of those sharp, triangular tire puncturing spikes that law enforcement use."

"I hadn't heard about that part on the news."

"I thought you weren't familiar with it at all."

"Oh yeah, I recognized it once you started telling me, but I never heard about how her car was disabled."

"You hungry?" Bobby had unzipped his bag and pulled out a bag of chips.

"Nah, I'm good."

"Apparently, he took her by surprise when she reached into the trunk to remove the spare tire and the jack. She was a daddy's girl and kept praying for him to find her... all the way up until the end..."

"How'd you find all that out?" Tom asked, his brows knitted quizzically.

"...Till the very last second when I *gutted* her."

"What? You what?" Tom turned to look at Bobby.

Bobby held a knife in his hand and, quick as a flash, he reached down to release his seatbelt.

Except the button wouldn't depress.

Tom smiled a wicked smile at him. He was holding a gun, pointed straight at Bobby. "Stupid fucker!" he growled. "Don't mess with an ex-Texas Ranger on a mission, especially one packing a Sig Sauer." In one swift motion, he thrust his arm out and cracked Bobby over the head with the sidearm.

Bobby slumped, unconscious, into his seat. Tom pulled over and removed two pairs of zip cuffs hidden under his seat. He secured Bobby's wrists and ankles together, and riffled through his backpack before driving on.

Bobby began to stir in the seat, moaning. "What the fuck? Where are you taking me, fucker?" Bobby spat. Tom didn't reply. Bobby looked around and realized they were climbing Austin Summit. "Answer me, asshole!"

"I don't owe you shit, except a world of hurt, just like you hurt me."

"I didn't do shit to you. I was about to, though." Bobby struggled in his seat, trying unsuccessfully to get free of his restraints. "What'd you do to that seatbelt?"

"I had it jerry-rigged 'specially for you. I've been looking for you, and I knew I'd find you eventually."

"Awww... I feel special now. Looking for little ol' me, Bobby Wilkes. And why is that?"

"I know who you are. I know what you've done. I've come to stop you."

"How did you find me anyhow? The whole police force of the state of Nevada's been looking for me for months. What's so special about you?"

"Determination. Intelligence. Experience. And a thirst for revenge. I saw your pattern. That you went up the highway and then came back down, making some people go missing and killing others. Sometimes using the hitchhiker disguise." Tom held up the hoodie and a paste-on mustache. "And other times looking like an innocent young man. I've been keeping track and just waiting for my opportunity. You fucked up this time."

"What do you mean?"

"That young couple by Carroll Summit."

Bobby's face fell, but only for a second.

"Who?"

"You know who! Against all odds, the police found them. Not only that, you were caught on camera in Middlegate by another tourist talking to them. That same goofy pornstache. I knew you'd be headed back this way. I took a chance and stayed in Eureka. Waiting. Hoping. And... then... there... you... were."

"How'd did you find out about them being discovered? There hasn't been anything on the news."

"I have a lot of friends on the force in Nevada. They've been keeping me up on *every single* missing person or death—other than from natural causes. I convinced them not to release it to the public."

"How come you haven't called your buddies yet to come arrest me? Won't you be in trouble for this?" Bobby held up his bound wrists.

"Who said you're going to prison?"

"Well, I'll be... And who made you judge, jury, and executioner?"

"I did, the minute you chose to kill my daughter."

"Daughter? Whatcha talking about?"

"Christine. My pride and joy. The light of my life. A purer, more giving soul did not exist, and that was her downfall. She trusted the 'Good Samaritan' who stopped to help her with a flat tire."

"No *fucking* way! She can't be. Are you pulling my leg? Your daughter was my little pig? What are the chances I open my big mouth about her... to you?" Bobby began to cackle like a wild man. "Well, I'll be goddamned! She's special to me too, being my first and all."

"Get that smirk off your face before I take it off myself." Tom had stopped in a pullout at the top of Summit Pass. He was brandishing the knife Bobby had pulled on him earlier.

Bobby held up his hands in surrender. "No disrespect, Daddy-o! That tender piece of flesh was U.S. Prime. And that voice of hers—it sent shivers down my spine. You ever been high up in the Sierras and heard the call of a vixen red fox? That's enough to scare the bravest of souls. But that little vixen of yours was mighty fine." Bobby licked his lips, staring off into space, reliving every moment.

Tom had the knife at Bobby's throat in the blink of an eye. "I oughta..." Another car was coming up around a tight curve just ahead.

"Don't have the *cajones*, Pops? 'To serve and protect' and all that bullshit getting in the way?" Bobby snickered.

"I've got the balls. I can and I *will* make you pay, but not here."

"Where you taking me then?"

"Right over there." Tom pointed out the window across the valley to a spot near the summit of the adjacent peak. A dirt road wound up the hill toward a large grove of brilliant green juniper trees and piñon pines.

"What's so special about that place?"

"There's a very old, secluded hunting cabin up there. Been in the family for generations. It's perfect for our purposes this evening."

"Ooohh, spooky!" Bobby didn't look afraid. He appeared to be deep in thought.

"You see all those Mormon crickets out there? They'll devour you—if the other scavengers don't get there first."

Bobby tried to suppress the involuntary shiver that ran up his spine. He always tried to avoid this area when those damn crickets were migrating in search of food. Any creature that looked like it was out of a scene in *Aliens*, that was cannibalistic and swarmed in the tens of thousands, spelled trouble in his book.

Tom drove down the steep twisty road to the bottom of the hill, and then made a left turn up the dirt road that led into the valley between. About a half-mile up, he stopped to unlock a fence before proceeding up the road.

If Bobby had been hoping to attract help from other drivers near Austin, he found the city as dead as it always looked every time he'd been there. It was supposed to have a population of 167, but he'd never actually seen any of the residents, other than the owner of the motel, who also ran the café; the Champ's Station attendant; and the docent at the tiny Austin Museum.

That was great when he had a victim in the vicinity.

Not so great now that *he* was being held captive.

They drove into the grove of trees, and Bobby saw a rundown plank cabin, just as Tom had said. It no longer had a door or any windows, and planks were missing from the walls. It was surrounded by a barbed-wire fence, adorned with antlers from numerous deer, elk, pronghorns, and bighorn sheep.

"What a happy little cabin of death you have here, Tom!"

"Soon to be much happier once I wipe your predatory ass off this planet. Maybe I should mount your skull."

Tom climbed out of the van and went around to Bobby's side, weapon in hand. He opened the door and jammed the high-voltage stun gun into Bobby's ribcage, discharging it until his body was wracked with painful muscle spasms. He climbed up onto the running board and leaned over Bobby to pop the secret mechanism that released the seatbelt.

Tom cinched the zip cuffs around Bobby's wrist until they cut into the flesh before dragging him into the cabin, thumping his head on every large rock along the way. With one great yank, he pulled Bobby up and slammed him down on an ancient wood kitchen table. It trembled under the force of his anger and brute strength.

Bobby's eyes widened, scanning the room and taking note of all the sharp implements within arm's reach. Tom grabbed a ratcheting tie-down from the floor and began to cinch it tightly around Bobby's chest, before doing the same with another around his pelvis.

"You're not going anywhere." Tom picked up a sharp blade, staring at Bobby with dead eyes and an evil grin on his face.

Bobby finally began to understand the gravity of his predicament. He threw his body against the straps, trying to break free or make the weak table collapse.

All it did was wobble.

"What should I do first? You seem to be quite fond of painful, gruesome acts. But I can't have you bleeding out too fast. It just wouldn't do to have you die *too* soon. Ahhhh! Oh yeah, wait! I've been planning this for a while." Tom turned away and walked to the other side of the room. "I've thought of everything." He held up a small propane blowtorch. "Cautery!"

"Please don't. I'm sorry. You can't do this. You said you were a Texas Ranger. You're supposed to uphold the law, not break it."

"You broke me the day you slaughtered my baby girl. I'm sure she begged for her life, but you didn't care. Just the way I don't... now."

Tom slashed with his knife, slicing open Bobby's stomach with one movement. Bobby yowled in pain and flailed on the table, or at least his legs did. The open wound puckered and began to stretch open as his intestines started to slide out from the movement. "This is how Christine felt that day. Anything you want to say?"

"HELP! Help me! Please stop. I beg you. Just call 911, and leave me here. I won't tell them who did this to me."

"All I can hear is my daughter's sweet voice, terrified and in pain, begging you to help her. Did you?"

Bobby began hyperventilating. His eyes scrunched closed, and he shook his head, refusing to answer.

"DID YOU?" Tom bellowed

"No! No, I didn't." Bobby whined, terror in his eyes.

Tom held up a finger. "Just one second. I'll help you though."

Bobby flinched when he heard the metallic click-click of the striker, and then the hiss from the flame of the lit blowtorch. His eyes opened, and he saw the flame move across the torn flesh of his abdomen. It bubbled and sizzled under the intense heat. The cabin filled with the smell of singed hair and burnt skin.

Bobby's screams echoed through the canyon, until they ceased when he passed out from the pain.

When Bobby awoke, his entire body felt like one nerve on fire, flashing up and down him, consuming him. Tom stood there smiling, holding smelling salts under his nose. Bobby turned his head, trying to avoid the pungent odor.

"Oh, you're finally awake!"

Bobby felt the breeze on his skin... all of his skin. He buried his chin on his chest, noticing that Tom had removed his clothing.

And much of the skin on his chest.

There was a large pool of blood on his groin. Apparently, his abdomen was still bleeding.

"Oh that? I noticed you liked body modification... with all your tattoos and piercings, carefully hidden under clothing. I thought you might like some more. I hear scarification is all the rage these days among you freakish types. Branding. Cutting. Chemicals. Forking of tongues and..."

Tom held up a mirror so Bobby could see the flesh that had been cut from his chest and abdomen in different shapes. And then the double lightning-bolt brands. "I must apologize. I'm not trained in this kind of thing. I tried to split..." Tom began to tilt the mirror more so the view went lower. "... your penis in half like I saw on the internet, but I'm afraid I made a mess of it."

Blood was pooled around the small mound of ragged flesh that had once been Bobby's penis, now charred and hanging by a thread.

"No, no, no! I get it. I'm sorry. Just let me go. Isn't this enough?"

"Enough? ENOUGH? Are you fucking kidding me? Nothing will ever be enough, unless you can bring her back. Can you do that, Bobby?"

"No."

"I didn't think so." Tom plunged the knife into Bobby's chest and pulled it out. "Whoopsie! You're not supposed to pull the knife out when you stab somebody. Sorry about that."

Tom sat down and watched as Bobby's breathing became more difficult. Blood had begun to pool up in the pleural space, putting pressure on his lungs... one had been punctured and had begun filling with blood as it collapsed. Bobby coughed and sprayed blood onto Tom's face.

Tom reached up to wipe away the fine blood droplets on his face, the gleam in his eyes never fading as the life did from Bobby's.

Tom dragged Bobby's body into the grove of trees and left it for the animals.

All except for one part.

The head.

He plunged that onto the fence post where one of the antlers had fallen off.

Tom drove off the property, headed for Mexico. With any luck, Bobby's body wouldn't be found for a long time. But if it was, Tom was prepared to pay the price. It had all been worth it.

"Road Hazard" by Sharon Marie Provost appears here for the first time.

Stephen H. Provost

Donner Time

"Would you like me to tell you a bedtime story?"
Old Clem stepped into Donnie's room and closed the heavy wood door behind him. Donnie's parents, Jalen and Bobbi, had gone to the late marathon of the Anthony Hopkins *Hannibal* trilogy down in Reno, and they weren't expected back until late.

Old Clem wasn't a relative, and he wasn't their usual

babysitter, either—Mariah Morgan had been grounded for failing a history exam—but everyone in Virginia City knew and loved him. Clem had lived there all his life, and though he refused to say how old he was, it was commonly assumed that he was in his late seventies at least.

Donnie, who was 6 years old and very precocious, frowned at Clem.

"Oh, you think you're too old for bedtime stories, do you?"

Donnie stuck out his tongue. "Mom and Dad tell me silly stories, like 'The Cat in the Hat' and 'Horton Hears a Who.'"

"What's wrong with those?" Clem asked, tilting his head to one side. It was impossible to tell if he was curious or merely trying to point his hearing aid in the proper direction for maximum clarity.

"Are you kidding?" Donnie said. "Those stories are for little kids. I wanna hear somethin' scary! It's almost Halloween!"

"I don't think your parents have any scary books in the house," Clem objected.

"We don't need an old book," Donnie chided. "Tell me a story about the city."

"Okay," Clem said, leaning over until his head was almost directly above Donnie's. "What would you like to know?"

"I dunno! Tell me about... tell me why there's that loud sound every day in the middle of the day."

"Oh, you mean the siren." Clem leaned back and scratched his head. "Well, most people hereabouts think it started back in the silver rush... and it did. When the miners heard the siren, they knew it was time fer lunch, so they'd break off diggin' and have a bite t'eat."

"Oh, that's not scary at all!" Donnie protested.

Old Clem smiled so wide it looked like his dentures were going to fall out of his mouth. "I said *most people* think that. But there's more to the story; another tale to tell, if you'd like t'hear it, one that might scare the bejeezus out of ya!"

Donnie sat up straight in bed and clapped his hands. "Yes! I *do* want to hear!"

Old Clem leaned so far back in the chair he was sitting in beside the bed that it looked like he might fall over. Then he commenced to staring at the ceiling and pondering, "Well, let me see now," he said, stroking his bristly white beard. "If I remember correctly, it goes somethin' like this..."

"Once upon a time, there was a group of pioneers who came out west from Illinois, lookin' for a new home in California. They had a grand total of fifty wagons with 'em, with a bunch of the migrants belongin' to the Donner and Reed families."

"Did you say Donner?"

"That's right. And Reed. They were all filled with visions of this great life in a state full of gold. But they got some bad advice from a fella named Hastings. He told 'em they could get through quicker if'n they followed a new route he told 'em about through Utah, rather'n takin' the California Trail."

"What happened?" Donnie asked excitedly. "Did the Injuns get 'em and cut off the top of their heads?"

Clem sighed. "There ain't no 'Injuns' in America," he said. "The Injuns are all in Indja! The people here had their own homes and countries afore we came an' took it from 'em. They weren't botherin' no one, 'cept maybe each other, till we came along an' stuck our noses in their business. But to answer your question, they made it across the Hastings Cutoff just fine, but it took 'em a lot longer than they reckoned. With winter comin' on, by the time they made it to the Sierra mountains, it was snowin' somethin' fierce, and they all got bogged down in it."

Donnie's eyes widened. "Did they get eaten by bears?"

"No, no. The bears were all smart enough to be hibernatin' in their caves when winter hit, but the Donner Party was out in the open. It was so cold that some of them started freezin' to death. They'd wake up one morning and find one of 'em froze solid with icicles hanging off his nose and ears. One night, someone might be all pink as a baby's butt, the next mornin', they'd be blue as a Smurf and stiff as a board."

"Smurfs are for little kids," Donnie objected.

"Sorry. Now, as I was saying..."

"And how come all the Smurfs are boys except just one who's a girl?"

"I dunno. Maybe a-cause all the other Smurfettes froze to death and were eaten by bears who were too stupid to be hibernatin'!" He threw up his hands. "Didn't you say Smurfs are for little kids? I ain't even finished answerin' your other question, and now you wanna hear about Smurfs. Does that make you a little kid?" He leaned forward and jabbed his index finger softly at the tip of Donnie's nose.

"Hey! I mean... no."

"Good, because I ain't no little kid neither, and I ain't gonna say another word about Smurfs. Now," he said again, "*as I was saying*, the Donners and the Reeds and the other folks with 'em didn't just start freezin', they ran out of food. So what do you think they did then?"

"They ate each other!" Donnie declared, thrusting an index finger into the air.

"That's exactly what they did," Clem said, nodding. "And because they ate each other, they survived, and the story got out about how terrible it was once they got to Sacramento. But they made everyone in the party swear that they'd omit one important detail from their story."

"Omit?"

"That is to say, leave it out."

"What was that?" Donnie was hanging on every word now.

"That they *liked* it!" Clem said, thrusting his own finger into the air. "They never imagined human flesh could taste so good. It was like chocolate and ice cream and birthday cake all rolled up into one and whipped into cotton candy. They couldn't get enough of it. But they had t'keep it a secret, because they knew no one else would accept it, and if they did, they'd find out how good it tasted and start eating *them*! This was their code: Never, ever, under any circumstances, would they let on to how yummy human flesh was."

Donnie shivered. "This *is* a scary story!"

"Do you want me to stop? I haven't answered your question yet."

"No, no!" Donnie objected, a fierce expression on his face. "I want to hear the rest!"

"Okay, then. Well, when the Donners had made it through, they returned to their normal lives in their new homes. But rumor has it that, every now and then, they'd invite a guest for dinner who didn't show up for work the following day. The coppers never went nosin' around, and nothing ever came of it, so they was probably *just* rumors. They wouldn't have been careless enough to start eatin' people again, would they?" He cocked an eyebrow to indicate it wasn't a rhetorical question.

"I dunno," said Donnie finally. "Would they?"

"Of course not!" Clem laughed, but then his face turned all serious again. "At least not most of them. You see, there was one family member who liked the taste of human flesh so much he couldn't contain himself. Everywhere he went, people started disappearin', and they said he was cursed because of it, never suspectin' that he was really eatin' 'em.

"Now, when Levi Donner—you won't find his name in any of the historical records, a-cause they've expunged it..."

"Expunged?"

"Erased... now, when ol' Levi had been kicked out of everywhere worth bein' kicked out of in California, he came over here to Virginia City. This was a few years after the Big Bonanza, an' ol' Virginny was a happenin' place. Saloons. Miners. Gunslingers..."

"And Injuns?"

"I already told you. There ain't no Injuns in America."

"Oh, yeah."

"An' at that time," Clem continued, "there was more'n twenty thousand people livin' here. But when ol' Levi arrived, guess what?"

"They started disappearin'?" Donnie whispered conspiratorially.

"That's right. But this time, Levi decided he wasn't about to get kicked out of another city, so he did somethin' none of the other Donners ever woulda done. He broke the code."

Donnie gasped.

"That's right. He started tellin' people that human flesh was a delicacy. That you could eat it sauteed, cooked over a fire, basted, broiled, you name it. He told 'em it went best with red wine, like most red meat, but that the drink of choice among the miners—whiskey—made it taste even better."

"And they believed him?"

"Well, he didn't just tell them straight out. That would have been pretty damn stupid. He'd invite his best friends over to supper, cook them up a leg o' man, and tell 'em it was a 'secret recipe.' Then he'd let 'em in on the secret afterward, having them swear they'd never tell."

"Did they?"

"What do you think? Of course they did! When whiskey starts flowin' mouths start a-runnin', an' people will believe sh... uh, things, they never would have given any thought to otherwise. So, pretty soon, word got around, and all sorts of people were swearin' that a human thigh or drumstick tasted ten times better than a chicken or even a filet mignon. Now, everyone thinks Virginia City shriveled up an' became like a ghost town because the mines stopped producin'. But the truth of the matter is, the miners got so busy killin' and eatin' one another that the work just stopped. It ain't that all those people *left* Virginia City. They ate each other."

Donnie was enthralled, and his eyes nearly bugged out of his head. "Wow!"

"Don't get too excited, son. My story ain't quite done yet. You asked about the siren that sounds at noon every day."

"Oh, yeah!"

Clem leaned in closer again. "Have you ever seen *The Walking Dead*?"

Donnie nodded eagerly. "Every episode. Even the spinoffs."

"Well, it's a great show, but they got one thing wrong about them zombies. In real life, zombies ain't the result of some plague or mutation or whatnot. They don't start eatin' people after they start walkin' around all stiff like Frankenstein's monster. It's the other way around. You see, eatin' human flesh has an unfortunate side-effect: The more you eat, the more you act like a zombie, just walkin' around bein' dumb and listless. It's like after you eat a turkey on Thanksgiving, except a hundred times worse. So after they ate up most of the people in Virginia City, these zombies just kept walkin' around like they didn't know where they were goin'."

Donnie frowned. "But what does all this have to do with that noise?"

"The siren, you mean. Well, I'm just now comin' to that. Hardly anyone ever came up to Virginia City for the longest time, a-cause they was afraid of the zombies. No one ever admitted it, but that was the reason. But sometime after the Great Depression, people started gettin' wise to the idea that they could make a buck off tourists comin' up to see the greatest silver town in all the West. So they started openin' stores, sellin' souvenirs, bringin' back the old saloons an' everything else you see today."

"What happened to the zombies, though? Did they just leave?"

"Are you kiddin' me? They gave everyone a helluva time before the new entrepreneurs..."

"Entrepreneurs?"

"People with stores tryin' to make a buck."

"Oh."

"...before the entrepreneurs came up with an idea. They started sounding the siren again like they had back in the boom times. An' when they did, it had a fortuitous side effect. But afore I tell ya what it was, I should mention this: Not only is human flesh absolutely delicious, but it's packed full o' nutrients that help you live a lot longer than the average bear."

"Bear?"

"I mean person. The point is that the miners who turned into zombies were still around seventy or eighty years after the fact. There weren't a lot of humans left in Virginny, so they'd go down and grab people off Highway 50, then return right quick... which is why they *really* call 50 the Loneliest Road.

"Now, these old miners were so stoned out of their minds after eatin' human flesh for so long that they couldn't think too straight anymore. A lot of those zombies had been eatin' humans for so long they didn't pay much attention to anything anymore, but one thing they remembered from way back was that a siren at midday meant it was chow time. So when that siren went off, all the zombies came a-running, and the entrepreneurs herded them all together so they wouldn't be botherin' the tourists.

That's where the people who wrote *The Walking Dead* got the idea of sound distractin' zombies. It all started right here in this very town."

"What did they do with the zombies when they got 'em all rounded up?" Donnie asked.

"They threw 'em all into an old mine and sealed it shut. That was the end of the matter. Now they sell a ton of candy and ice cream in Virginia City 'cause it tastes like human flesh, just to keep the zombies happy in case there are any of 'em still around. And that's my story. Scary enough for ya?"

Donnie leaned forward. "Yes!"

Clem was a bit discouraged that, rather than putting the boy to sleep, his story seemed to have rendered him wider awake than ever.

"I hope I didn't scare you too much," he said. "It's just an ol' legend: a made-up story."

He leaned forward again, rubbing his hands together. "After all that adventure," he declared. "I'm a little *hungry*."

Donnie shivered for a moment, then answered, "So am I."

When Donnie's parents came home, they were met with the sight of blood, human entrails, and bits of flesh strewn about the dining room and kitchen.

"Donnie!" his mother screamed. "Are you here? Answer me! Please tell me you're okay."

A moment later, a figure came down the stairs grinning, the tip of a big toe sticking out of its mouth.

"Do you want some?" he said, holding out a detached forearm dripping with blood. "It's mighty good."

"Donnie Donner!" his mother chastened him. "What have we told you about eating babysitters? We told you we'd bring you home some ice cream."

Donnie looked at the ground sheepishly. "Sorry, Mom, but Old Clem was so *gooooood*."

"Up to your room this instant!" his mother ordered. "And no ice cream for you tonight." She knew full well that he wouldn't want any. He'd had something better already.

She shook her head as Donnie headed up the stairs, looking at her husband. "What are we going to do with him?" Bobbi Donner lamented. "He's got to stop eating between meals. It isn't good for him."

Her husband just shrugged. "I don't think there's anything we can do about it," Jalen Donner said. "It's way past his Donner Time, and he *is* a fine young cannibal."

"Donner Time" by Stephen H. Provost appears here for the first time.

Sharon Marie Provost

The Kobayashi Maru Package

"You're kidding me! We're staying here?" Bobby asked, incredulous.

"Yes, isn't it to die for?" Chantel said in her faux snooty tone.

"Exactly my fucking point! No *fucking* way! I refuse to stay here. Drop me off at that motel up the street there."

"Oh, come on! Pleeeease! I swear on my life that you won't

die."

"You can swear on everybody's life in this town. It don't mean shit if we all die."

"Seriously! Big ol' 'Bobby the Hammer' Thompson is afraid of a few little clowns."

"First of all, I ain't afraid of nuttin'. Second, you say 'few' as if the population of China was a coupla dozen people. I see three dozen horrific depictions of those smiley bastards painted on the building, and I can't even see the whole place. I heard about this place on the Travel Channel. There's thousands more clowns in that museum in the lobby. Noooooo thanks!"

"You owe me, Bobby. How many crazy places have I stayed for you? I don't see Alex complaining."

"Alex is off in space. That herb he smoked has him orbiting Venus right about now. Not that he can hear us with those earbuds in anyhow."

Bobby reached in the back and slugged Alex in the side, startling him awake.

"Did you know about this shit?"

"What, dude? Oww... that really hurt, man." Alex was rubbing his side as he looked up. "No way, dude! This is fucking awesome. Please tell me this is where we are staying the night." He held his hands together while kneeling in the back of the van, praying to Chantel in the driver's seat.

"Finally, somebody with some sense," she retorted with a smirk at Bobby.

"Firing on all sixes there... all six brain cells left, that is." Bobby howled at his own joke.

"Apparently six is enough. Besides, how many do you have after all the 'roids you used to build up those muscles?"

Alex scooted into the back of the van, away from Bobby's grasp. He knew how much Bobby hated it when people accused him of juicing.

"Hard work and diet, man. That's all it takes to build up these babies." Bobby flexed in his tank top, two sizes too small in order to show off his muscles.

Chantel rolled her eyes. "So, what's the verdict?"

"Fine. Whatever. This is totally stupid. You're on your own. Don't expect me to save your asses. No dumbass clown is taking me down."

Bobby hadn't noticed Alex slip out the back of the van and come around to the passenger side window.

"Beep Beep, Richie!" Alex yelled through the window, making Bobby jump and gasp.

"That's it, dickwad. You're going down!"

Bobby jumped out of the van and began chasing after Alex.

"I thought I took two strong men with me on this road trip. Instead, I've got overgrown children." Chantel shook her head as she pulled up into a space in front of the office.

"Hey, idiots! Let's check out the museum before we register for rooms," Chantel called out as she exited the van.

"Fine. You guys have to make a deal with me though..." Bobby replied.

"I'm not sure I even want to ask. But *what*?" Chantel asked.

"On our trip up the Oregon coast next summer..."

"Yes?" Alex asked with a cringe.

"We go to the Itty Bitty Inn in North Bend."

"Okay, but what's the catch?" Chantel and Alex replied in unison.

"We stay in the Captain Kirk-themed USS Enterprise Room."

Chantel and Alex sighed loudly and started to turn away.

"You agreed! You can't back out now! It's only fair."

"Whatever!" Chantel waved her hand and walked into the motel office.

Alex, agreeable as ever, chuckled and fist bumped Bobby

before following her inside. "Epic manipulation there, bud," he called over his shoulder.

Chantel turned back around just inside the entrance. "And don't even think about claiming the bed after that. You two are in sleeping bags on the floor."

As she finished her sentence, she noticed Bobby didn't look right. His face had drained of all color. His eyes were flicking back and forth, scanning the room. He scarcely appeared to be breathing, only taking small, shallow gasps.

"Dude! What's wrong with you?" Alex snickered and slapped Bobby on the back.

"I... I... thought it was an exaggeration. *They're* everywhere. Thousands of them! What the actual fuck? I gotta go."

"Oh, come on! Don't be such a baby." Chantel grabbed his hand and pulled him toward the registration desk.

"Let me go, dammit! If you want me to stay here tonight, I am leaving this room. Now!"

"Fine. See you in a couple."

Bobby could hear his friends laughing at him as he walked out. He continued off to the left side of the parking lot toward a beautiful wooden gazebo. A few minutes sitting down in the cool fall air would help him relax.

That was when he noticed what was right next to the motel, just behind the gazebo.

The old Tonopah Cemetery.

Eternal residence to the original settlers of Tonopah. Resting place for 14 of the miners who died in a horrific mine fire in 1911 and the victims of the 1902 plague.

This is fucked! You've got to be shitting me. A fucking cemetery right next to the motel.

Bobby spun around and ran into Alex, who was nearly frothing at the mouth with excitement. "No fucking way! A creepy clown-themed motel that's haunted *and* has an eerie cemetery next to it. Boo-yah!"

Over Alex's shoulder, Bobby saw Chantel approaching with a sneaky, sheepish look on her face. "I see you found the cemetery."

"So you knew? I should have known. Who the fuck does that? Why would you build a motel, a fucking grotesque nightmare of a motel at that, right next to an old graveyard?"

She shrugged her shoulders. "Because it attracts visitors?"

"Macabre, twisted people like the two of you."

Alex slung his arm around Chantel. "Guilty as charged!"

Bobby sighed in disgust. "So did you get us checked in?"

"Sure did."

"Tell me... did you get one of them?" Alex asked, his voice dripping with enthusiasm.

"I'm sure I don't want to ask. But get *what* exactly?"

"Nope, you're correct. You don't want to know." With that she turned to Alex and nodded.

"What room number?"

"108."

Alex grabbed the key from her hand and galloped off toward the room, whooping out loud.

Bobby looked back at the gravesites, then turned to Chantel. "Let's get this nightmare started."

As he started to step away from the low cinder block wall surrounding the few steps down to the cemetery, he jumped when he heard a loud noise off to his right.

In the small strip of blacktop between the motel and cemetery was an old metal shipping container. He had been startled by the buzzing and metallic screech of what sounded like an angle grinder echoing from inside the container.

"What the hell was that?"

"Probably someone working. Maybe the owner is an artist or something."

"No... after that."

"It sounded like a whimper."

"You're bugging out. Seriously!"

Bobby strode off in the direction Alex had gone. "Let's just get in the stupid room."

Chantel paused, listening for a few seconds, then followed him, shaking her head. "Can you say paranoid?" she mumbled under her breath.

When Chantel reached the room, she wasn't surprised to find Bobby having another meltdown. His eyes were roving back and forth between the life-size Pennywise painting next to the bed and Alex.

"What now?" she asked, her impatience growing.

One look at Alex's guilty face, and she knew what.

"Why did you have to tell him?"

Alex put on his best innocent face and threw his hands up.

"You got us the goddamn ghosthunter package? Did some guy really die after placing calls to the front desk from this room? Calls that didn't go through?"

"Well, that's the story."

"Why would they lie?"

"At least she didn't pick the room where a guy actually died *in* it or the one with the spirit that taunted a guy until he committed suicide in the parking lot."

"Oh yes, cuz this is just so much better, right?"

"I *did* think you'd be more agreeable to it, Bobby." Chantel actually looked like she believed what she said. "It doesn't have to be sinister. Maybe the phone was just broken. He didn't die *in* the room, so I don't see why you are so upset."

"Whatever! I'm going to take a nap *on* the bed, not the floor."

"Fine. We're going to dinner at 6:30 and then doing the paranormal tour at 10. Alex and I are going to explore, and we'll wake you when we get back."

"I'm not so sure about the tour, but dinner sounds good. See ya later."

An hour and a half later, Bobby awoke to the sound of the doorknob wiggling as someone tried to open it.

"I'm up. I'm up. I'll be right out."

There was no reply. The doorknob clicked as it was turned roughly back and forth.

"Did you forget the key? Do you need me to grab you something as I come out?"

Again, no reply.

The door shuddered and bounced on its hinges as someone began to pound on it.

"Goddammit! What?" Bobby ripped open the door. The spring on the doorstop twanged as the door bounced off it.

There was no one there. Angry, Bobby stepped out and spun around, looking up and down the corridor for the culprit, but no one was around. He heard Chantel and Alex talking and laughing as they approached from the cemetery.

"Real funny, guys!" Bobby snapped.

"What's your problem, sleepyhead?" Chantel asked with a wink.

"Pounding on the door like that was *real* mature."

Alex gave him a sideward glance before turning to Chantel, a questioning look on his face. "I'm not sure what big boy is talking about, are you, dudette?"

"You guys didn't just about knock down the door a minute ago?"

"No," they replied in unison.

"Then did you see anyone else here before I came out?"

"There's nobody around except the front desk guy, and he went inside a few minutes ago after talking to us. I think everybody else staying here went out for dinner," Chantel said.

"That doesn't make any sense."

"Ever thought it could have been a nightmare? You've been pretty spooked ever since we arrived." Alex's impatient tone betrayed his frustration with Bobby's attitude. "I'm sorry this has bugged you so much. We didn't think it would be that big a deal. Can you just try to be a good sport? We do shit we don't like for you."

"Yeah, bro. I apologize. I'll try to chill. Maybe a few drinks will help. We still going to that Mexican restaurant we saw as we drove through town?"

"Margaritas for everyone!" Chantel said with a smile.

"Dude, I can give you some of that epic bud I got at the dispensary in Vegas when we get back too."

"I just might take you up on that, bro. Let's bail. I'm sure a few minutes away will do me good."

Bobby felt much better two hours later when they returned after consuming two pitchers of margaritas and countless tacos. It seemed like the rest of the motel's guests had returned during their absence. The bright neon lights on the motel's sign added to the circus atmosphere.

As they exited the van, Bobby heard the voices of a group of people standing in the back corner in the breezeway between the two perpendicular wings of the motel. As Bobby walked to the room, listening to the conversation, he realized the group was on one of the earlier ghost tours. It didn't sound as frightening as he had expected.

Alex and Chantel weren't paying attention as they searched their pockets for the room key. Bobby saw someone in a clown suit walk up behind the tour group. There was a machete in his raised hand.

Ain't no way I'm going on that shitty tour. It may just be a stupid jump scare, but I don't need to cut any years off my life.

Then everything changed.

"B... blood. Stab... uhh..."

"What in hell are you saying, Bobby?"

Bobby raised one shaky finger and pointed at the group as a blood-curdling scream pierced the night.

"Clown."

"It's a joke. Chill out."

"No. No, it's not. The clown just cut off her arm. Look!"

At that moment, two of the girls split off and began to run toward the open room two doors away. The third girl had collapsed to the ground, blood spurting from the stump where her arm had been connected. The severed appendage lay on the ground in a pool of blood.

The two young men in the group were trying to subdue the clown dressed in a polka-dot jumpsuit and wearing a bright purple, curly wig. A large, exaggerated mouth with blood-red lips and sharp teeth had been drawn on his face—except it *appeared* to be real. Droplets of saliva fell from his fangs and ran down his face.

The clown opened that mouth impossibly wide and bit down on the arm of the young man who had wrapped him in a headlock. Blood squirted between his teeth, splashing on the face of the other young man. The clown gnashed his teeth and shook his head as he ripped a large chunk of flesh and muscle from the man's arm.

Bobby spun when he heard another gut-wrenching scream from the direction of the metal shipping container. Once again, he heard the sound of power tools echoing within its cavernous interior.

Chantel screamed and grabbed Bobby's hand, pulling him toward their open room door.

But none of them had opened it.

There stood another clown. He looked just like Captain Spaulding from *House of 1000 Corpses*. He held a large meat cleaver in his hand. "Hey there, motherfuckers!"

Bobby acted on instinct, pushing Chantel out of the way as he gave the clown a brutal roundhouse kick to the face. Alex ducked under Bobby's foot and grabbed the door, slamming it shut when the clown fell backward.

"We've got to get out of here," Alex said, stating the obvious.

"Where, dumbass?"

"We got ourselves a situation here. Chantel signed us up for the motherfucking Kobayashi Maru package apparently. None of the options—motel, cemetery, or shipping container—seem like good places to hide."

Chantel put her hands on her hips, pissed off. "We don't have time for that *Star Trek* bullshit!"

"Run!" Alex screamed as he pointed behind them at another clown, approaching from the street.

The three of them ran toward the first clown, who had begun ripping out the throat of the second man. He didn't notice them as they ran past him between the two wings and around the back of the motel. They ducked down in the darkness behind a stack of pallets and other debris.

"Let's continue around the back here. Then sneak past the container and circle back around toward the front. We'll get in the car and get the fuck out of Dodge!" Bobby took control as usual. He acted like a few years in military school had somehow turned him into Rambo.

Where the fuck was that bravado a few hours ago? Chantel asked herself.

"Yes! Sounds good to me." Alex started to get up but stopped when he heard Chantel.

"Shitballs!"

"What?" Bobby whisper-yelled at her.

"The keys. I must have dropped them."

"You've got to be fucking kidding me," he replied.

"It's your fault. You pushed me."

"What happened to being a boss bitch, Chantel? You can't even hold on to keys? So help me, if you get us killed, I swear I will..."

"What, Bobby? What will you do, big man? Hit a girl? Kill me? Won't it be a little late for that?"

"Shut up, you two! Don't you remember there was a clown following us?"

Chantel was on a roll and ignored Alex.

"Go ahead. I dare you! I can take you." Chantel pulled off her stiletto heel and raised it like a weapon as the blade of a meat cleaver plunged into the top of her head from behind. "Gurggh... unnhhh."

She slumped to the ground, twitching as the clown from the street stepped forward, followed by the one that had killed the three people from the tour.

The clown from the street was rotund and wearing a billowy jumpsuit covered in red and white vertical stripes. He wore a black curly wig with goth makeup that made his eyes appear sunken in. A rivulet of blood tracked down from the corner of his mouth to his neck.

The clown held out a large old-fashioned bike horn with the black bulb and began honking it. "Who's next?"

"Either one of you takes one more step toward us, and you are going to be sorry," Bobby growled as he crouched in an offensive position.

"What you gonna do to us?" the Captain Spaulding clown

asked as he rounded the corner to join the other two.

"Fuck around and find out, shithead!"

Bobby reached down and grabbed a heavy pipe from the pile of debris they had been crouching beside. "Run, Alex!"

Bobby swung the pipe and smashed it into the side of the goth clown's head with a solid "thunk," dropping him to the ground. As Bobby prepared to battle the other two, a back door that led into the motel museum opened up.

Alex screamed, "Look!" The two men ran toward the door, hoping it would buy them a head start to reach the car and effect their escape. As they rounded the threshold, slamming the door shut behind them, they realized a small, vicious clown child stood before them, blocking their exit into the lobby.

The little girl, whose curly pink hair was done up in pigtails, was wearing Mary Janes and a yellow dress with red polka dots. The small clown growled at them as they approached, baring her teeth.

"Fuck this shit!" Bobby screamed.

With one swift, damaging karate kick to the throat, the clown girl's head snapped back, and she was thrown into one of the glass display cases.

Bobby and Alex brushed past and slipped out the front door without making a sound. A quick look to the right revealed several more clowns gathered near the motel rooms. They ducked down by a car parked near the office and tried to figure out where to go.

"Balls! Guess we have to go over to the last place in the world I wanted to go."

"Bobby, we can make it." Alex was cut off by another scream from the shipping container 15 feet to their left. "Don't tell me you're talking about going over there? The cemetery was great in the day, but I'm not so sure I want to see it now. And I don't even want to guess what's going on in there."

"We don't have a choice. Let's sneak around the side of the motel and hide in the darkness just in front of the shipping container. It opens to the back of the property, so as long as we're quiet, they'll never know we're there. That will give us the best cover to scope out the situation and figure out a plan of escape. Keep an eye on the cemetery. I don't know what the fuck else is out there. Got it?"

Alex nodded, and the two men ran around and crouched by the container, settling in the darkness.

"What the fuck is going on here? Is this like a fucking killer clown convention?"

"What do you mean?" Alex peered around Bobby's shoulder to see what he was looking at in the parking lot.

Gathered together near the cars that were parked there was a group of clowns that looked strangely familiar. They all had misshapen lumpy faces with exaggerated facial features, each with a bulbous, perfectly round red nose. Their hair was coarse like a Wishnik doll's.

They all wore loose-fitting jumpsuits with old-fashioned rounded clown collars, almost like jesters. Stranger yet, they carried items like impossibly large wooden mallets, oversized twisty straws, cream pies, boxing gloves on retractable arms, and what looked like ray guns.

Alex was shaking his head in disbelief. It was his turn to have a meltdown. "It can't be. It just can't. That was just a movie."

"Face it, Alex. Nothing is *right* here."

"But those are the fucking clowns in *Killer Klowns from Outer Space*."

"And that's Pennywise," Bobby said as he pointed over near their car. "What's your point?"

"What are we going to do?"

"We're going to have to fight our way out."

"Bobby, I can't fight my way through a long line at the dispensary. What do you think I can do here?"

"You better figure it out. Take this." Bobby handed him the large pipe he was still carrying.

"What about you?"

"I've got my guns," Bobby said as he flexed, displaying his large biceps. "Let's try sneaking into this thing. There can't be more than one of them in there, right?"

"What about just trying to run through the cemetery?"

"Are you fucking serious? Do you really want to find out what's hiding out *there*? Haven't you been paying attention at all? Can't you see the movement out there? I don't know who that is... what that is... but I ain't finding out if the miner from *My Bloody Valentine* is out there."

"Dude, you watch too many horror movies."

"You'll appreciate me if it saves your ass though."

"Have you forgotten what day it is?"

"It's Nevada Day I think."

"Right."

"So? What the fuck does that have to do with anything, dude?"

"And what day is Nevada Day?"

"Seriously fuck you! Fuck off! Come on! Are you really going there now?"

"It's Halloween, dumbass. The veil is thinner then. What if the ghosts of the dead miners and plague victims are roaming around out there? They're probably pissed off. They might want to kill us too. I ain't chancing it."

"You've lost it, dude. Which one of us was smoking the ganja? I'm taking my chances alone. You're crazy!" Alex had raised his voice with each word.

"Shhhh! They're going to hear you."

"Yes, we are," the Captain Spaulding clown said as he swung an ice hook, plunging it into the middle of Alex's torso from behind.

Alex's back arched as he reached out toward Bobby to help him. His eyes were wide and filled with tears. "Acccchhh... help," he sputtered as the blood gurgled in his throat. Captain Spaulding yanked him back by the hook and ran a boxcutter across his throat, slowly slitting it open, inch-by-inch, as blood flooded down his neck.

"Happy Halloween, motherfucker!" the clown cackled.

Bobby heard footsteps approaching from behind. He spun around to find the Killer Klowns and some of the others nearly upon him.

"Fuck it! I'll take my chances."

He ran to the ledge that overlooked the Tonopah Cemetery and placed one hand down on the cinder block wall to brace himself before leaping the four feet down to the ground. He bolted through the white wrought iron gate that led into the graveyard.

He saw the shadows of two people... clowns... ghosts... whatever the fuck moving about a hundred feet off to his left. He ran headlong through the graveyard, dodging and jumping over headstones and wooden markers as he made his way across.

He turned back to see if he was being pursued, and in that brief instant, he tripped over a broken headstone he hadn't seen partially buried in the dirt. His arms were pinwheeling as he fought to regain his balance. As he turned his back to look ahead, he blinked in the bright light shining directly into his eyes just before he was stopped dead.

Stone dead with six inches of a pickaxe buried in the center of the top of his skull. The pickaxe was held by a ghostly looking miner. Bobby's eyes rolled in his head for a second. "I knew it," he murmured just before he dropped.

The miner had a smile on his face.

"Fuckin' A, Marv!" Tony bellowed across the cemetery. He dropped Alex's body, which he'd still been holding, and jogged over to Marv, who was covered in all that white powder shit to make him look ghostly. "That was one spectacular move. I've never seen that shit before. He didn't even have time to react. I was sitting in my car when these idiots arrived early. I heard that stupid prick tell his friends he wasn't going to get killed by a clown. Guess he was right, huh?"

Marv ripped the point of his pickaxe out, making a wet slurpy sound and splashing Tony with blood. "Whoopsie! You got that right. Help me drag this asshole over to where you dropped that other one. We should get all those bodies loaded up into that container. How did the rest of the guys fare?"

"That little shit Sheldon took out three right as these idiots came back. Luckily, they didn't see anything go down before they got out of their van. We might have played hell catching up with them in a car without attracting attention. This is a sleepy town once the sun sets, but it's not totally dead. Unlike all these people," Tony guffawed as they dropped Bobby's body on top of Alex's.

Over the next few minutes, the rest of the clowns and miners, 11 in all, gathered around the shipping container. The goth clown was sitting on the ground with one of the Killer Klowns tending to a gash in his forehead. Pennywise was the last to arrive, carrying the limp body of the little girl clown.

A chorus of voices began asking questions.

"Let me help you with her, Ralph."

"Is Sally okay?"

"What happened to her?"

Ralph set Sally down on the pile of bodies. "We need to have discussions in our dark web chatroom before our retreat next year. We gotta iron out some kinks in our plan. Those last three jerkoffs hurt Stan. He has one hell of a head wound."

"What happened to Sally?" Stan asked.

"That lunkhead Marv took out kicked her in the throat. Collapsed her airway. Who in the fuck does that to a child?"

A volley of "Oh my God" and "Fucker" was heard through the assembled group.

"I'm real sorry, Ralph," Axe, another of the Killer Klowns, said.

"It's not a big deal except Billy Jo is upset. I'd brought Sally home to her from a camping trip when I took out some meth heads that 'bout burned down the park. I'll find another. Overall, though, I'd say we had a real successful retreat."

"It was great, Ralph," Tony replied.

"We only have about ten hours till daylight and a lot of cleanup to do. I made an assignment sheet delegating duties. I'll help Stan get the shipping container hooked back up to his truck, and we'll dump the bodies in the mine. The rest of you mop up all the blood and work on disposing of these cars out in the desert, at least three hours from here. No cheating!

"We can't have any of this come down on Steve's back. He's nice enough to host us here each year when he fills in during the owner's African safari. Which, by the way, Mark, did you collect the motel "registration book"? Can't leave that lying around... a handy little logbook of our victims, all the people who've gone missing in this area over the last decade.

"And last but not least, kudos to Andrea for her excellent idea to add the spooky theme since it is being held over Halloween this year. Got to incorporate ghosts as well as the usual clown theme. See you all next year!"

The Clown Motel is a real place in Tonopah, and it stands adjacent to the old city cemetery. Many people, including the author, find it extremely creepy. But everything else about this story is entirely fiction. "The Kobayashi Maru Package" by Sharon Marie Provost appears here for the first time.

Stephen H. Provost

Burning Love

It was the perfect opportunity for Lenny to hit the road. It was pushing triple digits in Carlin and the apartment AC was on the fritz, so he hopped on I-80 and headed west toward Tahoe.

Any excuse would have been good enough to get out of Carlin, though. Everyone who wasn't from Nevada seemed to think it had been named for *George* Carlin, the dead comedian. That would have been a lot more interesting than the truth: It had been named in honor of some general who'd been stationed there back in '58.

Eighteen fifty-eight, that is.

About the only thing that had happened worth remembering since then was a railroad crash in '39 (*nineteen* thirty-nine) that had left a couple of dozen people dead. Lenny didn't care about that. All those people would be dead by now anyway, so what did it matter? More people would die today, and more would die tomorrow. None of it affected him.

Judas Priest's "Heading Out to the Highway" blared on the radio as Lenny pulled onto the interstate. It was his theme song. He had nothing to lose, and he was going to do things his way, just like the song said. The bass from the amped-up quadrophonic sound system invaded his ears. He'd spent more on those speakers than he had on the rest of the car, a late-model 300ZX he'd bought used at Ruby Mountain Motors in Elko.

That the car had held up as long as it had was something of a miracle, but Lenny Furtado didn't believe in miracles. That was his parents' game, not his.

Traffic was crazy on I-80 heading toward Reno from Winnemucca, and it wasn't the normal kind of traffic, either. Most of the westbound vehicles weren't exactly economy cars. Lenny passed an old school bus painted to look like the one from *The Partridge Family*. There were VW buses pulling ATVs, Chevy Vans with dirt bikes on the back, and Winnebagos covered with stickers paying tribute to everything from the Grateful Dead to *The Evil Dead*. Nearly every vehicle he passed was piled high with water bottles, and most had been splashed with swatches of color that looked like something out of Woodstock.

Lenny wasn't old enough to remember Danny Partridge, Jerry Garcia, or the summer of '69—he hadn't even been born when Bryan Adams' song *about* the summer of '69 came out, and his parents hadn't been old enough to care about Woodstock. They wouldn't have gone anyway. They'd been indoctrinated by their own Baptist parents, a fate Lenny had been sure to avoid. As for Priest, his uncle had turned him on to them, and now Rob Halford & Co. were one of the four bands on his Mount Rushmore of Metal, alongside Metallica, Iron Maiden, and, of course, Sabbath.

Lenny glanced at his heat gauge, which had begun bleeding upward toward the red. He wasn't surprised. He'd put this old buggy through hell, and now it felt like hell, literally, as smoke started pouring out of the radiator at the upper end of the Forty-Mile Desert. He pulled off the highway at the Trinity Rest Area, cut the ignition, and hopped out and headed for the restrooms.

They were all full up, and when no one came out within ten seconds, he banged on one of the doors.

"Fuck off!"

"Fuck off yourself!" Lenny shouted back, banging his fist once for emphasis on the door.

Just then, another door opened up and he ran for it, just beating an elderly man who was walking up from the opposite direction.

"Here first," he said over his shoulder as he slammed the door behind him.

It was like a furnace inside. What was it Mark Twain had called this place? "Forty memorable miles of bottomless sand"? "Forty miles of bones"? His ass felt like a cracked egg sizzling on a skillet when he plopped it down on the toilet seat. He spent as little time there as possible.

He returned to his car, but he knew it wouldn't start for him. It was toast—burnt toast—and would stay that way until the sun went down at least. It was too hot to stay in the car, so he walked over to one of the picnic benches, mercifully shaded from the sun, and sat down, pulling out his phone to scroll the net.

"Fuck, no reception."

He looked up to see a banged-up Ford Ram pulling a trailer that looked like a red football-shaped space capsule. A guy wearing a kilt and a Green Day T-shirt rolled down the window of the cab and smiled, showing off a false tooth emblazoned with a marijuana leaf. "Need a lift?" he asked.

"Where you heading?" Lenny asked.

"Black Rock, where else?" the man chortled. "It's Burning Man, baby, and I'm ready to burn!"

A blonde with a Bettie Page haircut, clad in what looked to be nothing but blue jean suspenders leaned over him, almost lying in his lap. "He's a fire dancer," she said, then added when Lenny looked at her quizzically: "He twirls balls of fire around, you know? He's kind of a pyro." She shrugged. "Guess I am too."

"It's hot enough out here already," Lenny said.

The man laughed. "Hundred percent," he said. "But we got AC in the back."

Lenny nodded. "Sold."

"C'mon, I'll show you. I'm Kenny Catfish, and this is Neve Marie, like in Neve Campbell from *Scream*. 'Cept she's hotter."

"Shut up!" the girl in the suspenders said, bending forward slightly and jiggling her breasts... which nearly fell out. "Oopsie!"

Kenny opened the door and hopped out as his companion shut off the engine and exited the other side, joining him at the door to the earthbound spacecraft. "Welcome to the Uncensored Ship!" The man beamed as he held the door open for Lenny.

"Whattya call yourself, bro?" Kenny asked.

"I'm Lenny," Lenny said flatly.

"Hey," the guy in the Green Day shirt said. "We're Kenny and Lenny. Fire!"

Lenny tried not to wince. "You into Green Day?" Lenny asked.

"Bro, for me, every day's Green Day. Wanna go in an' fire one up?"

Did this guy ever stop talking about fire? Lenny shook his head and followed him inside, with Neve bringing up the rear. The interior looked like one of those party vans people rented for bachelorette parties, except everything was second-rate. The seats were cheap red-and-purple-striped fabric, and the armrests were worn where it looked like a cat had clawed at them. Kenny reached into a drawer under one of the seats and pulled out a couple of glowsticks, snapping them.

"How's this for atmosphere?" he hooted.

"First class, Kenny," Neve said, pretending not very hard to be impressed.

"Fire it up!" Kenny said, breaking out a bong with red and orange glass intertwined to form a surreal excuse for a dragon. He inhaled deeply and passed it to Neve, who declined. Lenny politely partook, coughing a little.

"Good shit, eh?" Kenny said, eyes wide as he nodded encouragingly. "Puff the magic dragon! Ha!"

Neve shook her head. "We'd better get on the road, boys. You can stay back here and party. I'll get us where we're goin' in no time. Yeehaw!"

She hopped out like she was eager to be gone, and Kenny pulled the frayed purple drapes across bubble-shaped windows that looked like portholes in a submarine. "Can't have the cops catchin' wind of this shit," he snickered. "Get it? Catching *wind*?" The snicker became a full-fledged laugh.

"You really think they're gonna look in here?" Lenny asked.

"Hey, between here and Black Rock is one big fat speed trap. Good thing we ain't dropping speedballs! Rawk-rawk-rawk!"

Lenny didn't find his bad puns funny and wondered if he

normally acted this way or was just stoned out of his gourd. "What the fuck is that?" he asked, pointing to the black tattoo of a winged goat on a throne that covered the back of Kenny's hand. It had a beard and a prominent set of breasts that protruded above a corset. The latter appeared to be held in place by a pair of snakes doing a pole dance.

"Oh, this?" Kenny said, lifting his hand to look at the black tattoo like he was seeing it for the first time. "That's Baphomet."

"My parents would say it's Satan." Lenny's voice was neither judgmental nor affirming. It was simply a statement.

"Nah, man, nah. Baphomet is like this old wise dude, but with titties. Gotta love them titties!"

Kenny inhaled liberally from the bong and offered it again to Lenny.

"I think I'll pass," he said. "Got any booze?"

Kenny reached into a small cupboard above the sink in the cramped Uncensored Ship and took a swig of Jack straight from the bottle. Lenny followed suit, wondering if his car would be okay back at the rest stop overnight. He shrugged it off and remembered his motto: He was going to do things his way, and he had nothing the fucksoever to lose.

The Uncensored Ship lurched and swayed as the pickup turned right onto an unpaved surface.

"Yeah, baby!" Kenny whooped. "The Playa! You don't wanna get stuck out here in the rainy season. It's like quicksand."

It rambled for about a quarter-mile before it came to a stop and Kenny leapt to his feet. Neve appeared at the door just as he was about to open it. "We're here, my lovelies!" she smiled. "Let the festivities begin!"

Lenny looked around and saw a couple of tents and a large firepit. Erected nearby was a large animal-skin canvas that served as a windbreak. It was adorned with a chalk outline that matched the tattoo on Kenny's hand. "Like it?" Neve asked, beaming.

"Bath mat, right?" Lenny snarked.

"Baph-o-MET," Kenny corrected him, clearly annoyed. At least he didn't giggle like a schoolgirl over *every* bad pun.

"Where's the rest of it?" Lenny asked. "I thought Burning Man was this huge place with thousands of people. I don't see anyone else."

Kenny smiled. "We have our own spot away from the rest of it. We'll head over when we feel like it for the partyin', but we prefer our privacy at night."

"But I can't even see Black Rock City from here."

Neve gestured casually over toward an area obscured by a low hill and several piles of stone. "It's over there behind that rise. They call it Meteor Rise because a comet or some shit killed a bunch of dinosaurs. Or coyotes. Or rattlesnakes. I don't remember which."

"That reminds me," Kenny said, adopting a tone that was as serious as he could muster in his current state of inebriation. "Be careful for them things. If ya see one, tell me. I got a noose on a pole, an' I'll catch the sucker. Venom's perfect for the ritual."

"The ritual?"

Kenny winked. "You'll see."

Lenny frowned at him. "Why don't we head over to the city now?" he suggested. "There's plenty of daylight left."

Neve shook her head. "I ain't up to that. I've been the one doin' all the driving, and I'm beat. I just wanna get wasted so we can watch the Man burn tonight."

"Tonight?" Lenny asked. "I thought that didn't happen till the end of the thing?"

"You ever been here before?" Neve asked him.

"No."

"I've been comin' every year since '17, except for COVID. So unless you know somethin' I don't, keep your trap shut."

Lenny raised both eyebrows, then almost choked when Kenny smacked him hard between the shoulder blades. "She's just funnin' ya, bro," he said. "I'm a newbie too. *She's* the priestess. I just do what she says."

"Uh... priestess?"

"Her ritual name's Sarah Salome, the high priestess of Baphomet. She's the one who'll be leadin' the ritual."

"Who else is coming?" Lenny asked.

"Oh, it's just us, bro. You're the third. There's always gotta be three. Maiden, matron, and crone. Father, Son, and Holy Ghost. Billy Joe, Tré Cool, and Mike Dirnt. Larry, Curly, and Moe." He laughed hysterically. "It's a kick. And the sex? Whoa, man. It's outta this world in a triple ritual. You'll see." He winked again.

Lenny played like he wasn't concerned, and he really wasn't. This Kenny was nutball, and the way he'd been consuming booze and bud, he'd be too wiped by nightfall to be of any use to anyone.

"Should we build a fire?" Kenny suggested, sounding purposely innocent in contrast to his obvious state of excitement. He *had* passed out, but he had come to again just after sunset. He was obviously hung over and frantically undressing Neve with his eyes... not that he needed to do much. She'd already ditched her top and was wearing nothing but a pair of very short shorts.

Lenny couldn't take his eyes off her either. Until, that is, she stepped around behind him and started massaging his shoulders. Her fingers burrowed deep into him, finding knots there he didn't know existed and untangling them, then putting her lips to his neck and softly sucking the skin into her mouth. He put his head back and stared up at the stars, which seemed to have been poured into the sky from some milky pitcher in a faraway galaxy.

He closed his eyes and felt something on his lips.

He opened them and let the whiskey flow over his tongue and trickle down into his throat. It had a bite, and he heard Kenny say, "just a touch of absinthe and a hint of snake venom."

"Should we take his clothes off now?" Kenny asked.

Lenny sat still in his seat, in a trance. Warmth radiated up his back from beyond where Neve had been standing before. She had moved somewhere else now. He wasn't sure where, but he could hear her breathing excitedly, the sound of it seemingly amplified in the silent desert.

"Yes," she whispered, and Lenny felt somebody undoing his shorts, then sliding them down...

"What the fuck?!" The voice was Kenny's.

Neve laughed uproariously.

"He's a... *she.*"

The fire was burning in a circle all around Lenny; Neve and Kenny were standing just outside it.

"But... it... won't..."

"Work if he's a woman?" Neve asked provocatively.

Lenny jumped to her feet. "No, it won't," Lenny said matter-of-factly. "The ritual calls for a burning *man.*"

Lenny jumped out of the circle and tackled Kenny, who was too hung over and shocked at the sudden turn of events to react. Lenny's loosened pants fell off, revealing a tattoo of Baphomet just below the small of her back.

Neve tossed Lenny a rope, and the pair of them quickly secured Kenny to the chair where Lenny had been seated a few seconds earlier. Lenny threw off her shirt and ran naked to fetch the gasoline from behind the Baphomet canvas, throwing it onto the fire—and Kenny, who struggled to free himself. In doing so, however, he tipped the chair over and landed in the fire, becoming an instant fireball.

Neve and Lenny danced around the burning circle, chanting something in another language as Kenny's howls rose into the night with the flames that were consuming him. Other chants and howls joined them from the distant revelers at Black Rock City, all of them oblivious to the human sacrifice being carried out in the distance, just beyond Meteor Rise.

Kenny's tortured wails became whimpers and groans, then, after a time, finally died. All that remained was the sound of the flames crackling, consuming his flesh and everything beneath it, down to the bone.

Lenny and Neve ceased their chanting and embraced, kissing passionately.

"I can't believe how well you played it!" Neve chuckled. "He never guessed that Lenny was really Lenore."

"It's been eight years now," Lenore said. "I've had enough practice." She laughed, taking a swig of the concoction Kenny had prepared before his untimely demise. "This isn't half bad," she admitted.

"Well, it is *your* recipe. I just passed it along to Kenny when we met at the open Samhain ritual."

Lenore spat on the desert. "All that cursed 'love and light.'"

Neve shrugged. "But you gotta admit, it's a great place to recruit our goths and wannabes for our annual sacrifice."

"Damn right!" said Lenore, kissing her again and biting her lower lip.

"Hail, Baphomet!"

"Hail, Baphomet!"

NEVADA NIGHTMARE'S EVE

"Burning Love" by Stephen H. Provost appears here for the first time.

Sharon Marie Provost

Sin City

What happens in Vegas stays in Vegas, right?
That's what I thought, but I was so wrong. I'd found my own gateway into hell. They called it Sin City for a reason.

It seemed so simple: I just had to find a couple of damned people for him. I knew just who to send his way. They'd earned their ticket in spades. In return, he'd promised me that he could keep me from dying

Alive? Yes.

Well? No.

Like they always said, when you make a deal with the devil, there's always a catch.

I'd made a gamble with my life. I'd gotten the payback I had been seeking. But I'd lost my integrity, and I was about to lose my soul along with my life.

The words still stung, like a slap to the face. To be honest, they wounded me to my very core, taking away all hope I had for survival.

"The rat is out of the cage."

I sat there in stunned silence, trying to process if I'd actually just heard those words.

"The horse is out of the barn. It doesn't matter about the delay. It was already too late the minute you had them in your lungs."

Aren't oncologists supposed to give it to you straight while still being compassionate and giving you all your options? I don't ever remember hearing one of those options being: Don't even try.

I was in the prime of my life, only 44 years old, and I had just been diagnosed with colon cancer. They'd done a CT scan before my surgery to stage my cancer, looking for signs of distant metastasis to my liver and lungs.

I'd been overjoyed when I'd gone to the gastroenterologist to get those results and found out there was no sign of spread. I just had to get through the surgery and possibly do a brief round of chemotherapy if there had been spread to any nearby lymph nodes.

Then I got a letter in the mail from the doctor.

No phone call.

No "I'm sorry I looked at the results wrong."

Just a very formal letter stating, "The results of your CT scan showed metastasis of your cancer, with multiple nodules being found in both lungs."

What the actual fuck?

How could the doctor do that? He'd told me I was fine only a week ago.

But I knew what this meant. I had Stage 4 cancer.

Incurable.

I called the recommended oncologist's office, and they scheduled me for a phone consult. The doctor looked over the notes and said there was nothing to be done until after I was completely healed from the surgery and released for treatment by the surgeon.

Five weeks later, I began a six-round course of chemo. When that was completed, I was set up for a recheck CT scan that found a few nodules had disappeared, and the others had decreased in size significantly. I expected that I would have to go through another course of treatment to make the rest disappear, but suddenly they said the nodules were inflammatory rather than being mets and ended my treatment.

Three doctors, because they kept retiring or moving on to other clinics, and two CT scans later at three-month intervals, and the nodules kept getting a little larger each time. Yet they still claimed that they were inflammatory, rather than cancer.

When I was finally assigned to Dr. Wallace, the head of the clinic, I insisted on an explanation of why I had been told these were mets originally but then, when they seemingly responded favorably to treatment, it had been decided they were inflammatory instead.

It was clear that he didn't appreciate a patient questioning his or his staff's treatment plan. But if I didn't advocate for myself, then who would? I knew I deserved an explanation. To placate me, he offered to do a "groundbreaking" new test that would look for signs of shed cancer cells, confirming if I did or did not have metastatic cancer.

I felt like I'd finally made headway. I'd know the answer one way or the other. I couldn't let cancer keep growing in my body unchecked. A few weeks later, the special blood test came back negative, but a short time after that, the next CT scan also came back—with even bigger nodules once again, plus new ones. This time, the oncologist angrily insisted I needed to go to a pulmonologist for them to explain the cause of the nodules.

A month and one lung biopsy later, I had my answer. They were colon cancer mets, just as they always had been. Mets that had been allowed to grow undeterred for nine months.

I was sent back to the oncologist for treatment to be resumed. When I questioned Dr. Wallace about the ramifications of nine months without treatment and how that might affect my long-term prognosis, that was when he had hit me with those words.

It doesn't matter. It's already too late...

Each one spit out angrily and utterly detached. He didn't care that they hurt.

It didn't affect him one way or the other.

Cancer runs rampant throughout our population. Cancer and medical care, in general, are big business. There would always be someone else to make a buck off. I could die tomorrow and someone new would take my place to fill Dr. Wallace's pockets.

My anger nearly boiled over. I wanted to scream at him, but my hands were tied. He had me over a barrel. I needed him to treat my cancer.

At least for now. At least until I could find someone better.

With time, my outrage only grew. I came to find out that his so-called magic test didn't work for colon cancer that has spread to the lungs. The shedding only occurs if it has spread to the liver. And after, I found a new oncologist, it came to light that the previous clinic had never ordered the proper testing on the tumor to detect any mutations or genetic markers that would dictate the proper treatment for *my* cancer. And I *did* need more targeted treatment.

I didn't know how to handle my resentment. My doctor recommended I go to a support group for chronic and terminal illness.

It was there that I found that my ire knew no bounds.

I heard one story after another about people being ignored, improperly treated, unable to afford medications because of Big Pharma, or denied treatment by money-grubbing insurance companies.

I started my own group to help patients like me. I found

people willing to donate their time and expertise to help patients with cost-saving programs to buy their medications, advocacy programs to fight for effective treatment measures, and file appeals on denied claims.

But it was never enough.

I watched as one friend after another suffered, then succumbed to depression or even suicide, or slowly died from their illnesses. Initially, I think the group helped give me a purpose and a reason to live. With the proper chemo regimen, my metastatic tumors decreased in size a bit and a couple even disappeared.

But as my own depression sank to lower depths, I think, so too did my will to live. Excitement over small reductions in tumor size turned into celebrations when my condition was unchanged. And that turned into a desperate clutching at hope when the tumor experienced a small amount of growth, but it stopped and stayed static when a new regimen was begun. At least for a little while. I knew I was running out of time.

Somebody had to pay. They had to learn the value of a human life beside their own. That would be my legacy.

I still don't know how I found Marbas... or if it was Marbas who found me. I had started frequenting the seedier areas of Vegas, putting feelers out into the underworld, searching for someone that could exact my revenge.

I had never really believed in any higher power or counted on anyone besides myself. But now I spent my nights praying to God or anyone out there who'd listen, begging for help. Help to save me *and* my friends. Help to get revenge on those who'd hurt us. I promised to do whatever it took. Give up my very life if needed to make things right.

I didn't realize the *depths* I'd reached into the underworld. I soon found out though one Saturday when I returned to my little rathole of an apartment after doing laundry down the street. It was all I could afford between the expensive cancer treatments and the meager number of hours I could still work effectively.

As I trudged up the last three steps to the third floor, my already nauseated stomach rebelled at the offensive odor emanating from there. I hadn't smelled something that rank since my family had visited the La Brea tar pits when I was a kid.

Mrs. Elliott had just scuttled out of her apartment, dropping trash down the chute.

"Hello, Malcolm." She pinched her nose as she turned to face me. "What's that awful smell?"

"I'm not sure, Mrs. Elliott. I just got home." My hand flew to my lips as I stifled a gag. "Have you talked to the super?"

"It's probably that young rock-n-roller boy at the end of the hall smoking the ganje."

I fought to stifle the giggle that almost burst of my mouth. Leave it to Mrs. Elliott to pull out the outdated terms.

I couldn't help myself from replying, "Well, they did make the wacky baccy legal now."

"I know. I know. Them hippie people think they can run the world now. But Stan sent out a notice that pot smoking was strictly prohibited and would not be tolerated here at the Three Palms."

"That's true. I'm not sure it smells like marijuana though, Mrs. Elliott. It smells like rotten eggs, but more pungent. Like... what is that shit called? Sulfur!"

"I'm sure Stan wouldn't like them burning stinky incense either. I'm going to go in and call him again right now. Thank you, Malcolm. I'll tell him it's making you sick. Poor man! Like the chemo isn't hard enough on you, and now you come home to this. I have half a mind to..." Her voice trailed off as she walked inside, shaking her head.

I turned the key in the lock and opened the door. I was nearly knocked over by the wave of heat and foul sulfuric fumes that wafted over me. In an instant, the contents of my stomach were racing up my esophagus and barely held behind my teeth. I ran to the empty copper planter in the hallway and evacuated the bitter bile that burned the sores in my mouth.

With any luck, Mrs. Elliott hadn't heard me and would blame this indiscretion on the young tenant down the hall. The only problem was: My apartment was the one that smelled like the bowels of hell.

I pulled a kitchen towel out of the laundry basket in my hands and placed it against my nose and mouth. I entered the apartment, but I couldn't see anything. All of my blackout curtains had been pulled shut tightly, not even leaving one crack of sunlight shining through. They hadn't been that way when I'd left earlier.

I left the door open as I walked across the room and grabbed the curtain cord.

"Leave that alone!" A voice boomed out of the darkness in the back corner of the room.

I jumped and spun around, banging my shoulder on the window frame. In my haste, I bumped into the small end table, sending a vase crashing to the floor.

"Wh... who are you? Why're you in my apartment?" I queried the darkness.

There was no response, but in the blink of an eye, the apartment door was shut, I was sitting on the couch, and the lamp beside me was on. I could barely see the outline of a very large figure in the shadows.

"How'd you do that?"

"Does it really matter? You summoned me, and here I am. Now you answer to me... not the other way around. Do I make myself clear?"

"Summoned you? I'm not sure what..."

"Silence!" The room reverberated, rocked with the volume of his response.

I was struck speechless for the first time in my life. All I could do was sit there as a gargantuan man stalked into sight, like a big cat on the prowl. His movements were unnatural.

Too smooth.

Predatory.

He had long, golden hair that shone in the meager light. His almond-shaped, amber eyes glowed red—the pupils' vertical slits as they locked onto my every movement. His body posture matched the energy of his stare, tense and ready to pounce on me at any moment. I felt like an antelope about to be mauled by the king of the jungle.

"Why did you summon me, mortal? Do you know who I am? Do you know what I can do to you? I am not one to be trifled with."

I couldn't understand how he could speak with such force. I could feel his words in my bones. His deep tones made my eardrums vibrate.

"Apologies for my ignorance. But *who* are you?"

"I am Marbas. I am a President in hell, and I rule over 36 legions of demons. I can both cause and cure disease. Transform man into whatever shape I desire. This is the last time I will ask. Why did you summon me? You do not want to anger me. Hell is the least of your worries at the moment."

"I... uh... I didn't know I had. I don't even know how one would do that. I've prayed... uh shit... forget that. I've called out to the universe—to whoever would listen—asking for help. Maybe that's how it happened."

"Help with what? I may be immortal, but that does not mean I want to spend my time *here* with you." Marbas looked around the room in disgust.

I shrank back into the couch. He was losing patience with me. I didn't know how to say it, but I concluded that directness was the best approach.

"I'm dying from cancer. My doctor is an asshat! He didn't treat it for months and performed the wrong blood test. I'm sure you don't want all the details. He just deserves to suffer. To know what it's like to be sick and then have no one care."

"I see."

"And my friends. They're in pain and dying. These shyster insurance companies and underhanded doctors who just want money, it's not right. I want my friends to get better, and these pricks to get what they deserve."

"So now you want help for others as well? You don't ask for much, do you? And what will I get in return?"

"Umm... that's a good question. Like I said earlier, I didn't call..."

"You most certainly did. You dare call me a liar?" Marbas rose up to his full height. The top of his head brushed the ceiling. Clouds of steam billowed around him, and the stench of sulfur became overwhelming.

I flew to the edge of my seat and grabbed the only thing nearby, an empty pizza box. I retched until I had nothing left in my stomach and still it cramped. Tears were pouring down my face.

I held up my hand in a defensive gesture and answered him in a hoarse voice, "I'm sorry. I didn't mean it that way. I just mean I didn't mean to... uhh... know how to summon you or any other..." I spread my hands out questioningly.

"Demon."

"Yeah, uh sure, demon. So I don't really know what's involved in making a deal with one. Hell, I don't even know if this is something you could or would help me out with. I mean you

SHARON MARIE and STEPHEN H. PROVOST

hear about demons hurting people... not about them healing them. At least not on TV. They always show a deal with the devil ending in the loss of your soul. Is that the price?"

"I am *not* the devil! He deals in souls, not me."

"Well sure, of course, I didn't mean any disrespect there. I'm an idiot. How about we make this easy? Can you help me, or should I say us, and what is the cost?"

Marbas rose up again, anger showing in his every move and expression. His eyes glowed only red, like laser beams, punching a hole through my heart.

"Not *can*, I meant *would*. *Would* you?"

Marbas settled back down and turned his back to me. "This is certainly within my power. As I told you before, I can both cure and cause disease. The men, at least as you described them, are damned souls who will be joining us in hell one day. It matters not to me if it's sooner rather than later."

He turned back, deep in thought, his fingers steepled together. "And I must admit, I have not had much fun lately. Oh! The things I can do to them would make your blood curdle. Pain, disease, death! Does that sound like you what you want?"

The smile upon my face was all the answer he needed.

"How would I know that you did..."

Marbas' eyes locked onto mine. My body was pressed back into the couch. The pressure on my chest made it hard to breathe.

I wheezed, "I only meant what." The pressure eased slightly. "I would love to know how they suffered. I wish I could see it. That's all." I gasped for air as he released his hold entirely.

"You will *know*." The whole room rumbled like an earthquake with the last word he spoke.

"Okay. Thank you. So I guess we need to get to the business part."

"Yes, we do. My services come at a high price."

"I assumed."

"If you provide me with four of the damned a year for me to play with, I will make sure that you don't die. In exchange for each one, I will cure the disease in your "friend" and transfer it to the party responsible for their suffering. You will bow down in awe at my powers of transformation. They will pay dearly for what they have done, and then they will be tortured forever more in the burning pits of hell. If you break our deal..."

"You'll stop, right?"

"Yes. But more importantly, you will die. But before you do, you will suffer untold torture and pain."

"Will I go to hell then?"

"That is not for me to decide. That's a risk you will have to take."

My heart skipped a few beats. That was a heavy burden to carry. I didn't know if I truly had a demon in my apartment, or if this was just some fever dream, and I definitely didn't know what he might be capable of. And as a lifelong atheist, I didn't actually know if I believed in hell and what unending torment might entail, but it would be worth it if those bastards paid.

"And what about the one who harmed me?"

"That one's on me. Call it a signing bonus." Marbas stood before me with a scroll unrolled on the coffee table. I hadn't even seen him move. He proffered a quill with a red-hot, smoking symbol on it. "Just sign on the dotted line as you mortals say."

I didn't dare take the time to read the agreement. I had already angered him enough, seemingly questioning him at every turn. I grabbed the quill and howled in pain as my palm was branded with the symbol, made up of two templar crosses and four circles connected by lines. My first instinct was to drop it, but I couldn't let go. Apparently, my choice had already been set in stone. I had to finish and sign my life away.

I scrawled my signature on the scroll and looked up at him.

I held out my hand. "What's this?"

"That's my sigil. It marks you as mine, but it is also imbued with great power. When you need to contact me, simply say my name and touch that symbol."

I nodded. "So how does this work now? Do I need to give you a list of names? My doctor is..."

"One step at a time. I will be back when I am ready for the first of the damned. Now that you have sealed our deal, I know who I need to take out for you. That is all for now."

"But wait! When? How will I know?"

In the blink of an eye, Marbas was gone. My living room had returned to its normal state. Sunlight streamed in through my wide-open curtains. The room temperature began to drop, and the foul odor started to dissipate.

"You'll know!"

I jumped when I heard those words behind me. But had I actually heard them out loud? It seemed as if they had just appeared in my mind, but once again they, reverberated through my body. I couldn't worry about that now. I had to figure out who needed my help... well, his help.

I awoke with a start, or at least I thought I had. My heart raced, and I could barely suck in air. I tried to grab my chest and sit up, but I couldn't move. It felt as if a great weight sat on my chest. I peered into the inky blackness of my room, but I couldn't see anything. Had I gone blind? Was I having a heart attack or a stroke?

Then I began to see the furnishings of the room and the sheets on the bed. But none of them were mine. I tried to sit up, but I felt too weak, and pain tore through my body. Yet the weird part was I could tell I had not actually moved. I groaned and rolled onto my side and finally managed to push myself into a hunched position on the edge of the bed.

It was like I was in one of those found-footage movies. I could see the world through my own eyes. Feel the pain. Smell the fetid stench of urine staining the sheets beneath me.

But it wasn't my body I saw. It was not my room or bed.

I, or I guess he, rose with great difficulty, swaying on unsteady legs, head spinning. We... Fuck! I don't know. Somebody! Somebody took quivering steps across the room toward a bathroom.

As the person turned the corner, his reflection appeared in the mirror. It was him! Fuck me sideways! It was Dr. Wallace, or it once had been. He looked like Jeff Goldblum in *The Fly* in the middle of his transformation.

Dr. Wallace's entire body was covered in oozing lumps and blackened masses. He looked six months pregnant with a giant tumor in his abdomen protruding from his otherwise emaciated figure. His chest heaved as he hyperventilated through his wheezing, diseased lungs. Blood-red feces dripped from him as he cried out in horror.

I heard a concerned voice from behind us.

"Dear! Are you okay, darling?"

We turned as a woman entered the bedroom. I heard his strangled voice, "Don't come in here." But it was already too late. The last thing I saw or heard was the woman's petrified screams. She said, "Oh, my God!" as she pressed her hand to her forehead just before she fainted.

I awoke, this time for real, in my bedroom. The sheets were soaked from my perspiration. Was that real or just some twisted nightmare? I didn't dare bug Marbas to ask him. He said he'd come to me when he was ready. I'd just have to wait until it was on the news, or they canceled my appointment on Thursday.

I didn't have to wait for long. The doctor's office called that afternoon changing my appointment to another provider for the following day. And then on the news that evening, there was a report about a beloved local doctor having died under suspicious circumstances.

Well goddamn! Marbas did come through for me. It was everything I could have hoped for and more. I felt gratified. Yet, I also felt overwhelming sadness and remorse for what I had put his wife through.

I pushed it to the back of my mind. I told myself that it was not my fault. And what about my family? I wouldn't be able to help my parents in their old age. What if I'd had a wife? Dr. Wallace deserved what he got, didn't he?

The next two weeks dragged by as I waited for Marbas to return. I'd been battling with myself as to whose issue was most serious... who needed our help first. I had finally settled on the answer, and I wanted to get it done. The longer I waited, the harder my shame came back trying to make me reconsider my deal with Marbas.

Then one day out of the blue, I returned home from the clinic after my chemo infusion to find him waiting for me in the apartment. I smelled him long before I reached my floor.

Did he have to come today of all days? My stomach had been in the back of my throat for the past three hours after they started the Irinotecan. I didn't know if I could get one word out without puking till the cows came home.

Luckily, I'd taken to carrying a handkerchief with me, so I pressed it to my nose as I reached the top step. Once again, I walked into darkness, and there he was standing by the window.

"Nice of you to join me."

"Excuse me for not being me ready for company. It's not like you told me you were coming today. I was getting my chemo. Which, now that I think of it, I probably don't need that anymore. Right?"

"Wrong. Unless you don't mind your cancer spreading."

"Wait! I thought you said..."

"I would keep you from dying. That is correct. I have, and I will continue if you fulfill your obligations."

"But you said you could cure people. That you would cure my friends."

"Yes, correct on both accounts. I said quite clearly that I would keep you from dying as long as you provided me with four damned a year. I never said I would cure you. In point of fact, you never *asked* me to cure you, just your friends."

I dropped my head in defeat. Fucking deals with the devil! There was always a catch. The saying was right, but so was he. I had neglected to ask for my own cure.

"I'M NOT THE DEVIL!"

I nearly jumped out of my skin. I hadn't said any of that out loud. I curled up on the couch in defeat, mumbling an apology.

"I trust we have this matter settled now."

I nodded, too weak to look up at him or respond out loud. I dropped the subject... there was no point.

"How did you like your revenge?"

I didn't dare tell him how I felt bad for Dr. Wallace's wife, instead expressing my approval of his demise.

"I thought you would approve. Are you ready to start our agreement?"

"Yes. I want you to help my friend, Brandy."

"What is the story with her?"

"She has a severe degenerative spine condition that requires spinal decompression surgery. She's in pain all the time, which makes it extremely difficult for her to walk. She's only 22 years old and about to start her career with an extremely important internship, but, at this point, she can't work. Her insurance has denied her claim repeatedly, even on appeal, despite multiple doctor recommendations stating this is her only viable treatment option.

"I run my own organization to help people deal with the struggles of chronic or terminal illnesses. I have a few very well-connected volunteers, one of whom knows the insurance adjuster involved in Brandy's claim. He repeatedly denies valid medical claims in order to save the company money.

"The more money he saves, the more money goes in his pockets with bonuses. It's criminal. I want her to have a successful start in life. She deserves it. And most of all, I want that man to understand the debilitating and depressing nature of a life with chronic pain."

Marbas had a wicked smile on his face. He stood there, deep in thought, twiddling his fingers.

"You trying to get on my good side? Oh, the things I will do to that man. Transformation, or should I say *deformation* in this case, is my specialty."

"And you'll make Brandy better?"

"Consider it done."

I was staring down at my hands, excited for her but uncomfortable about who else might be hurt by my actions. "You don't have to show me this time," I said in a breathless rush as I looked up. But he was already gone.

A wicked growl came from behind me, warm air ruffling my few wisps of hair, "Oh, but I do."

I went to bed that night anxiety-ridden, worrying that my sleep would be disturbed once again with nightmarish visions. Not that I cared what happened to that adjuster, but what if he had a family?

I had a fitful night's sleep, but that was from the side effects of the chemo. Hot flashes, night sweats, nausea, and severe heartburn were the order of the night. The next two nights passed the in the same manner. Maybe he'd decided to give me a reprieve after all. I considered calling Brandy to check in on her, but how I would explain my interest? I had no update on her case to report or any other news of interest. Instead, I waited on pins and needles.

On the fourth night though, I got my answer. I had been tossing and turning for hours, my whole body aching. As the hours passed, the pain grew to unbearable levels. I'd become accustomed to all my joints hurting, yet another lovely side effect of chemotherapy, but this was different.

I decided to get up and take a Tramadol, but I didn't know exactly how I was going to do that. The back pain had reached excruciating levels, and pains were shooting down my legs. When I opened my eyes and began to push myself into a sitting position, I realized I wasn't in *my* home again.

As he finally sat all the way up, a bolt of pain shot down *our* back. He yelped and slumped into a hunched position, his elbows digging into his thighs holding him up. He took a few shallow breaths, too afraid a deep breath would send him reeling again.

Why did I have to experience his pains, thoughts and fears? I never thought it would be this way. Wasn't I giving Marbas a damned man to play with? One deserving of all the pain and torture being inflicted upon his body. What had I ever done to deserve this?

Other than compromise all my morals to make someone else suffer. Fuck!

He struggled to stand, his legs shaking as he straightened them. He couldn't stand up straight and instead was stuck hunched over, throwing off his balance. Another searing pain +ripped up and down his back and then into his legs making them buckle. He grabbed his back and screamed, "Oh, God!" before falling to the ground.

Then I heard my worst nightmare: the scuttling of tiny feet on hardwood floors accompanied by the high voice of a little girl calling for her daddy.

Fuckballs! Not again!

My body was flooded with his feelings and panicked thoughts. He began to crawl across the floor toward his bathroom, desperate to lock himself in before he scared his precious little daughter. He couldn't let her see the fear and pain in his eyes. He needed to down a Tylenol or ten before he could show his face.

He climbed to his hands and knees just as he heard the door handle began to twist.

"Megan, wait, sweetie. Daddy will be out in a few."

"Dada, I wuvs you. Peek-a-boo!"

I scrunched my eyes shut, trying to block out the vision I feared to see... feared for her to see. But it didn't work. I was in his mind. There was no blocking it out.

I heard the click of the bolt slide past the striker plate at the same moment he gained his footing, straining to lift his head to look into the mirror. I'm not sure which scream tore through my head and heart first or more painfully.

He deserved all the pain he was experiencing, but no one deserved to horrify his daughter in that way.

And she was just an innocent child.

It quickly became apparent why he hadn't been able to straighten his back. To say it was misshapen and hunched was akin to saying the Hunchback of Notre Dame was normal. Not only that, but his spine twisted and turned like a snake slithering up his back. His neck was kinked to the side and so weak he could only lift it a fraction of an inch for a second or two at a time.

Tears streamed down his face, the pain in his body only exceeded by the agony in his heart for what his daughter had seen. She'd run, screaming, from the room, calling out to her mother.

Ideas began to flow into his head to end his torment. As a claims adjuster, he saw people's medical records all the time. Patients that had far less severe afflictions than he now had, and he knew how often they still felt pain. More importantly, he knew how difficult, or should he admit, impossible it would be to get his insurance to pay for the many complicated surgeries he'd need. One benefit of his employment had been discounted medical insurance through his employer, *the* company most notorious for denying valid claims.

I saw what he planned seconds before he lurched his way toward the nightstand by his bed. He ripped open the drawer, pulling it off the tracks, causing it to clatter to the floor. He threw himself to the ground, screeching and pulled out a locked box. He punched numbers into the keypad.

I screamed at him to stop, but he couldn't hear me. The connection only went one way. He pulled out the gun and placed it to his temple, pulling the trigger just as his wife rounded the corner and entered the room.

For only a second, I saw her and heard her wails as blood and bits of brain dripped down his face. Then all went black until I opened my own eyes, tears escaping in a flood. I curled into the fetal position and begged that man's family for forgiveness.

Three nights later, I was lying in bed, covered in sweat and weak, trying to take small sips of water. My nausea was at epic levels, and I'd been spewing from both ends for over 12 hours.

My chemo had caused some serious bowel inflammation, and I'd had pure water diarrhea at least once every hour. No amount of Imodium could slow it down, let alone stop it. I'd spent the day in the clinic receiving subcutaneous fluids and put on prescription medication.

I had just drifted off for a few minutes of restless sleep when

I felt the temperature rise precipitously. And then that god-awful smell invaded my burning nostrils.

"No, no, NO! Go away!" I screamed as I rolled onto my stomach, burying my face in my pillow.

"You had better not be speaking to me," Marbas bellowed, blistering heat rolling over my body in waves, singeing the few hairs I still had.

I rolled back over, weakness in body and spirit overwhelming me.

Why was he back again? I'd agreed to provide him with four people a year. I had thought there'd be a cooling off period in between. A little time to build anticipation or whatever you might call it for a cruel, sadistic bastard like him. But here he was again!

I could tell he was nowhere near done. He was going to want more and more. He was just getting started. Why hadn't I read that contract, especially the fine print? What evil clause had he cleverly hidden?

"What do you want?"

"Tell me the next person."

"So soon? Why now? Can't you see I'm sick? It's not like you helped me..."

Oh fuck! What had I just said?

"I only meant you didn't make me well. I'm on chemo with Stage 4 cancer. I can't keep up with your appetite."

"Pardon me! I forgot how much work you put into these little revenge schemes. Oh wait, that's me!"

Those last words came with such force I was knocked out of my bed, falling painfully to the floor.

"Give me the damned man, or hellfire will be licking at your feet before you can say my name."

"Allan. Help Allan. He needs a liver transplant. He's been waiting for over a year, and he's just about out of time. He's at the top of the UNOS transplant list, but organs that should be designated for him keep going to patients of means.

"He's on Medicaid, so he conveniently gets dropped down the list just at the right moment—the right moment to save the life of some rich motherfucker. Then he magically rises to the top again, only to miss out when it matters most. The director of the transplant list is a crooked fuckwad."

"Done!"

One last wave of heat blasted over the painful rashes across my body, and Marbas was gone.

I lapsed into unconsciousness for only an hour before I woke again in that same familiar way.

Or at least I thought it was... at first.

My eyes opened to see an unfamiliar room, and I felt someone lying next to me in the bed. I rubbed my eyes, trying to wake up. I turned to look and saw a man who was critically ill.

His scarred, sightless corneas stared off into space, but I could see the bright yellow tint of jaundice in the whites of his eyes. His mouth was open, and I, or whoever the woman was next to him, leaned over to see if they could feel him breathing. She could feel slow, shallow breaths.

"Martin! Martin, wake up!" she screamed at him.

He didn't respond. He was unconscious and appeared to be fading fast. She began to cry and reached across the bed, grabbing his cell phone off the bedside table. When 911 answered, she cried out, "Come quick! My husband is dying. I don't know what happened to him."

"Is he still breathing?" I heard through the phone.

"Oh God, no. He was a moment ago."

"Ma'am, do you know how to do CPR?"

"Yes! Please start compressions, ma'am. I'll walk you through it. You know the song "Staying Alive"? Give 30 compressions hard and fast to the beat of that song. Then give 2 rescue breaths and immediately resume compressions."

"I don't know if I can do this."

"You have to, ma'am. Help is on the way, but they are 10 minutes out. If you don't do it now, they won't be able to save him."

Why? Why did Marbas have to torment me so? Now I had to experience the death of this man from the perspective of his frightened wife.

I was forced to go through every moment of her trauma until the ambulance arrived and pronounced him dead. I awoke when she fell to her knees, sobbing, asking the first responders what had happened to her healthy husband. I didn't know for sure what had been wrong with him, but I could only presume he'd been given the diseased organs of all those patients whose claims he had denied.

I was traumatized by what I had witnessed, but not nearly as much as the poor family members. A few days after the man's death, I'd seen a GoFundMe page posted on Facebook for his family. His wife had cancer and couldn't work. Plus, he and his wife were the sole caregivers and means of support for his elderly, infirm parents. How would they support themselves? Who would take care of her?

I knew that Marbas would be back... and soon. I couldn't do this anymore. I was so stupid and selfish. Yes, I'd ensured that evil people had paid dearly, and fairly I reminded myself, for their wrongdoing. But I hadn't considered the collateral damage. I'd become just as bad as them if not worse. Selfish people like those damned men never thought about others.

But I did.

That was how this whole mess had gotten started. I'd been trying to watch out for the best interest of patients who'd gotten the shaft. But now I had hurt others who didn't deserve it.

It didn't matter what happened to my soul now. If there truly was a heaven or hell, I was most certainly going to the latter, regardless of any deal. I'd compromised every ideal I had ever held dear.

This had to stop now. I wouldn't participate any further. I rubbed the scar on my hand and screamed Marbas' name until my throat was raw and hoarse.

Marbas took his time showing up, and his anger was boiling over. "How dare you summon me, mortal? What do you want?"

"I quit. I can't do this anymore. Take my life, and my soul. I deserve to burn in hell."

"I refuse. You owe me another damned person for the time you've already had."

"I refuse as well. Do whatever you want to me."

"You are going to suffer more than any of them for this insolence. You will feel everything you would have suffered with your cancer *all at once.*"

With a loud crack, he disappeared. Seconds later, I dropped to the ground as pain shot through my abdomen. I could see it swell as ascites developed. I retched painfully, vomiting black material that looked like coffee grounds.

Fuck! My cancer must have spread to my liver—and now it was failing.

I struggled for breath. With each passing second, it felt more and more like I was trying to breathe in a fish tank. Fluid bubbled and rumbled in my lungs. I coughed hard, and bright-red blood shot across the floor.

I slumped on the floor, gasping and writhing in pain. I wondered how long he'd leave me there suffering. I feared he wouldn't be done with me for some time.

"We're just getting started, Malcolm."

I closed my eyes and prayed for someone to end it fast, but I knew no one would be coming to help me. As the hours, or maybe even days, dragged by, I began to worry about the horrors down in hell. I hadn't comprehended how much suffering Marbas would inflict on me here.

What would he do to me there? I'd had such good intentions in the beginning, but somewhere it had gone so wrong. Did heaven and hell exist? And how would all my actions balance out on the scales in the end?

I croaked out one last question to Marbas, "Am I going to hell?"

I almost wish he hadn't responded.

"Not my decision, mortal. You will just have to wait and see."

"Sin City" by Sharon Marie Provost appears here for the first time.

Stephen H. Provost

Retribution Road

ick Prager hadn't seen a gas station in nearly fifty
miles, and he was nearly running on fumes. Why
hadn't he filled up in Fallon? They didn't call U.S. 50
"America's Loneliest Road" for nothing. His fuel gauge had
shown he had enough in his tank to reach Austin with a few
miles to spare, but that was before he'd decided to take the scenic
route over Carroll Summit. He hadn't counted on all the twists
and turns, which guzzled his gas faster than a frat boy at a kegger.

Not that this analogy would have meant anything to him.
He'd never gone to college, let alone been in a fraternity. He was
an actor. Not a star—he lacked the matinee-idol looks of Brad

Pitt or the charisma of Pedro Pascal, with those puppy-dog eyes. He was more like Willem Dafoe or Steve Buscemi. Quirky and unforgettable. That got you steady work, which was all he cared about, even if it did mean doing those funky commercials for PestMaster Fumigators, Lager Lover, and Health-E-Surance.

He'd come out here to get away from all that. Most guys in his shoes would have been partying in New York or on some cruise ship, but he'd always been a loner. The parts he played were like shells that protected his true, shy, introverted self. He'd never had a girlfriend, a boyfriend, or an anything-friend. He liked interacting with his surroundings far more than the people who came with them. That's why he used his time off for solo adventures in out-of-the-way places, where pronghorns and wild horses outnumbered homo sapiens.

But being too far away from people had its drawbacks, especially if you were about to run out of gas.

Mick tried everything not to look at the needle tumbling downhill toward "E." Some bighorn sheep had come down to forage beside the road, leaving one behind to look down on the scene from a rocky precipice high above. Like it was watching him. Judging him. Waiting to pass some sort of sentence. It was so disconcerting that it succeeded in keeping his eyes off the fuel gauge—but also off the road.

The right side of the car started thumping and grinding, like a flat tire, but it was running over gravel and rocks off the side of the road.

Shit.

Mick eased onto the brake and turned the wheel, but he jerked it too hard. The Honda CR-V skidded out on the rocks, then veered away from the shoulder and into the opposite lane... where a truck was barreling straight toward him. He hadn't seen a single car on the road until now. But now... rigs that size weren't supposed to use the old highway. He knew in that split-second that he couldn't veer back without skidding to a stop and getting T-boned by that Peterbilt. He had too much momentum. He was headed toward a ravine, but it was either that or plow head-on into the truck.

He careened off the side of the road and directly into that group of juvenile bighorns, which had appeared again out of nowhere. The panicked animals tried to scatter, but it was too late. Fur and horns and hooves and blood filled his vision as he put his forearm up reflexively.

The window shattered.

Air brakes sounded somewhere nearby, but Mick had more immediate concerns.

The car bucked, and the right bumper crashed into a boulder, sending the rest of the Honda sliding sideways.

Mick came to a stop, his side of the car teetering on the edge of the ravine. He leaned slowly sideways toward the passenger side, wincing as a shard of glass sliced upward through his shirt sleeve and lanced deep into his shoulder, but he kept inching his way toward the passenger door, grabbing onto the far side of the seat cushion to pull himself along.

He was almost there.

He looked up through the window and saw the bighorn still perched high above him, judging him even more harshly now. He thought he saw red in its unblinking eyes, a threat that had given way now to fury. Condemnation.

He looked down and pulled a little more on the cushion.

The car rocked backward.

It was losing its grip on the ledge, and he braced himself to be hurled backward into the abyss.

Then he startled as he felt the car shift again beneath him— but not toward the precipice. Away from it.

He looked up at a broad face with a shaven head and stubbly shadow of a beard. "Want a lift, man?" he asked in a rough voice, then gave a short laugh and said, "Of course you do. I'm Tom Dethridge. I own the Texaco up the road a piece." He pulled open the door and grabbed Mick by the forearm, yanking him out of the car. Mick braced himself again for the car to fall away behind him, but it didn't.

"Scared, tiger?" Tom punched him in the arm. Hard. He had that blocky look of a linebacker who did *everything* hard. "Check it out." He pointed down, and Mick saw a winch attached to the Honda, securing it in place. The other side was attached to a tow truck.

Mick had been sure that the man who'd appeared in his car window must have been the big-rig driver. He hadn't seen anyone else on the road, and he distinctly remembered hearing the sound of the eighteen-wheeler's air brakes. But a tow truck? Wasn't it a weird coincidence that one just *happened* to show up when he was about to fall backward into a miniature version of the Grand Canyon?

He looked up at the top of the hill again, expecting to see the bighorn still there, glaring down at him, but it was gone.

"You might wanna step aside, man," Tom said. "Since she's sideways like that, I'm gonna have to scratch her up a little." He shrugged. "Sorry, man."

Mick moved out of the way and let Tom pull the Honda up and off the crumbling shoulder, the undercarriage, scraping over the rocks like granite pressed hard against a blackboard. As the winch pulled the car up over the lip, the back tire got stuck and started to hiss as it came loose from the rim. The front tire quickly followed suit.

"Sorry, man," Tom said, shaking his head. "Couldn't be helped. But we'll get you all fixed up at the station."

"We?" Was it more than just him? Of course it had to be. You needed more than one person to run a full-service station, right?

"Figure of speech," Tom said, detaching the winch and resituating the truck to hook it up again from the front. "Getting dark," he added. "You can stay at the station for the night. I'll have you up and running in the a.m." He winked and made a clicking noise with his tongue.

Carroll Summit Texaco wasn't that far up the road, nestled in against the hillside. It was a far cry from a modern truck stop. Just a couple of pumps and a detached toilet around the back. The Texaco star in a circle out front wasn't huge, but it almost seemed too big for the old-style building. Mick couldn't remember the last time he'd even seen a Texaco station—of any size. He'd filled up at one in Tonopah when he passed through there a few years back, but he remembered when you could find them everywhere.

Mick hopped out and stood in the glare of a single light attached to the front of the building. He tried the door to the station, but it was locked, so he waited for Tom to come around.

Before he got to the door, though, the station owner stopped in his tracks. "Well, how do you do!" he said.

"What?" Mick asked. It was chilly out, and he wanted to get inside, even though he couldn't tell how there was room for a living area in there, let alone a bed.

"You're that guy!" Tom said. "Don't tell me. I've seen you in them commercials."

Mick smiled and tried not to roll his eyes. His part in *Shoot to Spill* had got him a nomination for best supporting actor. Sure, it had been a while. But why did they always have to remember him from the stupid commercials? He just hoped he wouldn't have to draw an invisible pistol and say, "Kill 'em faster with PestMaster."

He didn't. Instead, he said, "You're that guy from that insurance scam."

Mick grimaced. He'd heard this before too. Health-E-Surance had been shut down after federal regulators indicted the company for refusing to pay out on valid claims. Mick hadn't had anything to do with the actual company. It had just hired him to do ads. But it didn't matter to the viewers who'd seen him as the face of the company, the yellow-jumpsuit-clad Health-E-Hornet who talked about "taking the sting out of health-care costs."

"Don't deny it," Tom said, snickering like he'd just discovered some secret treasure. "Those commercials were classic!"

Mick relaxed a bit.

"I mean, you were so damn funny. My mom loved you."

"Oh?"

Tom reached into a cooler behind the front seat and pulled out a Coors, tossing it to Mick. "Think fast."

Mick barely caught it, and when he opened it, it sprayed all over the place.

"Oopsie," Tom said with a belly laugh, popping a top himself "Yeah, man, I'm serious. She even went out and bought a policy from your company."

"It wasn't my..."

"Don't be modest. You really sold her on it. Too bad she couldn't get approval for that procedure she needed."

Mick cleared his throat. He felt obligated to ask, "Which procedure?"

"The one that woulda saved her from... you know..."

He paused, and Mick waited, shifting his feet awkwardly as he took a swig of beer.

Tom leaned in and mouthed the word slowly: "dy-ing."

Mick took a deep breath. "I'm so sorry, man."

Tom straightened up, threw back his head and laughed. "Got you, didn't I? You didn't kill her, man. The doc had already told her it was curtains. What good would a few more years have done her? Ha! We're all living on borrowed time, right?"

"I guess..."

"Hey, speaking of borrowing, I s'pose you got a credit card to cover the cost of the tow."

"Oh yeah," Mick said, grateful for the change in topic. "What do I owe you?"

"For the tow? Three-fifty."

"Wait... what did you say?"

"Three-fifty. Ten bucks a mile for thirty-five miles."

"I have a Triple-A card. Hold on a sec, and I'll..."

Tom shook his head. "You gotta show me that up front, sport. Ain't no good after the fact."

Mick downed the rest of his beer and tossed the can aside.

"Hey, litterbug," Tom said. "We recycle here. Drop it over there in that big barrel."

"Right." Mick jogged over and bent down to pick up the can, wondering how he was going to get out of this. He was just $100 under the limit on his Visa, and so he'd just have to use his debit card.

He dropped the can in the barrel, which had a weird smell about it, like a skunk had died in there. He plugged his nose and turned away.

Jogging back to Tom, he pulled out his debit card and stretched out his hand.

"What's this?"

Mick frowned. "My debit card. I assure you it's good."

Tom shook his head slowly. "I wouldn't know. We don't take plastic here. No reception to ring 'em up."

"But you said you took credit."

"Ah-ah-ah." Tom wagged his fingers. "I said, an' I quote, 'I s'pose you got a credit card for the tow. Never said I'd take it. You rich Hollywood fucks think you can just wave around plastic and make people go bowin' and scrapin' for you. Uhn-uh. Not here. I'll take cold hard cash on the barrelhead. *If* you don't mind."

"Look, fella, I appreciate the help and all, but I don't carry that kind of cash on me."

"Well, then we do have a situation, now, don't we? But I'm not an unreasonable guy." He spread his arms wide. "I'll just leave you out here, and you can change the spare and be on your way. You can come back and pay me on your way back through. How does that sound?"

It would have sounded just fine to Mick. More than fine. Except he only had one spare tire and *two* flats... both with bent rims that would need to be replaced before a spare tire—or a new one—would even fit on them. Then there was the matter of being almost out of gas. He doubted his car would get thirty miles down the road, even if the wheels and tires miraculously got fit. "I... I'm sorry," he said. "I just really need your help."

"Yes, you do." Tom nodded sagely. "The same way my mother

needed *your* help."

"Christ, man!" Mick exploded. "You said she was terminal anyway, and I'm not a fucking doctor."

Tom maintained his even tone. "But you played one on TV, right?"

"God no! I was just some idiot in a yellow jumpsuit earning a paycheck."

"And a pretty large check it must have been, too. Pity they paid you instead of covering mom's treatment, *like they said they would*. But since you have that money instead, you can pay me."

"I told you, I don't have it on me." Mick's hand flashed to the ground and scooped up a tire iron that was lying against one of the gas pumps. "Shouldn't leave this kind of thing lying around," he quipped. "Just let me call a real tow truck, one that takes debit, and I'll be on my way. Like you said, I'll just settle up when I come back through."

Tom spat on the ground. "Whoa, now pardner. Hold up there. I wouldn't be messing around with that tire iron... when the other guy has a gun." He pulled a pistol out from his waist. Mick hadn't seen it there before. He'd sworn it hadn't *been* there before. "But like I said, I ain't unreasonable—not like those fuckers who rubber-stamped mom's death certificate *while she was still breathin'*!"

Tom was shaking now, but he bit his lip and appeared to will himself to calm down. "Now," he said in a low and even voice, "come over here." He motioned toward the gas pumps with the barrel of his pistol. "I wanna show you somethin'."

Mick walked over to one of the pumps. They were the old-fashioned kind, with physical wheels that spun as you filled the tank. "Okay..."

"Look closer."

Mick leaned in and, on closer inspection, saw that the

wheels didn't mark the price of the gas and the number of gallons, as he'd expected. One *did* track dollar amounts, but the other was set up like a slot machine, with cherries, bars, lucky 7s, and other symbols typical of old-style one-armed bandits. There was even an arm to pull down and initiate the game.

"I suppose you're wondering how this works," Tom said.

Mick nodded slowly.

"It's a simple game of chance. You spin the wheels, and they decide how much you owe me. But if you get three of a kind, you don't own nothin'. *Right now*, you owe me $350, but if you get three on a line, consider it paid. Of course, if you don't hit a jackpot, ya gotta pay whatever the other wheels come up with, on top of your current balance. How does that sound, sport?"

Mick couldn't see any other choice, not staring down the barrel of a gun the way he was.

"All right," he said, reaching for the handle.

Before he could talk himself out of it, he grabbed it and yanked it back hard.

Both wheels spun around in a blur, and Mick pictured a couple of hamsters inside the pumps powering them with side-by-side running wheels. He tried to focus on the numbers and symbols as they whirred by, but it only made him feel dizzy, so he shut his eyes tight and prayed for the best.

When he opened them again, the wheels had come to a stop. Tom had put the gun down on top of the other pump and was slow-clapping. "Well, lookie there!" he said, sounding impressed. "You really are one lucky sonofabitch."

Mick stared at the three 7s staring back at him.

Tom washed his hands symbolically and patted Mick on the back. "There ya go," he said. "You don't owe me shit now. You're free to go, and happy trails to ya."

Mick just stood there. He noticed Tom's hand was resting

on the pistol again. He hadn't picked it up, but the threat of it was there.

"Oh. Right," Tom said, a dark expression settling across his face. "I guess you can't go anywhere in that buggy of yours unless you get 'er fixed, eh, pardner? Well, don't fret, sport. It's a pretty long walk to Austin, but you can make it there in a couple of days if ya hoof it. At least the first part's all downhill."

Mick had no desire to kill himself trying to walk all that way, and he could see Tom wasn't finished, so he waited for him to continue. He thought of a place he'd passed called the Shoe Tree—where hundreds of people had thrown shoes and boots up into the branches—as he wondered how many more shoes he was waiting to see fall.

"Of course, you have another alternative," he said finally. "I could fix your car right up for you, fill your tank up to the brim, and wash your windows to boot if you can hit three-of-a-kind again. That'd be a value of two-thousand big ones for another jackpot. If you're lucky. Whaddya think? Feelin' lucky, sport?" Tom picked up the revolver and spun the cylinder. "Or you could take a chance on Russian roulette," he said. "I ain't tellin' you how many chambers are full."

He pointed the gun at Mick and waited.

"Bang!" he shouted, and Mick jumped.

"Pull the lever," Tom hissed. "Or I pull the trigger."

Mick realized he wasn't being given a choice. He was stuck with some kind of sadistic bastard who was going to make him pay for his mother's death one way or another. He *had* to spin the wheel again, but even if he hit another jackpot, he suspected it wouldn't be over. The game would go on and on until the sonofabitch got the result he wanted.

Mick reached forward and pulled the lever, but this time, he forced himself to keep his eyes open.

The numbers stopped first, at 7-6-2-5. That was what he'd

owe if he lost. It didn't matter, he told himself. If he couldn't pay $350, he could hardly pay $7,625.

The figures on the right-hand wheel were still spinning, but finally slowing down.

The first one settled on a bar symbol.

Mick waited.

The second one fell to a bar as well.

He took a deep breath in and held it.

The last wheel slowed, showing a 7, a bell, a plum, a bunch of cherries, a bar, and...

Stopped.

"Three bars! Three fucking bars!" Mick shouted. "I win. You gotta fix my car!"

He couldn't tell whether the expression on Tom's face was a smile or a grimace. His eyes, though, flashed red like a neon bolt. "Do I *look* like a mechanic?" he said through gritted teeth, but his voice sounded strange.

Mick was shocked to see him drop the gun, but he hadn't done it on purpose. His body had begun convulsing, bones cracking and limbs skewing at impossible angles. He shouted in what sounded like agony, but could just as well have been rage. Perhaps it was both. His body was a grotesque mishmash of ribs protruding out of his chest, broken fingers retracting into a hardened wrist, which in turn was fusing into a smooth surface that looked like...

Mick dove for the gun, but as his fingers curled around it, it disintegrated into nothing. The light on the roof of the station flickered out, then fell to the ground with a clatter. He fixed his eyes on the symbols in the gas pump, but as he watched, the symbols melted away and the pump itself dissolved into the ground, fertilizing weeds that grew up where it had been in a matter of seconds. The Texaco sign fell over and disappeared as well. All that was left was the empty shell of a station, its doors torn off and its interior covered in graffiti.

The thing that had been Tom Dethridge sputtered in a gravelly voice that was barely understandable: "You killed my mother!"

"I told you!" Mick shouted back in horror. "I was just a guy in some commercials. I didn't kill..."

But then he saw it: what the tow-truck driver was becoming. The red in its eyes was nearly blinding, and those eyes were the same ones that had stared down at him from the ledge overlooking the canyon. His mind's eye replayed the visions of blood and bones, hooves and horns, being splashed and scattered by his car as it had hit those other bighorns. He had thought they were all juveniles, but now his memory revealed something else: the sight of an old female goat that had been escorting them up the road. Looking after them.

"Oh my god..." Mick breathed as the ram barreled toward him, hitting him full-force. Horns shattering his ribs. Carving out a bloody cavity in his stomach with its hooves. Leaving him a lifeless carcass in the road.

"Retribution Road" by Stephen H. Provost appears here for the first time. It is based in part on the author's experiences driving U.S. Highway 50 in Nevada, which served as the inspiration for his highway history travelog, America's Loneliest Road.

SHARON MARIE and STEPHEN H. PROVOST

Sharon Marie Provost

Ambushed

Destiny was excited to hit the road. It was 100 degrees out, but she couldn't resist a road trip, especially one filled with such a weird combination of sights to investigate: wetlands, abandoned ranches, the so-called "U.S. Navy Taco Bell," and decommissioned tanks in the Middle of Nowhere, Nevada. Plus, the best hamburger in the state at Middlegate before she set out down the long gravel road to Dixie Valley. What day could be better?

Destiny had loved looking at old tanks and other military vehicles ever since she was little. Her father, a career-Army colonel, had dragged her and the family around the world, and they'd spent his leave time on family trips visiting military museums along with the usual national parks. Destiny herself had been honorably discharged from the Army after twenty years of service when she was injured in Afghanistan.

Destiny's longtime friend, Allison, knew a lot about the history of Nevada's ghost towns. She'd been the one to tell Destiny about Dixie Valley. Settlers had come to the area in 1861 to mine borax, salt, and potash: Typical of mining booms, it had petered out in less than a decade.

After the miners left, new settlers had taken advantage of the plentiful natural springs, transforming the area into a lush ranching community. But the ranchers and their livestock didn't appreciate the loud sonic booms from fighter jets as they flew northeast from Fallon Naval Airbase.

The Navy had eventually acquired the land in 1995 and added it to the Fallon Range Training Complex, as a site for its pilots to practice bombing runs and for occasional mock troop assaults.

They'd demolished most of the structures in the area, except for a few homes and barns, an abandoned bus, and the old Domonoske place, nicknamed the "Hacienda," because it looked like a 1980s Taco Bell. Someone had even handwritten a special tongue-in-cheek U.S. Navy menu on an inside wall.

For air-defense training, they had moved in some old decommissioned tanks, including two M247 Sergeant Yorks, an M24 Chaffee, an M3 Stuart, and an M4 Sherman. Even though Dixie Valley was Navy property, the area wasn't closed to the public. Destiny couldn't wait to climb up on the old tanks and explore them.

Destiny left her house in Fallon and drove out to Middlegate Station to fill up her stomach before spending a long day in the desert. She stepped out onto the dirt parking lot and saw the heat rise in distant waves. It was only 10 a.m. and already a scorcher.

She walked inside and chose a table in the back corner.

"Be right there, hon, unless you know what you want." The waitress waited impatiently behind the bar, her eyebrow raised.

"Original hamburger, please. I never go by here without stopping in."

"I thought you looked familiar, but we get so many people coming by, it's hard to remember."

Ten minutes later, the waitress brought over her burger and set it down. "Need anything else?"

"You know anything about Dixie Valley?"

"Not too much, except that the airbase owns it. A lot of people stop in on their way out there. I've been myself, and it *is* pretty cool. Make sure you take plenty of water, though."

"Do I need four-wheel drive?"

"It's a gravel road; bit rough at times... a few shallow washouts in spots. That your Subaru Outback sitting in front?" The waitress pointed out the window to Destiny's beat-up forest-green wagon.

Destiny nodded as she took a bite of her burger.

"You should be fine. Any vehicle can make it out as long as it's not low clearance."

"Great. Thank you."

"You going out there alone?"

"Yeah. I can take care of myself."

"Well, anybody know where you're going?"

"Yes, my brother. He's expecting to hear from me tonight. Thanks for your concern though."

Destiny wolfed down her burger and grabbed some cold bottles of water and a couple of granola bars from the small attached convenience store. She paid the bill and got back on her way. She had to backtrack down the old Lincoln Highway about 7 miles before turning right on Dixie Valley Road.

The car bumped and jolted over the ruts of the graded road.

She'd hurt some discs in her back and shattered her pelvis, among other injuries, in an IED explosion in Afghanistan. After only a mile on the road, her body already felt like it had been ten.

Only 31 more miles to go! This better be worth it.

An hour later, she turned onto Settlement Road, a narrow dirt track that led over to the town. The area had become overgrown with weeds, bushes, trees, and tall grass. Abundant water made it an oasis in the middle of the desert. She wondered where to go to find the ranches and tanks because, as far as she could see, the area looked devoid of buildings.

Destiny was starting to feel discouraged when she saw a sign on a fence bearing the name of a ranch. She drove onto the property, following tire tracks still visible in the loose, sandy soil, then parked and got out of her car to look around.

She'd only walked about 75 feet up the drive when she saw the sandy brown and green camo tank tucked in amongst the foliage. She'd forgotten how effective camouflage could be. It was parked in the middle of a small clearing about fifty feet from a crumbling structure, seemingly made out of concrete with wood-framed window holes.

Destiny took pictures of the tank from every angle before using the wheels and treads to climb up on top and take a couple of selfies near the big guns. She was returning to the car when she heard some rustling in the brush. She turned to see who or what was approaching just when a scrub jay hopped out of the sagebrush nearby.

"You surprised me."

The bird emitted a high-pitched squawk at her before flying away.

Destiny climbed into her car and continued up the road before making a right turn and penetrating deeper into the ranchlands. As she peered through a dense thicket of trees and bushes, she saw the top of another tank. She drove into the lot and parked off to the side, avoiding the road's deep ruts.

She walked up the curving road and saw cattails peeking out from the thick patch of tall grass that surrounded a small pond. Next to the pond, nearly lost to sight, sat another large green tank. To the side of the tank lay the bleached bones and leathered hide of a cow.

Was it left behind in the move, or did it wander out here from a ranch miles down the road and get lost?

She had just begun to clamber onto the tank when she heard movement in the distance again.

A lot of movement.

"Hello?"

There was no answer. But she could hear hushed voices talking to each other.

"Is someone out there? This really isn't funny."

Her voice was met with twittering and the sound of flapping as a flock of birds took flight, startled, not far away.

Very near where she'd heard the voices.

The ground rumbled and shook as if a platoon of tanks were driving by. She spun around, surveying the area, but she couldn't see anyone or anything moving.

Her breath came out in sharp little pants, her heart thudding in her chest. She closed her eyes and told herself to stay calm.

Goddammit, Destiny! Chill the fuck out. It's been years since the PTSD gave you a panic attack.

The air had become preternaturally still. No sounds. The soft breeze that had been stirring the blades of grass had disappeared. The heat had become oppressive. The sun beat down on her pale skin mercilessly.

Destiny waited several moments in silence, but nothing

happened. When she opened her eyes, a bead of sweat ran down her forehead and into her eye, making it burn and water. Staring out into the void, she was surprised when a wisp of her hair blew into her face and a fly landed on her hand.

Everything had returned to normal. As if nothing had ever happened.

But it had... hadn't it?

Destiny forced herself to return to what she'd been doing, taking another selfie from atop the tank. She chose panorama mode on her phone and turned slowly, capturing the whole vista surrounding her. She squinted, shading her eyes with her hand, straining to identify the object reflecting a metallic glint from the sunlight streaming onto it.

Destiny jumped off the tank and took a few more pictures from the ground before returning to her car. It looked to be about a mile or so away, just past a line of trees, so she decided to walk over. Destiny placed a pin on the Google Maps app at her car's location, then grabbed a bottle of water off the floor by the passenger's seat.

She exited the lot and turned right. She'd only walked a couple of hundred feet when she found another narrow dirt track to the left that led toward the trees. She downed the water in her bottle with one long slug, then trotted down to the trees.

She had just entered the trees when she saw the old school bus covered in graffiti. She'd taken a few pictures and walked around it to get another vantage point when she noticed another large tank painted in sandy brown and green camo sitting in the shade underneath a tall tree.

This tank was exceptionally tall, and she stood there, contemplating how to climb on top when she noticed a chair sitting down the road. But as she started toward it, the air seemed to close in around her. The sound of the breeze and the chirping of the birds disappeared, replaced with crunching and squeaking noises.

The tanks were rolling toward her.

From every direction.

She was surrounded. She could feel it, although she couldn't see them yet. She began to back up and tripped over a tank 50 feet behind her—the one she'd just walked away from thirty seconds earlier.

But now it was within arm's reach, its gun trained on her.

Destiny began to hyperventilate, and her head began to spin. She grabbed the tank to steady herself. She closed her eyes, fighting off the attack of vertigo, determined to get her breathing under control before she passed out.

She pretended she was deaf while she hummed "Row, Row, Row Your Boat." She couldn't let herself acknowledge the thundering sound of hundreds of boots marching in time right toward her. She counted to 100... then opened her eyes to find herself surrounded by four tanks: the three she had seen plus a small desert tank, like she'd seen in Afghanistan. Its gun was being lowered.

It stopped when it was level with her face.

Destiny screamed and threw herself into the space between two of the tanks, falling to the ground. She clambered to her knees and took off running back into the line of trees.

"There she is!" Destiny heard a voice bellowing behind her. "Get her! Fire at will."

She cut across the field in a diagonal path in the direction of her car. She burst through the bushes at the far end, but she was not on the road she'd expected.

The map showed she was only 20 feet from where her car should be, but there was no entrance to the ranch or car parked there. Instead, she saw a large open area in front of her occupied by a brick house, devoid of windows or doors, that looked exactly like a Taco Bell from the '80s.

She'd found the so-called Hacienda, better known as the U.S. Navy Taco Bell. There was nowhere else to hide, so she ran over to the empty building. It had been ransacked, but there was a stone hearth along one wall of the main room and a wood countertop in the center.

As she crossed the threshold, she couldn't believe what happened. The place where she was standing morphed into an entirely different room: one with tan walls and tabletops alongside swiveling chairs affixed to the tile floor. The fireplace was still there, but she couldn't remember ever having seen a Taco Bell with that décor before.

She spun around to see if she was being followed, only to find twin glass doors shut behind her and a menu affixed to the wall behind the wood countertop. Off to her side, the typical orange and yellow logo was painted on the wall, but it read "U.S. Navy Taco Bell" with a yellow tank, rather than a mission bell behind the words.

Destiny jumped when a voice spoke to her from only a few feet away. "Welcome. May I take your order?"

Destiny stared at the man, eyes wide as she took in his Navy dress blue uniform and the menu handprinted on the wall behind him.

20 mm Burrito
50 cal Taquito
105 mm Quesadilla
Sidewinder Tamales
Drop the Chalupa

Destiny busted through the doors and took off running back toward where her car should be, but everything looked different again. The road she'd just run up a few minutes ago was gone. Instead, she was surrounded by sagebrush and bushes. In the distance, she saw a large scrap-metal barn off to her right, and ducked down as she ran toward it. She could hide there.

The troops weren't visible, but she could hear them coming.

Destiny slipped through an opening in the side and sat down in the corner. She took slow, quiet breaths, trying to calm herself. Staring off into space, concentrating on the sounds around her, she began to notice faint words printed on the scraps of tin that made up the shed.

Cyanide! What the fuck are cyanide tins doing out here?

The soldiers had arrived. She could hear them fanning out around the area searching for her. After what felt like an eternity, she heard a man call out, "All clear!" She couldn't understand why no one had checked the shed.

Maybe they thought it was too obvious, that no one would be stupid enough to hide there.

The men moved off in the opposite direction, and Destiny let out a small sigh. But just then, she heard faint rustling noises outside the shed. Someone was creeping up on her location. She rose to a tense, crouched position, ready to spring at anyone who came in after her.

She waved a hand in front of her face. The soldiers' movements had stirred up a lot of dust that made it difficult to see and breathe in the dimly lit shed. She couldn't hear the furtive movements outside any longer, but it was getting harder to breathe.

She began to cough, covering her mouth in an attempt to deaden the sound. Her head began to spin, and she found it difficult to maintain her crouched position—the more it spun, the more nauseated she became. She clutched at her head as pain began to thunder through it.

She looked around her in a panic and realized it wasn't dust in the air.

It was gas.

The fuckers must be using the cyanide gas on me. Me! A U.S. citizen in my own country!

Destiny rose to her feet unsteadily and stumbled toward the crack in the shed's wall. She fell to the ground when her foot caught a rock just outside the door. Destiny took great gulping breaths of fresh air, crawling away as fast as she could toward a crumbling wooden shed not far away. She couldn't see or hear the troops or tanks moving any longer.

They must've just left me here to die.

Destiny crawled deep inside the ramshackle structure and collapsed onto her side. Her body began to seize and flop on the ground, spittle frothing from her mouth.

After a time, the tremor ended, and she lay on the ground, unconscious.

The ground shook, and the rhythmic metallic rattle returned. Destiny awoke feeling disoriented and terrified. She could tell it was more than one tank, and she could feel the vibration all around her. They had surrounded her again.

A fifth tank had joined the others in a line in front of the shed. All the tanks were lowering their guns and targeting the wooden shed where she was hiding.

"Please stop! I'm sorry. I didn't mean any harm. There weren't any signs saying it was government property and to keep out."

Destiny screamed and cried, but she received no response.

The tanks fired their cannons, and the wooden shed flew to pieces around her. The thunderous explosion of the tanks' guns discharging was the last thing she heard.

Harry drove into town, unsure where to start looking for Destiny. She'd been expected back in Fallon last night, but she'd never checked in. Nobody else had heard from her either, and she hadn't been home when he went by her house in the morning. He'd called Allison, and she'd offered to come with him to help look for her.

He decided to search the area systematically, the way their father had taught them. He turned up Settlement Road and pulled into the first lot. There were fresh tire tracks leading in, but no sign of Destiny. She'd clearly been there at some point.

"There was a tank right here when I came out a week and a half ago. I wonder what happened to it. I know they hold training out here, so they probably moved it. Maybe Destiny just lost her way looking for them," Allison said, forcing her lips to part in a reassuring smile.

They spent the next forty minutes searching through town before they found her car parked near a pond. Bottles of water had been left in a bag on the passenger-side floor. Harry climbed a nearby tree to get a better view of the area. He knew she'd come out here to see the old tanks, so if he found them, chances were she'd be there too. Allison walked around the pond to see if Destiny was near the tank parked there.

"That's so strange. The tank that was here is gone too," she said when she returned.

Off in the distance, about a half a mile away, Harry saw sunlight glinting off some large metallic objects near a bunch of trees.

"There's something big over there." Harry pointed off to the east.

"The old bus and another tank were parked there. She must have walked to them. Maybe she twisted her ankle or something on the way. I'm sure she's fine."

They returned to the car and drove over, turning into a clearing near the grove of trees.

To their surprise, they found several tanks... five, parked next to each other, near an old wooden shed on its last legs. It was still standing, but it looked like a stiff breeze could bring it down at any moment.

"They must have moved the tanks right after I was out here. There's not even any tread marks left. Or maybe one hell of a storm washed them away... Wait! Look!" Allison pointed excitedly to the left of the shed.

"There's footprints!"

The two of them ran over to the shed, calling out Destiny's name. Flies buzzed in a large cloud around the building. As they rounded the doorframe, Allison cried out in shock. Harry ran to Destiny's side and dropped to his knees. He began to shake Destiny, but she slumped to the ground, completely limp.

Her unseeing eyes were wide open, and her face was pulled back in a grimace of terror. He felt for a pulse, but there was none. Even in the heat outside, her body was cool to the touch. The flies were being drawn by the smell of early decomposition that hung in the air. Allison pulled out her phone and called 911.

"Doc, she'd only been out there about 28 hours.

Shouldn't she have been in rigor still?" Detective Moran asked, notebook in hand.

"Typically, yes. Rigor starts setting in after about 2 hours and is complete in about 8 hours," Dr. Phillips said. "Then it can last up to 24 hours after that. But that all changes depending on the temperature. It's been over 100 degrees the past two days. That speeds up the process greatly. I'd say she died shortly after she arrived."

"What was the cause of death then? We didn't find no signs of foul play out there. In fact, we didn't see any tire marks or footprints other than hers, the brother's, and her friend's."

"It was a heart attack."

"Then why did she look like that? Her face? It was unnatural. To be honest, it spooked the hell out of me. I've seen a lot of weird shit in my time, but this takes the cake."

"I can't explain that exactly. True, we would've expected her muscles to relax. Her face shouldn't have been stuck in that tense expression. Her eyes wouldn't necessarily have closed, but they should've been in a more natural state. I don't know how to account for any of it other than to say strange things happen sometimes. Just the same, it was natural causes. Nothing more."

"But why would she have been so scared?"

"Wouldn't you be scared if you were having a heart attack alone in the middle of nowhere?" the doctor asked. "When the body is shutting down, a person can have seizures or experience visions during a hypoxic state."

"Her brother said she'd had some pretty severe PTSD after getting back from Afghanistan. Could that be related?"

"Sure. That's definitely possible. The stress of a panic attack could have been the tipping point for an undiagnosed cardiac issue."

"So I can tell the family and the Navy that it was just natural causes then," Moran said, shaking his head ruefully. "Great! I don't think either one of them will believe me. Her brother insisted she was the picture of health. Meanwhile, the Navy is royally pissed because somehow their tanks were moved. Decommissioned, inoperable multi-ton armored vehicles moved mysteriously, and a body shows up the same day. Fuck my life!"

"Ambushed" by Sharon Marie Provost was inspired by a trip to Dixie Valley. It appears here for the first time.

Stephen H. Provost

The Turn
of a Deadly Card

"Whatever you do, don't use it."

She was speakin' of the amulet, and I wasn't about to argue. I had it with me as a lucky charm, nothin' more.

Claire was hard to resist, but I could be as all-fire stubborn as she was. Truth of it was, the church mouse still had the kind of spell over me no run o' the mill leggy blonde coulda pulled off. She didn't want me goin' at all, even if it *had* been her idea for me to get away from all the Azrael bullcrap.

She just hadn't figured I'd be headin' out west to Vegas, which they was already callin' Sin City. Not exactly the kinda place a former church secretary would approve of. She'd gotten out from under daddy-o's thumb, that self-proclaimed "prophet" who didn't want his little girl livin' her own life. I wished it coulda happened some other way, but that's a story for another time.

These days, Claire was runnin' a Christian community center outta the place that used to be the church. Before ya go gettin' any ideas, her and me ain't exactly romantical—not that I would've objected, the age difference be damned. When it came right down to it, though, we was closer than that. Claire'd helped me crack my toughest case, or I'd helped her, with her bein' my client and all. A serial killer who hadn't been caught in half a century? Now that was a doozy, but we'd solved that crazy mystery together, an' I couldn't have done it without her. We had each other's backs, no matter what. Didn't matter that she was a believer and I wasn't, or that I had my own way of goin' about things that didn't actually square with the scriptures. We was closer'n blood, the two of us, an' that was that.

Now, when I told Claire I was thinkin' of a vacation, she was all for it. She shoulda known I didn't *take* vacations, unless there was work involved, and when she found out about that, she was none too pleased. Then, when it came to light I was goin' to Vegas to do a job for Vinnie's son—well, *then*, she blew a gasket.

Vinnie Lombardo was one of the "family" bosses in town, the biggest cheese on the cutting board. He ran the local numbers game, fixed fights at the auditorium (which he also owned), and had his filthy fingers in who knows how many peccant pies. Operatin' out of my two-bit town gave him the look of a two-bit crook an' kept the FBI off his tail, whilst in the meantime, he was stretchin' out his tentacles in all sortsa places on the hush-hush.

Them places now included Vegas, where he'd sent his kid to act as his proxy and set up shop there. I knew Vinnie's kid, Zito, and we weren't exactly on speaking terms. I'd knocked him out cold once, and I'd thought Vinnie'd be all bent outta shape about it. But instead, he'd been all forgivin'. Said the kid had it comin' and needed to be taught a lesson. Still, I couldn't help thinkin' Vinnie was enjoyin' the idea of sending me out to watch over him. What if he wanted to teach him another lesson, like how to get back at someone who'd screwed him over?

I couldn't overlook that potentiality, but I also couldn't say no to Vinnie—not if I knew what was good for me. We'd been scratchin' each other's backs for so long, datin' back to my days as a cop and through my whole career as a P.I., that he now seemed to have a perpetual itch—one I didn't dare ignore. So I'd packed up my stuff and driven cross-country on Route 66, not knowin' what to expect.

One thing I did know: It sure as hell wasn't this. Vegas was like an oasis in the desert without the oasis part. Just a bunch o' sand an' tumbleweeds an' dust an' heat. Yeah, some o' the motor courts had pools, but who wanted to fry your skin off by the time you got halfway there from your room? The place was a desert with a bunch o' neon on Fremont Street that dripped on down what they called "The Strip" until it dried up like a prune-faced gambler south o' there. Bugsy, who'd been tight with Vinnie back in the day, had opened the Flamingo there in '47, but he hadn't lasted long enough to enjoy the fruits of his labor. Some goons bumped him off at his squeeze's place in L.A., an' the law never figured out who done it.

Vinnie said he knew, and he winked at me when he put me on this job. That meant one of two things: Either Vinnie'd had him whacked, or he wanted people to *think* he'd done it so he could move in on Bugsy's territory. That territory was Las Vegas, which was why the kid was here.

Vinnie'd set me up at his new resort, the Sandpiper, which he'd opened up across from the Tropicana. He'd put me up in the Presidential Suite, which wasn't exactly the best way for me to keep a low profile if I was going to dig up info. What kind of info? He hadn't told me. Yet. But then there was this envelope sitting on that glass table in the middle of the suite, propped up against a Champagne bottle.

I opened it.

"*Compare*," it began, usin' the customary word for "old pal"... "This here is your 'portfolio.' It's who you are, for the duration."

Ben Dryer. I was supposed to be some joker named Ben Dryer. This smelled funny to me. I was used to comin' up with my own disguises, not havin' someone else go writin' the script for me. But it was Vinnie's game, and it was my job to play ball. That didn't mean I couldn't try to sniff out what his angle was. Was this Dryer a real person? By assumin' his identity, was I makin' myself a target... or maybe bein' used by Vinnie to smoke someone out? Those were questions for later.

I looked closer at the "portfolio." It came complete with a fake ID, a fistful of dollars, a ticket to someplace called the Bloody Ol' Bucket, and... what was this? Ben Dryer's last will and testament, with the whole kit and kaboodle signed over to... Vinnie's kid! This was crazy as hell. Accordin' to the will, this Dryer guy was richer than a double ice cream sundae piled on a brownie with sprinkles an' marshmallows. If Vinnie wanted to clip the guy and have his kid get the windfall, that made sense. What didn't make sense was involvin' me in the shindig.

There was more to the letter: "Open the box."

I hadn't noticed the cardboard box sittin' on the other side of the four-poster bed. I'd been distracted by the Old Glory bedspread and the picture of Uncle Sam smilin' down on me from the ceilin'. I'd heard of mirrors in them lovey-dovey rooms, but this was a whole new level of kinky.

The box. Right.

I opened it with the boxcutter lyin' on top and closed the blade up, stashin' it in the front pocket of my trousers. You never could tell when it would come in handy. Inside the box was a disguise: glasses, a fake goatee, some skin tone, and a black wig. That made sense. Vinnie's kid would remember the real me, so I needed to look... different. And this was sure as hell different.

I looked back at the letter. "The ticket will get you in the game, if you got the password too. The password is 'insomnia.' It's for the concierge at the front desk. He'll lead you to a vehicle, where the driver will blindfold you and transport you to the Bloody Ol' Bucket. Once there, you will present the ticket to the doorman, along with your last will and testament, and this will grant you access to the game. Once you have read this message, please burn it in the fireplace. Hold on to the rest of it. You'll need it, bucko."

If that wasn't an invitation to a trap, I didn't know what was. But whose? Vinnie's? The kid's? Or...? I was just gonna have to play it through and find out.

They didn't take the blindfold off until I was there in the room and had fished out my ticket. The muscle, who was about six-foot-nine and nearly four hundred pounds of pure muscle, frisked me, found the boxcutter I'd stashed, and tossed it aside.

"No weapons," he said. "Them's the rules."

Then he pulled the amulet out of my pocket and held it up to the light. The silver symbols glinted in the light as he turned it over in his fingers.

"What's that?" Zito asked.

"Lucky token," I said. "My little girl gave it to me."

The kid nodded and told Sasquatch to let me have it back,

then turned to me. "You'll need all the luck you can get, sugarfoot." I'd heard him use that before. It was what he called people he didn't like. But I could tell by the look on his face he didn't recognize me... or did he? I shook my head and put the amulet back in my pocket.

I nodded, scannin' the room for a way out in case things went bad, but the door I'd come in through looked like the only one. I'd expected some high-roller hangout with fancy furnishin's and a big wheel of fortune or some such. But there weren't none of that. It was kinda bare bones, lookin' like an old octagonal barn with straw on the floor that had been converted into a poker room. They'd put eight chairs around a red felt-covered table in the same shape, so it looked like a stop sign. That weren't too comfortin', I'll tell ya that much. I was the third one there, not countin' Vinnie's kid, who was standin' at the end opposite the door, leaning forward with his knuckles on the table and a big ol' grin on his face like a vulture straight outta Looney Tunes.

"Welcome to the Bloody Ol' Bucket, Mr. Dryer," Zito said, clapping his hands together once and holding them clasped there, like he'd killed a mosquito. "Please take your seat." He gestured toward one of the chairs, and it was clear by the way he said it that I wasn't gonna be given my choice of seating.

"What's the buy-in?" I asked, seein' no chips on the table.

"You did bring along your will, I trust."

I pulled the manila envelope from inside my coat and handed it over. No skin off my nose. It was probably as bogus as my Ben Dryer alter-ego.

"Aren't you the eager beaver," the woman sitting beside me said. She was dressed all in black, the kind of willowy gown that hugs the curves before drippin' off ya at the bottom. 'Cept she didn't have a whole lotta curves to hug. She was one o' them straight-up-and-down gals, all legs, no hips, and an A-cup top. She reached out a bony hand, and I took it. "Shondra Elephante," she said, nodding.

"Ben Dryer."

"Hmmph," she said, shrugging. "Never heard of you."

I had heard of her, though. Everyone who knew anything about the families did. She was Terry Graciano's moll, and she never went anywhere without him. Except she was here now, and he wasn't. "I'm here to make sure this is on the up-and-up," she said, seein' the question in my eyes. She lowered her voice and leaned in. "If anything happens to me, he's gonna fuck this joker up, and he knows it."

"So you're the bait," I said.

She scowled. "Don't say it like that. I'm the insurance. And I don't come cheap." She winked.

"That's not what Morty Hedgpeth says." The voice belonged to Buddy Clay, who I recognized too. He was sittin' across the table from the two of us, a polished oak cane with fancy engravin's on it and a fat round head, just like his, 'cept it was gold. He was crackin' his knuckles like they were goin' out of style. Nerves? Or was he tryin' to intimidate us? It was hard to say. Clay was known as kind of a wild card in the business. He liked to go it alone, which made him a bunch of enemies, but it gave him the advantage of defying expectations, and staying one step ahead of the crowd. He liked to bet big so he could win big, so I wasn't surprised to see him here.

"Morty Hedgpeth don't know shit," Shondra snapped. "Fuck off an' mind your own business, Buddy."

Buddy touched his thumb and forefinger to the brim of his snakeskin cowboy hat an' smiled. "Whatever you say, ma'am."

The others filed in one at a time over the next few minutes. There was Sammy Quivver, the gas station tycoon, who'd been buildin' a bunch of big truck stops with slots inside around Vegas, Boulder City, an' Searchlight. But he'd made his fortune as a high-end pimp, luring kids off the street and sellin' 'em off to the highest bidder in Beverly Hills, Malibu, or out in Palos Verdes. Scum of the earth, that one.

Jeannie Gardner was the other dame in the game. She'd inherited Ripley Gardner's Magic Lamp Casino when he'd disappeared mysteriously a couple of years back. He'd named the place in her honor, with her name bein' Jeannie and all, so it seemed only fitting. She'd been the prime suspect in his murder, but without a body, they couldn't prove squat. Jeannie was good at coverin' things up... except when it came to her cleavage, which was on full display.

Mikey Alonzo had flown in from Long Beach, where he'd just built a new racetrack. What was good for Bing in Del Mar would be just as good for Mikey—or so his thinking went. He tried to ignore what folks were sayin' about Long Beach not exactly bein' Del Mar, or even Santa Anita. One thing was for sure, though, these players were all thoroughbreds, which made me kinda antsy about my own resume. Ben Dryer, I had a hunch, had been made up out of whole cloth; no one here knew him, which meant he was shady by definition.

I was waitin' for the eighth player to show up, but our host wasn't. "'Fraid Mousey won't be joinin' us tonight," he announced. "But he sends his regards." He threw a manila envelope into the pile at the center of the table, which I deduced must contain Mousey McGee's last will and testament. Were these guys—an' gals—all putting their entire fortunes on the line, and risking gettin' capped, just for a game of cards? Talk about high rollers.

Zito nodded to the muscle, who opened the door and shouted through to someone on the outside. The door closed again, an' I heard a click from the outside: They'd bolted the door so we couldn't get out.

"Now," Vinnie's kid said, turning' to the players and leanin' forward on his knuckles again. "Let's get down to brass tacks. You might think it's a little, eh, over-the-top for me to be askin' yous to ante up your will. But the way I sees it, a game ain't worth playin' if the stakes ain't right. I'm sure you agree."

People around the table started murmurin' their agreement, except for Buddy Clay, who gave a hoot and yelled out, "Damn straight, pardner!"

"Fine." The kid glared at Buddy, who clicked his tongue and made a motion with his hand like he was firin' a six-shooter.

"I'm sure you all know everyone here," Zito said, his eyes moving from one person to the next.

"Everyone except him." Buddy pointed at me.

Here it comes.

"He's good," Zito said, and everyone just seemed to accept it.

"So here's the rules," the kid announced. "We're all here for a friendly game of five-card draw, same as always. Your wills, well, they're the ante."

"What about the chips?" Sammy asked. "We ain't got nothin' to bet with."

"Ow contraire," Vinnie said. "You got yourselves."

"I don't get it," Jeannie said, rolling her eyes. "Just spill it."

Shondra shot a sideward glance at me, like she was worried. Did she know something I didn't?

"All righty, then," Vinnie said. "I'm sure you're all familiar with a game called strip poker."

The bunch of them nodded.

"Hold up, there, buttercup," Jeannie said. "I ain't takin' off my clothes for nothin.' I think I'll call it a night." She stood and went over to the door, tryin' the handle.

It wouldn't budge.

"'Fraid you're here for the duration, *buttercup*," Zito said. "But

I got good news for ya. I never said we'd be playin' strip poker. I said it would be *like* strip poker. You see..." He cocked his head sideways like that terrier stickin' his nose in the RCA to hear "his master's voice." "...Instead of losin' an article of clothing, you'll be leavin' a little piece of yourself behind."

"I still don't get it," Jeannie said.

"You won't be bettin' with chips," Zito said, letting the syllables slither out. "You'll be bettin' with body parts. Your body parts."

"What the fuck?" Sammy shouted. "What kind o' sick sonofabitch...?"

"Somethin' wrong, Sam?" Buddy chuckled. "Ain't up for it?"

"You *knew* about this?" Shondra said, her face white.

Buddy raised an eyebrow. "Well, no, not exactly. But when Zito here told me the stakes couldn't be higher, I figured it had to be somethin' kinda wild."

"This is a scam!" Sammy shouted. "I ain't playin'. I'm outta here."

"That's a shame," said Zito, shaking his head slowly. "But I can't make you play." He pulled a Glock out of his belt and shot Sammy in the head.

He fell over backward from the force of the impact, his head slamming into the wooden wall behind him and his body kickin' up sawdust as it hit the ground.

Zito reached into the pile and pulled out Sammy's will. "This is mine now," he said. "Which is quite convenient, since I didn't bring my own. Now I got a stake in the game."

I kept up my poker face, but inside I was just like the rest of them—as shaken as a 007 martini. When I'd known Zito, not that long ago, he'd been a screwup who couldn't hold his own against the pizza delivery guy. Now, he was lookin' and actin' all different. Like he'd flown right over the cuckoo's nest and landed in the torture chamber down the street. He'd always had a screw loose, but now all the bolts that had been holdin' this nutjob together had fallen off completely. No wonder Vinnie had wanted me to keep an eye on him. But there wasn't a whole lot I could do in my current predicament, not without a weapon and with some six-foot-nine muscleman starin' me down.

Oh, yeah. And with a meat cleaver in his hand, which he was in the process of scrapin' against a whetstone.

If there'd been any doubt in my mind he'd gone batshit, it was erased by the fact that he was gonna be playin' this game himself. He coulda just sat back an' watched. He had the only gun in the room—no weapons, my ass. He coulda just orchestrated how everything went down and collected everyone's will when the dust cleared. He'd be the richest sonofabitch in Vegas. Hell, west of the Mississippi.

"There are seven of us here now. Lucky, don'tcha think? But for who?" He laughed maniacally. "This game, my friends, is winner take all. Last man standing—unless it's a woman, of course. For each hand, I'll deal the cards..."

"You?" Shondra said. "Shouldn't it go around the table?"

"My house," Zito said, spreading his arms across the red felt, "my rules. But as a show of good faith... Carlo?"

Sasquatch came over to the table, and Zito put the palm of his left hand out in front of him, flat with his fingers splayed. "Little finger, first joint."

Squatch nodded, raised the cleaver, and brought the blade down full force on Zito's finger.

Zito screamed like a baby, jumped up from the table and started hopping around on one foot like Bugs Bunny on a pogo stick. This was the Zito I remembered. Couldn't take a punch, and couldn't take havin' the tip of his finger chopped off, either. I sat there stone-faced, starin' at that little piece of flesh an' bone just lyin' there on the table. A little bit of blood dripped from it, blendin' in with the color of the felt table.

The kid winced, cradling his hand and gritting his teeth as he managed to grunt out, "There... Nothing... to it... What the hell are you waitin' for Carlo? First aid! NOW!"

Bigfoot reached under the table and pulled out a med kit, dabbin' some peroxide on a cotton ball and pressin' it up against the end of Zito's finger. The kid bit down so hard I thought he was gonna bite right through the bottom of his face, tryin' not to hyperventilate through those clenched pearly whites of his. It was all very dramatic, unless you were like me and had seen a guy get nailed to a cross and impaled. Now *that* was some nasty shit.

Squatch wrapped gauze around Zito's finger an' escorted him back to his seat.

Zito let what he'd done sink in—and the pain ease up— for a couple before he finally raised his head and started talkin'. "Now that we have that out of the way, I hope you're feelin' a little better about our situation."

Jeannie put a hand to her mouth, then leaned away from the table, an' I saw her body convulsin' as she heaved and retched, spillin' the contents of her dinner onto the floor. She pulled a cloth napkin out of her purse and dabbed her mouth but didn't say nothin'.

"The rules are simple," Zito rasped. "When the hand is dealt, you either place a bet, or you fold. If you fold, you lose a body part—whatever one ya want, unless you'd rather Carlo here chose for you. If you place a bet, you bet a body part. Again, your choice. If there's any... er... dispute over which body part's more valuable, Carlo here will make the call. An', in case I forgot to tell ya, Carlo here's a lawyer, so at the end of it all, he'll make sure those wills'll be signed over to the winner, all legal like. Fair enough?"

No one said anything until Buddy Clay grabbed that cane o' his an' slammed it down against the floor with a crack. "Hell yeah!" he bellowed. "Let's get 'er ON!"

"Let it never be said that I'm a shitty host," Zito said. "Carlo? The Chateau Renard, 1883, if you please?"

The big man stepped over to a cabinet an' pulled out a bottle of blood-red wine, poppin' the cork and distributin' some glasses that he had in there too.

"Liquid courage!" Zito shouted, raisin' his glass for Sasquatch to fill it.

The big galoot went around the table, depositin' some of that merlot or cabernet or whatever the hell it was in each player's glass. When he came to Buddy, the guy said, "Got any whiskey?" Squatch went back to the cabinet and pulled out a bottle of Jack, settin' it down in front of him with a shot glass.

Buddy ignored the glass, twisted the top off, and downed a swig. "Now *that's* what I'm talkin' about!" he said with a satisfied "Ahhhhh!"

"I'll take some of that," Mikey mumbled. He looked like he was about to send his own dinner chasin' after Jeannie's.

When Carlo came to me, I just shook my head and covered the wine glass with my hand. I could hear Claire talkin' at me in my head: Now was *not* the time to go fallin' off the wagon. Hell, it was probably my own voice. Claire woulda told me to get the hell outta there so as not to go puttin' my sobriety on the line in the first place. Not that I had any choice at this point. Claire woulda blown a fuse if she'd knowed I was in Sin City with a buncha goombahs with a closet full o' booze and a 1 in 7 chance I was even gonna walk outta there with my skin.

"Deal the cards," I said.

"Gladly." Zito shuffled two decks of Bicycle cards together, the kind with the red backs and the kind with the blue, then sent 'em flyin' across the table at us. He weren't no trained dealer, and one of the cards caught on the felt as it headed toward Shondra, turnin' over to show a 6 of spades.

"Burn it," she said, and he dealt her another.

I picked up my cards and had a look at them. Two kings, hearts and diamonds; a seven, a five, and a two, all diamonds. I could draw for a flush—25 percent shot, give or take. I could ditch the low cards and try to build on the kings, but that was a longer shot. Still, if I ditched one of the kings and didn't get a diamond, I'd be stuck with a nothing hand.

"Bets," Zito called.

"I'm in for a pubic hair," Shondra said, smirking as she laid down her cards. "And I'll take two."

Mikey smiled. "I'll see that and stand," he said.

Zito was next. "You pansy-ass wimps," he said. "I see your hair and raise you a ring finger. And I'm takin' a card." He looked at what he picked up and beamed. Either he was lousy at holdin' things close to the vest or he was even worse at tryin' to throw us off the scent.

Jeannie sighed and threw all five of her cards back at Zito, who dealt her five new ones. "I'm in for the hair," she said.

"That ain't the bet now," Zito said, leanin' in to her and staring down at the three-carat princess-cut diamond she was wearing. "It's the ring finger. Good thing your hubby's..." He drew a finger across his neck slowly. "He might not like you losin' that weddin' ring of yours if he was still gracin' us with his presence, eh? 'Course, you took good care o' that, didn't ya?"

He winked at her, and she spat in his face. "Fuck off."

Zito wiped his face with the back of his hand, then whirled to grab the cleaver from Zito, who was standin' behind him. "I'll take that as insurance!" he shouted at Jeannie. "Hold her down, big guy!"

Sasquatch did as he was told, grabbin' Jeannie's hand and holdin' it down to the table so hard I heard her wrist crack. He pulled her fingers wide apart as she squirmed there, tryin' to pull away. She couldn't.

The cleaver came down, slicin' that finger of hers clean off. Blood started spurtin' out of it as she screamed, fallin' backward in her chair.

Zito took the finger, eased the ring off, and tossed it into the pot at the center, then threw the finger across the room. Shondra ducked just in time to dodge it.

"Bet's to you, Clay," Zito snarled.

Buddy grinned and leaned forward. "Well, you heard the ol' sayin'," he said. "I'd give my right arm. So, what the hell. My right arm it is. I'm gonna stand."

Mikey just shrugged, but Zito blanched. He hadn't counted on this. Buddy Clay was every bit the poker player he wasn't. He might have one honey of a hand. Or he might be bluffin'. I don't think anyone else at the table coulda pulled off a bluff like that, but Buddy was one of them "put up or shut up" kinda guys. You never really knew what he was thinkin', which was how he stayed a step ahead.

The bet was to me now. "Right arm it is," I said, wonderin' how the hell I was gonna extricate myself from this. "I'll take one."

Zito dealt the card, and I had a look.

Shondra said she was in for the right arm, too—what else *could* she say? Then it was Zito's turn. He'd made his bed, an' he was lookin' none too pleased about havin' to lie in it. For all his spoutin' off like some big-mouth tryin' to be like pops, he still wasn't much more than a spoiled 2-year-old in a starched shirt an' a pinstripe suit. Like he was dressin' up to look like Mickey Mantle but didn't have the stuff to be a batboy in the dugout.

"Fold," he said finally.

"You can't fold," Jeannie sniped. "That's the rule *someone* made."

"She's got ya there," Buddy guffawed.

Then, predictably, the Glock came flyin' out. "I said *fold*," Zito shouted, wavin' it back and forth between Jeannie and Buddy.

"I reckon I been called," Buddy said an' flipped over his cards before anyone could say a thing. "Full house. Queens over sevens. Read 'em an' weep."

He weren't happy for long, though.

I flipped my cards, and there for all to see was that fifth diamond I'd been lookin' for. "Ain't a straight, but beats your full boat, Buddy," I said. "I reckon."

Sasquatch whipped out the cleaver, fast as that, an' brought it down with all his strength on Buddy's right shoulder. He squealed like a pig as it sliced clean through, the arm droppin' and floppin' away beside the table like a dead fish outta water. Carlo set the knife aside and fetched the first-aid kit, tryin' to stem the flow of blood with a big ol' towel as it gushed out everywhere. But he'd cut the arm off right at the shoulder, which meant there weren't no place to apply a tourniquet.

Buddy was writhing on the floor, makin' it all the harder.

"Fix him up!" Zito shouted.

For the first time, Sasquatch answered back. "I'm a lawyer," he growled. "I ain't no doctor!"

"You shoulda cut off his fuckin' forearm!" Zito screamed.

"He said the arm!" Sasquatch snarled back.

"For godssake!" Shondra shouted. "Open the fucking door and call an ambulance!"

"No dice!" Zito shouted. "I ain't givin' away our location, and I sure as hell ain't bringing the cops down on our head."

"*Your* head," Shondra corrected him.

"Aaaaaaaghhhhh!" Buddy yelled. Bigfoot was tryin' to press a big white towel up against his bloody stump, but he was pressin' so hard it was defeatin' the purpose of it. Buddy kept thrashing around, which meant Squatch couldn't get a good hold on him until he finally sat on the sonofagun. By that time, the white towel looked like somethin' a matador might be holdin', the floor was covered in a syrupy red muck.

I couldn't believe Zito hadn't thought all this shit through... but what was I sayin'? This was Zito Lombardo we were talkin' about here. Not only hadn't he thought about havin' proper medical aid available, he hadn't noticed that, when Bigfoot had put the cleaver down, Jeannie had stepped around behind him and picked it up. Shondra had seen it, too, an' was tryin' not to draw any attention to it as she watched Jeannie raise it high over her head, gettin' ready for the killing blow.

But whether Zito had seen her lookin' or just had some sorta sixth sense workin' for him, he musta realized what was about to happen and, at the last moment, wheeled around and fired his gun point-blank between the dame's fleshy headlights, knockin' her backward and into the wall.

By this point, Buddy had passed out, Shondra was shakin' like a maple leaf, and Zito was standin' there like some crazed maniac, wavin' his gun all around.

Mikey was still sitting at the table, tryin' his best to blend into the woodwork. He'd been in over his head from the beginning, an' you could tell by lookin' at him he'd rather be out on the golf course. Of course, Zito weren't havin' none of it. He turned toward Mikey and pointed the barrel of the Glock in his direction. "Show 'em!" he demanded.

"I think the lady's next," he said, noddin' toward Shondra.

"Ah, right you are. Whatcha got, toots?"

"We're done here," I said, at which point Zito shifted the gun to put me in his sights.

"We're done when *I* say we're done, Elijah," he shouted.

So he *did* know who I was. Vinnie musta tipped him off. It was like I thought: He wanted me to be an object lesson to the kid about how ta deal with a knucklehead who crossed him—me being the knucklehead whose knuckles had been part of that right cross, which he'd been on the other end of.

Claire's voice rang in my skull: "Whatever you do, don't use it."

I sure as hell didn't wanna use the goddamn amulet, but I was outta options. Who knew what was gonna happen when I tried it? What I did know was that, if I didn't use it, it would be curtains for Shondra, then me, an' Mikey too. I fingered the thing in my pocket an' pictured myself back at home a week ago, when I'd been takin' stock of the guns in my cabinet an' checkin' on my ammo. I grabbed Shondra's hand, an' shouted, "Hold on!" just as the bullet came flyin' out of Zito's gun. I closed my eyes tight and winced as I braced for impact.

I slammed face-first into the floor of my bedroom, with Shondra landin' on top of me. Well, that answered two questions: One, I could make the amulet work for me, and two, I could take someone along for the ride.

"What the hell?" Shondra said, dustin' herself off as she got to her feet.

"Just a little detour, dollface," I said. "You won't remember a thing." *With any luck.* I grabbed my old bowling trophy off the shelf and cracked her over the head with it. The gold-plastic bowler's arm came loose and fell on the ground. Meh. It had been a runner-up trophy anyway, an' Shondra's noggin had gotten the worst of it.

Now that I was a week ahead of myself, I had some time to think. I drove Shondra to the Greyhound station, bought her a ticket to Miami, and left her sittin' there on a bench. Then I turned around an' bumped straight into... Claire.

"What are you doing here, Elijah? You're not still thinking of going on that trip to Nevada, are you?" She walked up to me an' flung her arms around me, pullin' back and fixin' me with that Colgate smile of hers. No kiss, though. It wasn't like that, though I had my share of not-so-honorable intentions.

Great. Everything was a week earlier than it had been, so she thought I was still gettin' ready to hit the road.

"Who's that?" she said, nodding toward Shondra.

"Just a... client," I lied. "Can you do me a favor an' make sure she gets on the bus to Miami OK? She's got family down there who'll be waitin' for her." Another lie, but I sure as hell wasn't gonna tell Claire I'd done the very thing she'd told me *not* to do.

"Sure thing. What's her name?"

"Shondra."

"That's pretty. She is too." She fixed me with a sly smile. "Anything going on between the two of you?"

"Ah, dollface," I said. "You know I only have eyes for you." I said it playfully, but that one *wasn't* a lie.

We said our goodbyes, an' I prayed Shondra wouldn't remember all the gory details an' spill 'em to Claire. Well, I didn't exactly pray. That was Claire's department. But I was hopin' really hard. Claire figurin' things out was the last thing I needed.

I headed back home an' grabbed what I'd need: a pistol, a shotgun, an' a throwing knife for my bootstraps. I couldn't be leavin' anything to chance when I headed back. An' yeah, I had to head back. The only question was when? If I picked things up where I left off, Sammy Quivver would still be dead, Jeannie would be shot in the chest and missin' a finger, an' Buddy Clay would be dyin' on the floor. But if I popped back in before everything started goin' to hell, it would raise a ton of suspicion, an' Vinnie would be hard on my case about it.

I did some quick-ass rationalizin'. The world was better off without Sammy Quivver. An' Buddy? He was bound to wind up on the wrong end of a big bet sooner or later. Jeannie gettin' shot was just what she deserved for offin' her old man. Nope, I'd pop back in right where I left, but loaded for bear this time. I stuck a knife in my boot, drew the pistol, shouldered my shotgun, an' rubbed the amulet for all it was worth.

Pop!

"What the...?"

"Drop it, Zito."

"Where's the dame?"

"Shondra? She cashed in her chips before you could do it for her, Lombardo. Now drop the piece, or I drop you."

I saw a flash of silver from the corner of my eye, which distracted me enough to see Bigfoot hurling that massive piece of cutlery straight at me. I ducked, an' Zito fired. He was as bad a shot as he was a host. I hunkered down under the table, retrieved the meat cleaver, then rose up and threw it at him, knockin' him back off his feet. I grabbed the shotgun off my shoulder an' whirled around, blastin' the lock on the door to kingdom come.

Jeannie went runnin', an' Sasquatch tried to tackle her, which was a good thing because it meant he was distracted for just the moment I needed. I dropped the shotgun, pulled the knife from my boot an' lunged at him, burying it in the side of his neck.

Blood started sprayin' out like a gusher from a well down in Texas as Squatch started clawin' at his neck to stop the bleedin'... which only made it worse. The congealed blood from Buddy's shoulder fountain mixed with the new stuff, and it looked like we'd have a whole new Red Sea on our hands before too long— one that actually lived up to its name.

In the meantime, Zito had crawled back up on his haunches, found the Glock again, an' was firin' it.

I aimed my own pistol and fired back.

He missed.

I didn't.

An' suddenly, just like that, the whole place was so quiet you could hear a dormouse tiptoe out, if one had been there.

I heard slow clapping from behind me and turned around.

"Well, look who it is," I said, starin' at Vinnie's ugly mug, which was smilin' back at me. I pointed the pistol at him, but he just held up his hands in protest—although he didn't seem too worried. He knew me shootin' him would only set in motion a whole lot of repercussions that neither one of us was eager to face.

He walked over to where Zito was lyin' an' kicked him hard in the face, makin' him grunt. Then he expired ignominiously.

"Stupid kid," he groused. "Couldn't do anything right from the day he was born. Even came outta his mama wrong-end first." He laughed.

"So this *was* a test," I said flatly.

"'Course it was, *compare*. I was testin' him to see if he knew how to take out the garbage..."

"Me."

He nodded.

"But I was also testin' you to see if you were up to puttin' that sorry excuse for an heir out of my misery. You passed. He didn't. Now I know who not to entrust the business to."

I stared at him. "So what happens now? All those wills— that's what you wanted, right? To clean up from all these suckers?"

"True enough. I knew they was just like yours truly. They couldn't resist a pot that big, the risks be damned."

"Real high rollers," I scoffed, shakin' my head. "But there's just one problem with your plan, Vincente." He hated bein' called Vinnie, an' I humored him to keep the peace. "There's one thing you didn't figure on: Those wills were all made out to Zito, an' he's dead. So's Bigfoot, an' he was the lawyer, right?"

Vinnie burst out laughin' so hard I thought he was about to bust a gasket. "I thought you'd figured that out, *compare*. Maybe you ain't as good as I gave ya credit for—at least not without that li'l churchmouse o' yours." He reached down and gathered the pile of wills into his arms. "You *know* I got other lawyers, right? An' the only will made out to Zito was the fake one I gave you. The rest all got *my* name on it. If the kid had passed his test, I'da given him a hefty take. But he didn't, so I guess it's all *mine* now, eh, compare?"

Vinnie'd been orchestrating the whole thing from the beginning. I oughta've know that Zito couldn't be the brains behind it. He didn't *have* enough brains to come up with nothin' this crazy.

"There's just one thing I can't figure out fer the life o' me," Vinnie said, fixin' me with one of those suspicious looks that told me he didn't like not knowing how I'd put one over on him. "I set the rules to this game, and one o' them rules was no guns allowed. Zito had one, in case somethin' went wrong, but no one else managed to smuggle so much as a toothpick in here. But you got a whole fuckin' arsenal. What gives? I gotta know how you did it."

I smiled. "We're in Vegas, baby," I said. "And a magician never reveals his tricks."

I palmed the amulet, pictured myself back home, and vanished into thin air, leaving Vinnie standin' all by his lonesome in that Bloody Ol' Bucket.

"The Turn of a Deadly Card" by Stephen H. Provost appears here for the first time. The events in this story

take place following the events in the novel Azrael's Assassin: Testament in Blood, *a collaboration with Sharon Marie Provost. The title was inspired by the Alan Parsons Project song title, "The Turn of a Friendly Card."*

SHARON MARIE and STEPHEN H. PROVOST

Sharon Marie Provost

When Fate Comes Knocking

C alliope felt anxious as the week that led up to her birthday began. It should have been like any other week, except anybody "normal" would have been excited. She was finally turning 21.

If she were anybody else, life would actually begin now. Nobody would be able to hold her back from doing whatever she wanted anymore. The responsibilities of adulthood began at 18, but somehow this stupid society thought it was proper to

269

withhold the fun until 21.

All her friends had huge blowout parties on their 21st, and they'd been pestering her about making plans for hers. But she knew it was useless. It wasn't meant to be for her.

There would be no party.

No drinking.

No gambling.

She'd never be 21 at all.

Lidia screeched to a halt in front of Calliope's apartment and lay on the horn.

"Your chariot awaits, my queen!" she bellowed out the window.

Calliope ran to the window and waved for Lidia to quiet down. She grabbed her purse off the counter and skipped down the stairs.

"Hey there, loudmouth! Thanks for picking me up."

"Of course. So where are we off to first?"

"Meadowood Mall. I need to go to Rue 21 and get a dress."

"Oooh! What are we shopping for? A hot date?"

"No."

"Are you finally going to let us throw you a party?"

"No, not that either." Calliope frowned and looked out the window.

"Chill, bitch. I didn't mean to be nosy."

"It's not that."

"Then what?"

"You wouldn't understand."

"Callie, I'm your best friend. You can talk to me about anything. For god's sake, it's just a dress. What can be so upsetting about that?"

"I don't want to talk about it. You'll just think I'm crazy. I've already fought with my mother about it enough."

"Talk to me. Please. I love you."

"Fine. Let's go somewhere quiet for coffee, and then we can talk."

"How about Bibo Coffee in Midtown?"

"Perfect."

The two girls ordered lattes and chose a table in the shade on the patio. Calliope couldn't look Lidia in the eyes. She cleared her throat and began, twirling the tassel hanging from her purse.

"The dress... the refusal to celebrate my birthday... it's all related."

"I assumed from how weird you were acting. But how?"

"I guess I have to start at the beginning. When I was 5, I went to stay with my grandma in Las Vegas for the summer. While I was there, something happened. When my mom found out, she refused to let me see her again. My parents had been fighting a lot, ever since I could remember, but that seemed to be the last straw. They divorced the next year, and I only saw grandma once after that when I was spending time with my dad."

"Wow! What the hell happened, girl?"

"My grandma was a psychic. She believed in all that metaphysical stuff, and..."

"Did she have a crystal ball and dress like a gypsy?"

"Lidia!"

Lidia held up her hands in surrender. "Okay. I'm sorry. You know I get excited and run off on tangents."

"No, she wasn't a gypsy—and they like to be called Romani now. No crystal balls for her... although that doesn't mean she discounted their use. She would take me to her little shop down by Fremont Street during the day while she worked. She taught me all about her beliefs. If people didn't mind, I even got to sit in during their psychic readings with her."

"That sounds cool. What's the big deal?"

"Well, one night I went to bed, and I woke up screaming. I was inconsolable. My grandma called my parents, and they couldn't even calm me down over the phone. She ended up taking me to the hospital, and they sedated me and kept me overnight. The next morning, I woke up to find my parents there. I never even got to say goodbye to my grandma."

"Shit, Calliope! What happened?"

"I had a vision in my sleep."

"That sounds like it was a lot more than a bad dream."

"They called it a night terror, but it was more than that. I woke up knowing that I would never see my 21st birthday. Something tragic and unexpected is going to happen to me just before my birthday."

"You just said is... you don't mean to say you still believe that? Right? That's crazy. Shit! Sorry. I mean that's not rational. It was just a fucked-up nightmare of a small child who had been exposed to too much 'woo-woo' shit at a young age." Lidia raised her hands and waggled her fingers in the air to accentuate her statement.

A tear welled up in the corner of Calliope's eye. She turned away and rubbed the back of her hand across her face.

"Yes, I do still believe. I always have. It never went away—even after all the counseling my parents dragged me to for years—but it's more than that."

"What do you mean?"

"It wasn't... I mean *isn't* a nightmare. It's not like I saw what happened to me and that it scared me. I just saw my parents and friends—you—talking about what a tragedy it was. I saw my headstone bearing the date of October 17, 2025."

"That's Friday, only three days from now. The day before your..."

"My birthday."

"Why did you change it to the present tense, *isn't*, a nightmare?"

"Because that was only the first time it happened. It's never stopped. I have them every six months or so."

"And you said you saw *me* though. That doesn't make any sense. We didn't even meet until we were 10 years old. How could you have seen me when you were 5? Did the vision evolve to become me once we became friends?"

Calliope chewed on her lip, her gaze downcast.

"Talk to me, Cal."

"You promise you'll believe me?"

"Of course." Lidia made a motion with her finger across her chest. "Cross my heart and hope to die. Shit! Guess that was in poor taste. Maybe I'm still 12."

Calliope laughed and gave Lidia a big hug.

"I wouldn't have you any other way. You know how some people look just the same as adults as they did when they were kids... just older. You're like that. You know how shy I was when I was a kid. When I saw you in the classroom that day we met, that's why I came up to you and introduced myself. I recognized you. I knew we were best friends, or soon would be.

"I saw my parents as they look now. Mom with her gray hair and bad nose job. Dad with his male pattern baldness. I saw Alex."

"Your little brother that's ten years younger than you?"

"Exactly. I couldn't possibly have known that Dad would remarry and have a child with his new wife."

"I don't even know what to say, Callie. You're blowing my mind. How is this even possible?"

"I don't know. I never got a chance to ask my grandmother. I believe she truly did have psychic ability. She believed that some people could foretell future disasters. I think this is probably the same kind of thing, except it's my future alone."

"So why don't you ask her now? You're an adult. Your parents can't stop you from contacting her."

"Unfortunately, though, death can."

"Damn it!"

"Have you tried talking to anybody else? There must be someone who can help."

"No, I haven't. You can't cheat death. Haven't you watched enough of those *Final Destination* movies to know that?"

"But that's a movie for Pete's sake!"

"Regardless, I still believe you can't change the future."

"What's the harm in trying?"

"The heartbreaking disappointment I might feel if it turns out that I can't. And now, you would feel it too. I'm afraid too. You fuck with death, death fucks you. What if it gets worse?"

"What's worse than death?"

"I don't know. I don't want to find out."

"I'll chance it. I can't lose you. You are my rock. My port in the storm. You keep me sane in an insane world. You keep me out of jail when I go wild."

"Don't get me wrong, Lidia. I haven't totally given up. I'm not walking out to meet my death. I will be careful and try to avoid any danger. No walking under ladders or breaking mirrors or Evel Knievel stunts. I hope, more than anything, that I'm wrong, and we can both laugh about what a fool I've been on Saturday when I take *you* out for drinks to repay you for dealing with this shit."

"So, do you know what happens to you? A plane falls on your head? Hit by a car? Murdered? Disease? I mean... you are healthy, right?"

"No, I don't. To be honest, I don't want to know. It would be so much worse if there was no way to avoid it. And yes, healthy as a horse. I just know everybody was talking about it being a tragedy. That could be any of those options you mentioned."

"I'm afraid to ask now, but why are we buying a dress? And if you say for your funeral, I swear to God I will..."

"Then shut up and don't ask. I just want to save Mom and you some of the work planning for my... for it. Besides, she'd never pick something that I'd want to wear."

Lidia hung her head down and began to sob. "Calliope, you can't do this to me."

Calliope stood up and stepped around Lidia, pulling her phone out of her pocket. "I'm sorry. I didn't want to tell you, but you insisted. I can take care of this myself. I'll just call for an Uber."

Lidia jumped up and grabbed Calliope's wrists.

"You'll do no such thing. You're my ride or die—even if we both get old and marry our soulmates—so we will face this together. Two heads are better than one, they say. You'll stay at my house starting Thursday night. We'll be stuck like glue to each other from the moment the clock strikes twelve on the day before your birthday until the moment we ring in your 21st. Got it? We're conjoined twins now."

Calliope laughed through the tears that had begun streaming down her face.

"Deal! But can we still go get a dress? Just for my peace of mind..."

"Yes, we can, my dear. Because we *are* having a 21st birthday party for you at my house where I and all our friends will keep you safe from planes, trains, and automobiles... or anything else that might be coming for you.

"It'll start on Friday at 7 p.m. and end when we all fall down in a drunken stupor. Then Saturday, when you're official, we're going out to the LEX Nightclub in the Grand Sierra to dance, drink, and gamble to our heart's desire.

"It will be the celebration to beat all birthday parties ever. Fire dancers, ice sculptures, fine wine, Cristal champagne, caviar, you name it. Who says money doesn't buy happiness? I wouldn't be a Montgomery if I didn't throw money at a problem."

"Slow down there, Paris Hilton! How about just all our friends, beer, margaritas, Mexican food, and confetti cake? What will your parents think about all of that?"

"Party pooper! But whatever the princess desires, she shall have. Your wish is my command. Don't worry about my parents. They're in the south of France for the next month, and I don't have a cap on my Gold Mastercard." She laughed giddily. "I'm so excited. You do realize you've unleashed a monster, right?"

"Yes, unfortunately, I do. I'm a little scared to see what you have planned. But I would love to go out to the LEX on Saturday, if..."

"Not if. When! Now to decide who to invite. Maybe we should ask tall, dark, and mysterious over there. He hasn't taken his eyes off you the entire time we've been here."

Calliope started to turn and look at who Lidia was referring to.

"Wait!"

Calliope leaned back in her chair and hazarded a look when Lidia gave her the signal.

"Umm no! Try dark and scary. Not my type at all. Let's just stick with our friends. We'll work on a boyfriend starting on Sunday. Fair enough?"

"Now that's what I want to hear. Plans for your *future*."

The rest of the afternoon passed quickly with Calliope trying on innumerable dresses before finally settling on a candy-apple-red knee-length bodycon dress. It flattered Calliope's figure while still being modest enough for a funeral. They agreed that even though fiery red is not a traditional color, everyone knew it was Calliope's favorite. But more importantly, she'd look hot at her birthday party. There'd be no funeral this year or for many years to come.

Calliope walked out of her Econ class on Thursday afternoon and found Lidia waiting for her.

"Twinsies, remember? You're mine now." Lidia smirked as she linked her arm through Calliope's elbow. "I stopped by your apartment and packed some stuff for you, including that hot dress that'll have all the guys drooling. Ready, Freddie?"

Calliope shook her head in amazement. "You weren't kidding. Lead on, McDuff."

Before heading to the Montgomery house for some movies, the two girls stopped at Ijji 2 to enjoy teppanyaki for dinner. Ever since Lidia's 13th birthday—which had been held there for 40 of her *closest* friends—they both loved the teriyaki chicken with tuna appetizer, and the entertaining show put on by the chef while cooking.

Calliope flushed with embarrassment when all the people assembled at the table surrounding the grill broke out singing "Happy Birthday."

"Bitch! It's not my birthday yet."

"Close enough. And we are here *celebrating* it. Payback is a bitch. You sicced the Ruby River Steakhouse people on me last year. Hurry up and eat your ice cream. I want to pant after Brad Pitt in *Legends of the Fall*. I never get tired of that movie."

"Do we get to watch any movies I want? It's *my* birthday."

"We have all night. The rest of the evening you choose."

"Woohoo!"

"But no *Sleeping with the Enemy* or any of those other tiresome stalker slasher movies. You have an unhealthy fascination with those."

The next day, Calliope rose before the sun. Part of her was surprised when she'd awoken at all that day. The rest of her dreaded waiting for the moment that would bring the end of her life.

Would she see it coming and have time to be afraid?

Would it hurt?

Would her family and Lidia be okay afterward?

Deep in her heart, she couldn't help but hold out a sliver of hope that Lidia and her mother were right. Everything would be okay. It was all just the terrible nightmare of a child that had been overwhelmed with ideas beyond her emotional and intellectual capacity to understand.

Calliope nodded off on the couch while watching videos with Lidia and started having the same vision. She saw her headstone with the same date. Her mother came into view crying... and then Lidia woke her up. She'd received no more information than the dozens of other times it had happened. She felt even more convinced that she wouldn't reach 21, despite all Lidia's preparations.

There was a light knock at her door.

"Come in."

"I knew you'd be up. Let's go have breakfast. You're going to owe me after all this. You know I'm not an early riser."

Calliope swung her arm over Lidia's shoulders and walked down the hall with her.

"I can't thank you enough. I'm sorry to be such a pest."

"So what did you make us for breakfast?"

"Did you hit your head? Do I need to take you to the hospital? Is it a hematoma on your brain that's going to kill you?"

"Har-de-har-har, bitch!"

"You know I don't cook. Don't know how. Daddy's money

willing, I'll never have to learn. However, I did ask Mrs. Withers to make us eggs, bacon, and waffles with strawberry compote."

"You're a saint. Cancel that. Mrs. Withers is a saint, but you've thought of everything. Thank you! Let's hurry up!"

Calliope bounced down the stairs, with Lidia right behind her. They burst into the kitchen, giggling.

"Good morning, Miss Montgomery and Miss..."

"Calliope, Mrs. Withers. Or Callie if you prefer."

"Have a seat out in the garden. I'll be right out to serve you. Happy Birthday, Miss... uh Calliope."

Mrs. Withers rolled out a cart with a steaming tray of scrambled and poached eggs, crispy bacon, golden-brown Belgian waffles, fresh strawberry compote, hand-whipped cream, and Vermont maple syrup.

"You've outdone yourself, Mrs. Withers. Thank you so much!"

Lidia turned to Mrs. Withers. "After you're done with breakfast service, you can take the rest of the day off. We'll be ordering in for lunch, and then the party will be catered. I hope you have a great day, Mrs. Withers. I appreciate you having this ready so early."

"Very well, Miss Montgomery. I appreciate your kindness. I've been meaning to go see my new granddaughter."

Lidia turned to Calliope and smiled. "I thought I'd have our favorite pizza from Grimaldi's delivered for lunch. Then I've got to go out for an hour or so to run a few errands to pick up some *special* party supplies. I'll be back by 5 to get ready for the party."

"I thought you Montgomerys had people to do that kind of stuff for you." Calliope gave her a mischievous smile.

Lidia socked her upper arm. "We do, thank you very much. But this is special. It takes a personal touch."

"Now I'm scared."

"You should be. Do you feel comfortable staying her alone in my family's mansion? Or I can have someone come over to sit with you if you like."

"I'm not a baby. What could possibly happen to me here?"

"Are you sure?"

"Positive. Besides, if it's meant to be, there's nothing we can do to stop it."

"Never mind. You've got me all spooked now. You're going with me, and you'll sit in the locked car while I run inside to get what I need. You're not going to spoil my surprise, but I'm not leaving you here alone. I don't know what I was thinking. Twinsies all the way!"

"You're ridiculous! But that's why I love you. Whatever you say. I'm not going to argue. Is there someone in the rose garden? You didn't plan something crazy for the party, did you?"

"I'm sure it's just Marcus, the gardener. As for your other question, you'll just have to wait and see."

When the girls returned just after 4:30, they found that Mrs. Withers and the gardener had departed. A large white party tent had been set up on the property near the garden.

"Guess the deliveries arrived on time. Marcus said he would oversee them before he left. I'm going to check on the food in the kitchen. No peeking!"

"I swear I won't. I'm going to run upstairs to take a quick shower and put on my dress. I'll see you in a bit."

"I'll help you with your hair. You need a sexy updo to go with that smoking hot dress."

"Thanks. I'm really getting excited about tonight. I hope..."

"You hope you find the man of your dreams tonight? That better be what you were going to say next."

Calliope smiled and nodded. "Of course."

Calliope took a long hot shower to try to relax. She heard a couple of thumps downstairs. She was too afraid to hazard a guess about what Lidia might be setting up now.

When she stepped into her dress and pulled the zipper up in back, she realized just how inappropriate it would have been for a funeral. Lidia had obviously insisted on this dress for this party. It hugged her curves in all the right places. She'd never let herself see how fit and attractive she really was—it'd never seemed important since she thought she'd never have time to marry.

As she was admiring herself in the mirror, she heard a scream that cut off abruptly. She ran to the top of the banister and called out, "What did you do? Cut yourself?"

She didn't hear a response.

"Lidia, are you okay?"

The house was eerily silent.

Calliope ran down the stairs, calling Lidia's name. When she turned into the kitchen, she saw Lidia lying on the floor, a large pool of blood blooming around her. She was still, her chest not rising and falling with her breaths. Her eyes were vacant, the pupils fully dilated.

"Lidia! Oh my God!"

Calliope ran to her and knelt by her side. She felt for a pulse, although she knew she wouldn't find one. Lidia had been stabbed repeatedly in the chest. Her shirt was soaked red with blood.

Calliope sobbed silently. Her lungs ached as she fought to take a breath. She willed herself to rise and call for help.

A voice from behind her said, "You look gorgeous in that dress, Calliope."

Calliope spun around and met the eyes of a man she didn't know. He held a Bowie knife, dripping with blood. She stood there in stunned silence as recognition dawned on her.

"It's you. You were there that day... when we got coffee."

"Bravo! Good memory, Calliope. Your beauty was so captivating that day. I couldn't take my eyes off you."

"So why didn't you ask me out?"

281

"I heard what you said about me that day. Besides, I wanted to be part of your destiny. You said you didn't know how you would die. I wanted to be the instrument. I had to feel your blood on me."

"Why did you have to kill *her* then?"

"The meddlesome bitch was causing trouble."

"What do you mean?"

"I listened to the two of you that day. I heard what you said about being fated to die before your 21st birthday. She wouldn't listen to you. She was determined to interrupt your destiny. I couldn't let her do that."

"But you didn't have to hurt her. She couldn't have stopped it. Nobody could have. I knew I would die today no matter what she tried. It wasn't supposed to be this way. She was supposed to be one of the people mourning me. I saw her. I always have. Why didn't she just let it be? I told her death fucks you. I just never imagined it would happen this way."

"Well, the bitch shouldn't have gotten in the way."

"Of what?"

"I was here earlier just waiting for my chance. She had to change her mind and insist on you going on those errands with her. If she'd just left well enough alone, I would have killed you while she was gone. Nobody else had to get hurt. Don't feel bad. It's her own fault."

He spoke with such conviction, the emotion galloping through his words. Calliope had been backing inch-by-inch toward the side exit from the kitchen while he was lost in his own speech.

"Why do you want to kill me? Who says you're not interfering with my destiny by taking this upon yourself?"

"We have a connection, Calliope. We are bonded. I was meant to hear you that day. I'm the only one that could intercede on your behalf and stop that bitch.

"I could hear the excitement and anticipation in your voice. I know you've been waiting for this your whole life, just as I've been waiting to find just the right woman for my first victim. This is going to be so special, for both of us. Can you feel it, Calliope? Are you ready?"

He had closed his eyes, relishing his own twisted words.

She turned her back to him, slipping off her shoes as she prepared to bolt from the room. "Yes, I'm ready. Thank you."

As she said the last word, she began to dash across the dining room, willing her bare footsteps to be silent.

But he had opened his eyes and saw her take off, and he was right behind her.

He grabbed a fistful of the long blond hair streaming out behind her and yanked her back, slamming her to the ground. Her head bounced off the hard oak floors. Her mind swam as she fought to remain conscious. He had knocked the wind out of her. In one swift movement, he stepped over and straddled her, pinning her to the ground.

"Baby, I've been looking forward to this for days. The pain will be brief but exquisite. I'll never forget you. Thank you for sharing this momentous occasion with me."

He leaned down and kissed her lips softly. The knife slid across her throat leaving a large smiling gash from ear to ear. Blood spurted from her carotid arteries onto him. He nuzzled his face into the gaping maw as blood bubbled and gurgled with Calliope's last gasping breaths through her torn trachea. The cut was so deep that only her spine and a bit of flesh still kept her head attached to her body.

As the life faded from her eyes, he smeared the blood down his body, moaning in ecstasy.

"Happy early Birthday, Calliope."

SHARON MARIE and STEPHEN H. PROVOST

"When Fate Comes Knocking" by Sharon Marie Provost appears here for the first time.

Stephen H. Provost

For the Greater Good

The gelatinous glob rolled across the floor of the cave, toward the end of the darkness. This was its natural and preferred form. Unlike the natives to this planet, it didn't need to rely on specialized orifices and appendages. Every part of its body was equally attuned to each of the five senses, so it could see in every direction. No need to turn one's head around like an owl to see if something might be sneaking up on you.

There were other advantages, too. Asexual reproduction was far less messy and more immediate than the clumsy copulation most of the species here used, and its malleable form afforded it extreme adaptability to any environment. No broken bones. No worries about "breathable atmosphere." No limitations from extreme temperatures—at least up to a point.

Its chameleon-like abilities were an added convenience, although comparing the creature to a chameleon would do it an injustice. It was infinitely more capable of blending into its surroundings than that Earth-born reptile.

The creature had ventured forth from its lair in the Lehman Caves before: always at night, when it would attract the least notice. It needed practice in mimicking the qualities of the primitive beings that had developed here, especially the humans, who were under the impression that they had "tamed" the planet when they had, in reality, raped it. It had traveled far on these journeys, its body unconstrained by fatigue and easily adaptable to speedy travel, and the results had been encouraging: It had gone unnoticed in a variety of guises. Now, it was confident that it was time to emerge in the light of day.

Derrick LaMont had been working as a tour guide at Lehman Caves for twelve years now. Great Basin National Park, just west of the Utah-Nevada state line, received fewer visitors than Yellowstone or Yosemite, but he'd had plenty of practice honing his skills. He knew his presentation by heart, and he knew that he always needed to recount the visitors who'd entered the caves as they exited at the end of his tours. It was common for a precocious child to go wandering off or a photo bug to linger, looking for the perfect shot. He'd even seen a couple or two explore the thrill of sexual intimacy in complete darkness, the same way some people were all hot to do it in the graveyard. He wanted to tell them they could just use a blindfold, but he knew that wouldn't go over well. He had to stick to the script.

But for all the times he'd been forced to head back and track down dawdlers, he'd never seen *this* happen. Twelve people had gone down into the cave, and thirteen people had come out. Had he counted wrong? He went over the tickets in his pouch again, and then a third time, but the count was always the same: twelve. He would have chalked it up to a lost ticket except for two things: He'd *never* lost a ticket, and he had a memory for faces. He didn't recognize the man who'd emerged with the others. Not from this tour. Not from anywhere.

His eyes kept returning to the man who stood behind the rest of the group as he wrapped up the tour just beyond the entrance to the cave. He was shifting his weight nervously from one foot to the other, and when LaMont called for questions, he understood why: He'd been waiting to ask something.

"Excuse me," he said, "but I've noticed, during my travels, that many of the trees in this place called Nevada are dead. It looks like they have been burned. Did you do that?"

"Me?" It seemed like an odd question.

"No, all of you."

"Well, yes. The Forest Service has found that it's best to let nature take its course. If we tried to put out every fire, the forest would become overgrown, and the environment would be thrown out of balance. We even conduct controlled burns to help things along if we think it's necessary."

"So, you kill the trees?"

"Umm, yes."

Some of the others in the crowd were starting to fidget. Visitors always wanted to be on their way to the next attraction—or to get lunch. LaMont took it as a cue to shift the focus away from the stranger's uncomfortable line of questioning. He shifted his eyes purposefully to the other side of the crowd. "Any other questions?"

But the Stranger wasn't finished. "How do you justify this?"

A guy wearing a Mustang Ranch T-shirt piped up from the back. "Because we don't want the damn fires spreadin' and burnin' down our houses, that's how, dumbass."

Other voices murmured in agreement.

LaMont was losing control of the crowd. Like it or not, he would have to steer the conversation back around... so he could end it. "It's for the greater good," he said, then quickly moved to wrap it all up. "I'm afraid that's all we have time for today. Thank you all for joining me on this tour of the Lehman Caves. I hope you enjoy the rest of your visit here at Great Basin National Park."

The Stranger knew what he had to do when he left the park that day. He would need to ingratiate himself to these humans, to earn their trust. From conversations with those he met, he learned that a settlement called Las Vegas was the best place to make connections with "those who mattered." Celebrities and people called high rollers made a habit of visiting this settlement, where they often consumed large volumes of alcohol and would, thus, be susceptible to suggestion.

When he arrived, he knew he would have to practice blending in before he made his move. The place was entirely foreign to him. His own kind did not live in settlements; they did not need shelter to protect them from the elements. And this settlement was different than any other he had encountered. Towers of light crowded the thoroughfares their vehicles traveled on. Women dressed in skimpy outfits approached him on the street, shoving pieces of cardboard in his face. "Girls Galore." "All Naked All the Time." People stepped out of doorways to places without windows, inviting him to try the best slots in Vegas and the cheapest buffet on the strip.

He quickly concluded that these were not the people he needed to impress.

But first, he had to find a place to stay. Money was no object, as he could morph bits of himself into perfect facsimiles of the currency used here and hand it out. It would revert to its natural state after a short time, but that was none of his concern. He concluded that the taller buildings were probably the most likely to provide what he needed and quickly settled on one with the word "TRUMP" emblazoned across the top. He knew this was a word associated with card games and concluded it was likely the destination for some of the high rollers he had heard about.

He was quickly disabused of this notion upon checking in: When he asked where the trump games were, he was informed that trump, in this case, was not a word but the name of an extremely influential man. This was working out better than he hoped.

"When can I meet him?" the Stranger asked.

The concierge laughed. "He is not here. He just owns the hotel."

"What would it take to arrange a meeting with him?"

"Well, a donation of a few million dollars to his campaign fund might do the trick."

"All right," the Stranger said, but upon being informed that this Trump was all the way across the country, he decided against it. If Trump was so important, there had to be others here who were connected to him who were influential as well. Now, all he had to do was find them.

Lorraine Mink wasn't her real name. She had taken it on as a stage name and had wound up pole dancing in the hope that it would lead to a big break. So far, it hadn't. But she had earned enough of a following to make a decent living, and one of her "sponsors," as she called them (the term was less offensive to her than "sugar daddies") had set her up in a suite at the Trump International.

That's where she met the Stranger. For some reason, he never told her his name, but it didn't matter. He obviously had money if he was staying at the Trump for an extended period.

She gave him her usual coquettish spiel: flirting, showering him with compliments, basically telling him whatever he wanted to hear. It always worked with men. She just hadn't met the right one yet... except now, maybe she had.

She invited him to her room and locked the door discreetly behind them.

"Do you know Trump?" he asked her.

"Of course I do, sweetie," she lied.

"Then you must be very important."

"I am," she said, squaring her shoulders and raising her chin. "And maybe, if you play your cards right, I can become very important to you." She raised her hand and ran a long, purple nail lightly down his cheek. "Would you like that?"

"Yes."

"I think I might like that too." She snuggled into him, pressing her curves in to match the contours of his body.

Usually, it was just that easy, but not with him, and that, together with his air of mystery, only made him more enticing. He was awkward, but not in the way a pimple-faced fifteen-year-old might feel awkward in these circumstances. His attitude was brusquer and more perfunctory, like he was negotiating a business deal. She supposed that made sense, with them both staying at the Trump. On a certain level, everything was transactional, she just wasn't used to someone acknowledging it so openly. It threw her off a little, but it intrigued her even more.

Perhaps if she matched his no-nonsense approach, he would get the hint. "Shall we get down to it then?" she said, taking a seat on the bed, uncrossing her legs, and patting the spot beside her. "Will you help me with my top... and my bra?"

"Of course."

At least he figured out how to undo a woman's bra, which was more than she could say for most men.

Then he said something that surprised her: "I'm not sure we should do this."

"Oh? And why not, sugar?"

"You will get hurt."

She laughed. "Do I look like a virgin? I hate to break it to you, if you're looking to be a cherry-poppin' daddy, I'm afraid you're a little late to the party."

"I didn't mean..."

Recognition dawned on her face. "Ohhhhh. You think you're gonna hurt me *that* way." She tapped the palm of her hand on her chest. "You don't have to worry about that, baby. This doesn't have to be anything you don't want it to be. But if you do want more, that might be arranged—if you're a good boy."

He looked indecisive, but she knew how to wipe that look off of any man's face. She put both hands on his cheeks and pulled him to her, nibbling at his lower lip before allowing her tongue to slither into his mouth. Deftly, she pivoted over and sat on his lap, pulling his arms around her, and started rocking. "You like that, sugar?" she said. "Oh, yeah. That's it. Maybe we should get a little bit more... comfortable."

She reached down between his legs and found what she was looking for, teasing him briefly before she pulled back and got down on her knees in front of him. Reaching for his zipper, she pulled it slowly down, then rested her head in his lap, nuzzling him like a kitten. She could feel him start to respond, so she moved her mouth around, letting her warm breath cascade across his underwear...

The Stranger left Lorraine's room quietly while she was still sleeping and headed back to his own, grateful that he hadn't given her his room number. Copulation was overrated, but this species was obviously designed to pursue it, despite any danger it might place them in. He had observed that back in the cave with one couple who had stayed behind on the tour to, as the male had put it, "get it on." Or, rather, he had heard it in the darkness. The moans of pleasure. The accelerated breathing. It had made no sense to him then, and he'd thought that perhaps he could become enlightened by having the experience himself. His body, in human form, had responded just as any other male of the species might. But he had *felt* nothing, and remained mystified about why this activity held such irresistible appeal for humans... until it suddenly came to him. His own kind was drawn, at regular intervals, to reproduce by division. It was an urge linked to the survival of the species. It had to be, he realized, the same for humans: an inducement to engage in an activity that might otherwise seem onerous.

For the greater good.

He felt that urge now and, in the privacy of his own room, reverted to his natural state and began to divide. The process continued through two, four, and then eight offspring, each genetically identical to the parent. They adopted different forms—some male, some female, but all human. The parent, who could not truly be distinguished as such, sent them on their way to fulfill their mission.

Subdue the humans and, if necessary, destroy them.

Something was wrong.

Lorraine looked in the mirror at her jaundiced face. The constipation had become intolerable. The pressure. The throbbing pain. She hadn't been able to move anything in three days.

She couldn't stand anymore. She flopped down on the bed, writhing like the pet goldfish that had jumped out of her aquarium as a child. She hadn't realized it, and had recoiled when her foot had found the slimy, scaly thing that she had called Goldie. She hadn't stepped down hard enough to squash it, and when she bent down, she found it was still alive, quivering as its mouth puckered in and out, its gills searching in vain for the life-giving water.

Unwilling to bend over to pick it up, she had run to her mother—and had watched in horror as she flushed Goldie down the toilet.

"It's just a fish," she had said. "God gave us dominion over all the animals."

"Does that mean I won't see her in heaven?"

"That's right. Heaven is reserved for the children of God, not base creatures."

The memory of her mother's voice faded as Lorraine felt a new stab of pain in her abdomen. Her mind raced frantically over the past few months. She always made her sponsors use protection, but there had been one time... the Stranger. That had been a huge mistake. She'd never seen him after that, but he had certainly left his mark upon her. Or inside her. This wasn't a case of massive indigestion. She'd lost her lunch, or dinner, more than once by going overboard with the tequila, but this didn't feel like that. She wanted to be sick, but trying to induce vomiting only made things worse.

But how *could* she be pregnant? Their encounter had been less than a week ago, and her stomach was distended like she was six months along. She'd never been *that* pregnant before—her sponsors always paid for abortions—but she knew it shouldn't feel like *this*. The extreme pressure inside her was unbearable, heaving up like ocean waves inside her. She tried to reach for the phone. She had her doctor's number saved in there somewhere. But any movement only multiplied the pain.

She groaned in agony as the thing inside her churned and

began thrashing around, as though searching for a way out. It pressed up against her lower ribs—her ribs! She didn't know much about physiology, but she did know her womb didn't extend *that* far up.

She felt a rib crack and screamed in agony.

But then the pressure moved. Lower. Whatever was inside her was searching for the easiest possible exit. Soft tissue. An orifice...

Her back arched involuntarily as it pushed against her birth canal. Her body tried desperately to accommodate it, but it was too large. Tissue began tearing inside her, and blood began to flow out of her. This was not like her period. This was a crimson river bursting through a dam that was failing.

Lorraine felt faint and was on the verge of passing out, but she had to see *what* was doing this to her. She looked down and saw it begin to emerge: an amorphous gray mass of tissue that throbbed as it appeared, plopping onto the floor with a squishing sound, drenched in its "mother's" blood. Her blood.

She stayed conscious just long enough to see it begin to change form, until it stood before her.

The Stranger.

I must... be... hallucinating...

It was the last conscious thought of her draining life.

Two years later...

The Strangers gathered around the table at Camp David. They had successfully infiltrated the government at all levels: Congress, the Executive Branch, the Joint Chiefs... but they hadn't been able to consolidate power.

"Unless we are able to eliminate any opposition, we will not be able to secure our place as rulers of this planet," one said.

"But how should I... we... do that?" Even, now, having undergone multiple reproductive events, the Strangers occasionally lapsed into the memory of their former unity. It was, in truth, more than a memory. It was still reality. They shared the same genes, unlike the baser humans, who diluted and contaminated their progeny by intermingling their DNA.

"We need to ensure their loyalty," another said. "I have been studying their historical records. The most effective rulers have placed loyalty above all else—above truth, above science, above everything."

"How have they accomplished this?"

"By threats, false promises, and ultimately, by force."

"This is barbaric."

"Yes," they all said at once.

"They *are* barbarians," one said. "What else should we expect?"

Heads nodded knowingly. They had judged it prudent, if inconvenient, to maintain their human form while conducting official business. They had made it clear they did not want to be interrupted, but humans were not always reliable when it came to following directions. It was better not to take the chance.

"We have never lowered ourselves to such things as force or deception to ensure what you call 'loyalty.'"

"There has never been any reason to do so. With us, there is no such distinction. This 'loyalty' is part of who we are. We are one."

"Then perhaps we need to become one with *them*."

The others murmured. They had, naturally, all come to the same conclusion at the same time.

"There was, of course, the unfortunate incident with the human called Lorraine."

"We tried to warn her she was putting herself in danger, but she would not listen."

"They will listen to me... to us... now."

More murmuring and nodding of heads.

"If we were to insert our genetic material into them, without actually replicating ourselves inside of them, we could avoid further 'unfortunate incidents.'"

"This has never been attempted."

"It has never been necessary."

"But I believe it is possible."

"There is one impediment."

"These people are disorganized. They rebel against one another for the sake of doing so, even though collaboration would serve them much better."

"Yes. They consider prevailing over others more important than arriving at truth."

"Indeed. Their love of discord could make them resistant to our efforts."

"Precisely."

"I have been looking at their historical records in regard to this, as well. Leaders who seek resources for their military ambitions always do so by persuading the people to sacrifice."

"For the greater good."

A chorus of laughter.

"They do not even understand the meaning of that phrase."

"Or perhaps they do."

"I know what you have in mind."

"Naturally."

"The man at the cave told me... us... that they allowed trees to burn, or even set fire to them, for the greater good. Left to grow unchecked, they would upend the ecosystem and destroy other life in the forest."

"Just as they themselves have done to this planet."

"Yes!"

"If they accept this principle, we cannot be faulted for applying it to them."

"It is even in one of their historical records: 'The good of the many outweighs the good of the few. Or the one.'"

"The rulers who have been most effective at galvanizing support..."

"They call them dictators."

"...have always been undermined by those who feign loyalty and wait for the opportunity to rise against them."

"We must not allow this to occur."

"Those who are disloyal must be eliminated."

"And if we become one with them, we will *know* whether they are truly loyal."

"Yes! Yes!"

They rose as one.

"It is time to implement our plan."

Derrick LaMont stood in a long line of people who were waiting at the government clinic in Ely to undergo "the procedure." It wasn't as though he had any choice. The government had offered low-cost medical insurance to anyone willing to sign up for one of its Health Now packages. Which was everybody. The deal was so good, you just couldn't say no, and it had put private insurers out of business.

No great loss, he thought. No more number-crunchers overruling doctors because something was too expensive. No more penalties for "pre-existing" conditions. There were packages tailored specifically to diabetes, cancer care, heart disease, even ED—all offered at the same low, flat rate.

The only condition was that you had to undergo "the procedure."

All he knew was it supposedly involved receiving an implant to monitor your vitals in real time. Cutting-edge technology. The idea was to detect any warning signs long before a doctor could find them at a regular checkup—*if* they could detect it, and not pass heart disease off as indigestion or dismiss colon cancer symptoms as IBS or constipation. It put a lot of general practitioners out of work, but fewer checkups meant lower costs, which the government passed along to the consumer.

The line was long, but it went faster than expected. The government had anticipated the demand and opened up half a dozen spaces for the procedure, so LaMont reached the front in a mere fifteen minutes. A man in blue scrubs and a facemask escorted him back to what looked like a dentist's chair that had been set up in a room barely larger than a cubicle. He couldn't help but notice the restraints attached to the arms of the chair, but before he could think any more about it, the man in blue shoved a clipboard in front of him and tapped it with his pen. "All we need is your signature authorizing the procedure," he said in a voice that was strangely dispassionate.

It also sounded vaguely familiar, but try as he might, he couldn't place it.

"Sure sure." LaMont scrawled his name. "Let's just get this over with."

"By all means."

That voice. Where had he heard it?

"This procedure is simple, but will be somewhat painful. We need to insert the implant directly into the brain, and this procedure will give us the most direct access to the frontal lobe."

"The frontal lobe?" LaMont was getting nervous, but there was no backing out of this now. The man in blue was securing the restraints on his arms. He put pressure on them, but they held firm. Was the man talking about a frontal lobotomy? No, that was impossible. The government would never do anything so vile to the people it was sworn to serve. It would be... inhuman.

That's when he saw the man produce an instrument that

looked way too much like an icepick for his liking.

He squirmed in his seat.

He tested the restraints again, this time using all his strength.

They didn't give. Not even a millimeter.

"Now just try to relax," the man said. "When this is all done, you won't remember a thing."

He raised the icepick and positioned it an inch from his eye, so close that LaMont's vision of it blurred. He strained to focus on it, as if holding on to this one image could somehow keep him from losing his mind. His will. His freedom.

He winced, closing his eyes tight and bracing for what was to come.

But it didn't.

He opened his eyes and saw the man in blue staring down at him, his mask pulled back to reveal a creepy, sickly-sweet smile on his face. "Thank you," the man said simply. And in that moment, LaMont remembered where he'd heard that voice before. It has been more than two years ago, at Lehman Caves, and it had belonged to the nameless stranger who had asked him about burning trees.

"For what?" LaMont stuttered.

"For your assistance in saving you, and this planet. Just as your kind ordered... what did you call them?... 'prescribed burns'—yes, that was it—to eliminate threats to the forest, we are ensuring that we can eliminate those of you who would destroy Earth."

His own words came back to him then. "For the greater good," he rasped.

"Precisely."

He screamed as the man in blue raised the icepick and, with a single violent thrust, jammed it into the corner of his eye.

"For the Greater Good" by Stephen H. Provost appears here for the first time. The title was inspired by one of the author's favorite Twilight Zone *episodes, "To Serve Man."*

Did you enjoy this book?

Recommend it to a friend. And please consider **rating it and/or leaving a brief review** at Amazon, Barnes & Noble, and Goodreads.

About the Authors

Sharon Marie Provost is an award-winning author who specializes in horror, thrillers, and speculative fiction. Beginning her career in late 2023, she has published a novella, two short story collections, and two collaborative collections of short stories with her husband. Her first novel, *Dark Arts: Love Me Tinder*, was published in 2024. It has received acclaim for its detailed and chilling story of a serial killer who turns his victims into works of art. In 2025, her "Shadow's Gate" received the Imadjinn Award for Best Short Story Collection, and she published two collaborative novels with Stephen H. Provost: *Azrael's Assassin: Testament in Blood* and *Evermore: Dark Soulmates*. Sharon is the chief operating officer of Dragon Crown Books. She has lived in Carson City since 1987.

Stephen H. Provost is a former reporter and columnist with more than 30 years of experience at daily newspapers. Over the past 11 years, he has written or co-authored more than

60 books. In addition to six novels and three novellas, he has produced an extensive collection of nonfiction works on topics ranging from Nevada's pioneer days to the history of retail in the United States. He has written more than 20 books on U.S. history in the 20th century focusing on highways, towns, and culture. Stephen is the founder and publisher of Dragon Crown Books. He lives in Carson City.

Books by
Sharon Marie Provost

Dark Arts
Shadow's Gate
Shades of Love, Vol. 2
The Last Train to Clarksville
Evermore: Dark Soulmates (with Stephen H. Provost)
Azrael's Assassin (with Stephen H. Provost)
All Hallows' Nightmare's Eve (with Stephen H. Provost)
Christmas Nightmare's Eve (with Stephen H. Provost)
Nevada Nightmares, Vol. 1 (contributor)
The ACES Anthology 2023 and 2024 (contributor)

Books by
Stephen H. Provost

Fiction

Evermore (with Sharon Marie Provost)
Azrael's Assassin (with Sharon Marie Provost)
The Memortality Saga
    Memortality
    Paralucidity
Meteor Ridge
Academy of the Lost Labyrinth
    The Talismans of Time
    Pathfinder of Destiny
The Only Dragon
Identity Break
Identity Forge
Crimson Scourge

SHARON MARIE and STEPHEN H. PROVOST

Nightmare's Eve
Christmas Nightmare's Eve (with Sharon Marie Provost)
All Hallows' Nightmare's Eve
    (with Sharon Marie Provost)
Shades of Love, Vol. 1
Need
Death's Doorstep
Feathercap
Madeline the Redheaded Witch
    The Reluctant Little Witch
    Madeline's Dragon Quest
The Adventures of Mark Twain in Nevada
Waffles the Poodle Dragon
Nevada Nightmares, Vol. 1 (contributor)
The ACES Anthology 2023 and 2024 (contributor)

Nonfiction

Mark Twain's Nevada
The Comstock Chronicles
Virginia City Then & Now
The Legend of Molly Bolin
A Whole Different League
California's Historic Highways series
    Highway 99
    Highway 101
America's Historic Highways series
    America's First Highways
    Yesterday's Highways
    Highways of the South
Highways of the West series
    America's Loneliest Road
    Victory Road
    The Lincoln Highway in California
        (with Gary Kinst)

NEVADA NIGHTMARE'S EVE

Sierra Highway
Bonanza Highway
Roadside Illustrated series
Happy Motoring!
Signpost Up Ahead: The East
Signpost Up Ahead: The West
The Great American Shopping Experience
What I Tell My Friends, Vol. 1 (with Lief Sorbye)
Fresno Growing Up, 2024
Martinsville Memories
The Century Cities series
Cambria Century, Carson City Century
Charleston Century, Danville Century
Fresno Century, Goldfield Century
Greensboro Century, Huntington Century
Roanoke Century, San Luis Obispo Century
The Phoenix Chronicles
The Osiris Testament
The Way of the Phoenix
The Gospel of the Phoenix
The Phoenix Principle
Forged in Ancient Fires
Messiah in the Making
Please Stop Saying That!
50 Undefeated

Praise for Other Works

"The writing was superb, the attention to detail shows she knows what she's doing when it comes to police procedure, and the kill scenes are very detailed and disturbing... For fans of serial killer stories with plenty of graphic imagery. Highly recommended."
— Justin Boote, author of *Soul Searchers*,
on Dark Arts by Sharon Marie Provost

"One of the best books I have EVER read! Messed-up, cringy, tense, sickening, thrilling, exciting, disturbing and complete!"
— Kim Sloan, author of the *Billy Bob Adventures* series,
on Dark Arts

"Haunting and beautiful. This book is so good! All the stars!!!"
— Angel Van Atta, author of *In the Tall Trees*,
on Dark Arts

"I love this book. The different stories leaves you wanting more. Takes your imagination in places that leaves you just WOW. Sharon Provost is in my top 3 as now. If you haven't read this book yet, get it. You will not be disappointed. Hands down Amazing."
— Kristy Chandler, Amazon reader,
Shadow's Gate by Sharon Marie Provost

"I read this book in one sitting, something I rarely do. The story is fast paced and crisply written, the description of the crimes, though tough to read, are expertly and vividly written. There are plenty of believable twists and turns. The ending is fabulous."
— Catherine Riddick, former *Fresno Bee* assistant managing editor,
on Dark Arts

NEVADA NIGHTMARE'S EVE

"Heartwarming, heart-wrenching. The romance broke my heart and then mended it."

— Carol Purroy, author of *Tiara*, on
The Last Train to Clarksville by **Sharon Marie Provost**

"Keeps you on your toes! Thrilling adventure from an eccentric mind! Twisty-tales to get your heart pumping and your mind wandering! Don't read in the middle of nowhere, alone, and in the dark."

— Steven J. Ponte, Amazon reader,
on **Shadow's Gate**

"I loved the story and the twist at the end. It's my kind of book! I had no idea and I love to be tricked and intrigued by an ending! Highly recommend it if you are a fan of everlasting love!"

— Sue C. Dugan, author of *A Slow Climb Up the Mountain*, on
The Last Train to Clarksville

"Sharon and Stephen will pull you into this page-turner from the very beginning. **Evermore** will take you down the dark side of soulmates and the desires that exist from one life to the next. Each time making them more mad, desperate to get it right or move on again to the next life to try it all over again. Will they finally find love and conquer it, or will they die trying? Read the book. You won't be disappointed.

— Maureen, Amazon reader

"Stephen and Sharon Provost did an incredible job preserving this piece of history. Thanks to their research and storytelling, this place won't be forgotten. A hundred years from now, people will still be able to read about it—and that's something special."

— Jeadene Solberg, cofounder of
Northern Nevada Ghost Hunters, on **Chinese Camp**

"The complex idea of mixing morality and mortality is a fresh twist on the human condition. ... **Memortality** is one of those books that will incite more questions than it answers. And for fandom, that's a good thing."

— Ricky L. Brown, Amazing Stories

"Punchy and fast paced, **Memortality** reads like a graphic novel. ... (Stephen H. Provost's) style makes the trippy landscapes and mind-bending plot points more believable and adds a thrilling edge to this vivid crossover fantasy."

— Foreword Reviews

"From time travel to karma earned, these short love stories range from thought-provoking to heartbreaking."

— Blue Bookwyrm Reviewer
on **Shades of Love, Vol. 1** by **Stephen H. Provost**

"A collection of so many good little short stories that pull you in and show us the ugly side of love, the dark, jealous side. How love can wind into every fiber of your life and grow into an obsession, not love. It shows how love can hurt, the pain of one-sided love that is a slow descent into madness. You'll see so many different stories... legends, grief horror, stalkers, slashers, paranormal, myths, revenge, and so much more."

— Micki-d, Amazon Canada reader, om
Shades of Love, Vol. 2 by **Sharon Marie Provost**

"The genres in this volume span horror, fantasy, and science-fiction, and each is handled deftly. ... **Nightmare's Eve** should be on your reading list. The stories are at the intersection of nightmare and lucid dreaming, up ahead a signpost ... next stop, your reading pile. Keep the nightlight on."

— R.B. Payne, Cemetery Dance

"The story feels so close, so intimate, we as readers experience the emotions, the events, and the conflicts, in what feels like real time. Gut-wrenchingly so."

— Stephen Mark Rainey, author of *Blue Devil Island*,
on **Death's Doorstep** by **Stephen H. Provost**

"Among the greatest what-ifs ever conceived—the power to bring back loved ones! This story defies genres by taking that question to its next level. You really can't put this book down.

— Ruth Goyne, former wire desk editor at *The Tennessean*
on **Memortality** by **Stephen H. Provost**

"**Memortality** is a terrific science fiction thriller that imprints on your mind like an unforgettable snapshot."

— John Palisano, award-winning author of *Nerves*
and past president of the Horror Writers Association

"**Memortality** takes a concept we've all dreamed of and turns it into our worst nightmare."

— Michael Knost, Bram Stoker award-winning author

"Provost sticks mostly to the classics: vampires, ghosts, aliens, and even dragons. But trekking familiar terrain allows the author to subvert readers' expectations. ... Provost's poetry skillfully displays the same somber themes as the stories. ... Worthy tales that prove external forces are no more terrifying than what's inside people's heads."

— Kirkus Reviews on
Nightmare's Eve by Stephen H. Provost

"Stephen H. Provost has nightmares to sell. But be wary, this is no ordinary merchant of dark dreams. These are tales and poems of every sort from a writer to watch."

— Mark Onspaugh, author of *The Faceless One*
and *Deadeye Jack*, on **Nightmare's Eve**